FULL OF MONEY

FULL OF MONEY

Bill James

This first world edition published 2009
in Great Britain and in the USA by
SEVERN HOUSE PUBLISHERS LTD of
9–15 High Street, Sutton, Surrey, England, SM1 1DF.
Trade paperback edition published
in Great Britain and the USA 2010 by
SEVERN HOUSE PUBLISHERS LTD

British Library Cataloguing in Publication Data

James, Bill, 1929-
    Full of Money.
    1. Drug traffic–Investigation–England–London–Fiction.
    2. Gangs–England–London–Fiction. 3. Journalists–Crimes
    against–Fiction. 4. Police–England–London–Fiction.
    5. London (England)–Social conditions–Fiction.
    6. Detective and mystery stories.
    I. Title
    823.9'14–dc22

ISBN-13: 978-0-7278-6813-8   (cased)
ISBN-13: 978-1-84751-177-5   (trade paper)

Except where actual historical events and characters are being
described for the storyline of this novel, all situations in this
publication are fictitious and any resemblance to living persons
is purely coincidental.

All Severn House titles are printed on acid-free paper.

Typeset by Palimpsest Book Production Ltd.,
Grangemouth, Stirlingshire, Scotland.
Printed and bound in Great Britain by
MPG Books Ltd., Bodmin, Cornwall.

One

Obviously, she didn't want to be called out some day to find Gerald beaten unrecognizable, except via one of his foul bow ties. Or things might turn even darker. Already there'd been a couple of deaths, admittedly one only a trite turf war shooting, but the other a young investigative journalist who'd . . . who'd got investigative. Esther Davidson had the profile note on him in front of her now.

STRICTLY AUTHORIZED READERS ONLY
{In part personal★}

Gervaise Manciple Tasker, aged 31 (deceased).
- Born July 1967, Grantham, Lincolnshire. Died August 1998.
- Parents: Brian and Margaret Tasker, retired teachers.
- Gervaise Manciple educated locally until scholarship (Classics) to Oxford University. Graduated 1988.
- Entered journalism. Reporter on giveaway newspapers in Dagenham, London. By 1994 established as freelance specialist in 'exposure' topics. Bylined articles *The Times*, *Daily Telegraph*, *Mail on Sunday* and *Daily Mail*.
- Final project: examination of command structure and operational methods of drugs firms on Whitsun Festival and Temperate Park Acres municipal housing estates. It was rumoured Tasker persisted with inquiries although warned off by staff of Adrian Pellotte (Whitsun Festival). Of motivational relevance? But also researched Temperate Park Acres trafficking.
- Tasker hobnobbed with a middle-class, professional group who did 'slumming' trips to drink at Whitsun Festival and Temperate Acres pubs. (★For special attention of Detective Chief Superintendent Davidson: group sometimes included her husband, Mr Gerald Davidson.)
- Two members of Pellotte firm arrested and released. Evidence did not support charges.
- As income-boost sideline, possible Tasker also a small-scale dealer in illegal substances for one of the firms. But perhaps

an assumed role only, for access to company leaderships and
to material for intended article(s). May have been suspected
of 'skimming' from a firm's takings or 'stretching' the product
and personal revenue by undue additive quantities (procaine,
boric etc). Death punitive?

Did Gerald realize how bad things might become, and how fast? As
tactfully as it could, the profile mentioned the large, braying crew
of acquaintances he liked drinking with these days. It was not the
sort of thing Esther could raise with him, and not the sort of thing
he would raise. Often, she watched Gerald to see whether the journo
slaughter especially terrified him. However, his moods always skit-
tered so crazily that you couldn't read anything from his face or his
body angles. Or you could read *everything*, which added up to the
same. There'd been those couple of formal arrests for the killing, but
of people who knew how to handle interrogation, how to stymie
interrogation.

Witnesses? Scarce. Scared – sceptical about protection schemes.
The arrests failed. For gang crime on Whitsun and Temperate this
routine was . . . routine.

The funeral. She thought Gerald possibly went. But that might
be no more than formal respect for someone he did know, though
not closely: a bit of a rally-round to convince his relatives he'd been
grandly popular, except with the hoodlum, or hoodlums, who killed
him. Esther herself didn't go. That reference in the profile to possible
dealing kept her away. She did not give send-offs to pushers, even
to mock-up, masquerading pushers, though, in fact, no confirmation
ever came that Tasker traded drugs, neither as an earner nor a cover.

But funerals of the murdered could be tricky for police. Death
had its divisions and subdivisions. Only if victims rated as wholly
blameless would officers on the case attend, out of respect; not if
the life snuffed had been dubious, quasi-criminal, criminal. Esther
could enjoy funerals: the hit-or-miss stab at dignity, phoniness in
brilliant bulk, the loud, brave, creaky expressions of hope. But she
avoided this one and didn't send anybody else.

She could have wished Gerald hadn't gone either; supposing he
had, that is. His role as principal bassoon with prestigious orches-
tras brought a certain fame. People noticed him, and he *would* wear
those incandescent bow ties, possibly even to a funeral. Many knew
his wife to be a big-time cop. At present, Esther's role as Detective
Chief Superintendent in the Metropolitan Police put the criminal

life of a large, undocile slab of London under her eye. Later, she would leave the Met and take on even bigger pieces of geography when she'd been raised to Assistant Chief Constable and worked in two out-of-London forces.[1] For now, though, this. Gerald's possible attendance at the funeral might not look as bad as if she'd appeared there herself, but it was an embarrassment. Gerald specialized in embarrassments. He regarded it as the duty of an artist, such as himself, to come up with them. Artists shocked. For instance, Van Gogh's ear.

They weren't all artists in Gerald's social group. He might be the only real one – though there'd be some amateurs and dilettantes – having a go at music, writing, painting. But she assumed they'd all be educated, male, big thinking, large talking, opinionated, stupidly and perilously blurt prone. They might well have welcomed in a freelance journalist who sold to the major papers and who'd been at Oxford on the Humanities side, not engineering, or anything useful – 'banausic,' as Gerald would say. They liked to pub crawl by taxi and especially to pubs in dodgy areas, including on the Whitsun and the Temperate Park estates. He and his mates believed this showed they were bold, not timorous or narrow or miserably bourgeois. They *were*, of course, bourgeois, but not timorously, narrowly or miserably bourgeois, in their view.

Esther regarded that kind of carry-on as OK, but Gerald with drink in him was liable to open his gob a bit wide, and could say things in these risky bars that might not be life enhancing – for his own life, that is – or even tactful. Others in his lot might do similar. Being arty they thought they could speak their piece at full volume if they wanted to. And such people, liquored up, *would* want to, convinced that loudness helped prove they were not timorously, narrowly or miserably bourgeois.

For example, they'd most probably sound off with frank, and therefore deeply unsafe, comments on the death of one of their number in bad circumstances – Gervaise Manciple Tasker, investigative journalist. Esther wished they'd give such pubs the go-by, at least for a while. It wasn't likely, because Gerald would wish to signal he could do whatever he chose to do. Call it artistic licence. Call it senseless. Call it naive. These pubs would be listening posts, among their other roles. Wild, unedited conversations between Gerald and

[1] See *Tip Top* and *In The Absence Of Iles*.

his chums might get mentioned upwards to people running the firms – people like Adrian Pellotte and Harold Perth Amesbury on Temperate. This could easily turn out troublesome.

It shouldn't be troublesome, easily or otherwise. Esther had to recognize that. Pellotte and Amesbury and their firms ought to have been squashed a long while ago. But, of course, Pellotte and Amesbury and their firms successfully hid their real and booming substances trade behind one or more of the usual type of respectable commercial fronts: courier services, scrapyards, builders' merchants, leisure equipment, garden furniture supplies, chandlering. Esther, new to the patch, would try to expose and destroy the true core game of these outfits. To date, though, Pellotte and Amesbury and their teams survived – survived and threatened. Gerald must know this, yet would not, could not, kowtow, due to his special, gifted, unconfinable soul, which, during piss-ups, probably became less confinable still, on whisky.

All right, she was used to Gerald's unique nature. For years he had gone through spells as an all-round, egomaniac, blustering nuisance who could play first bassoon to top concert standard. But she'd admit he definitely had many loveable aspects, as well as the rubbish:

(1) non-golf
(2) apolitical
(3) anti-soccer
(4) anti-JS Bach
(5) but fond of other eighteenth-century stuff
(6) sweet breathed
(7) skilled, imaginative and staminad at sexual violence
(8) tap-dancing flair almost to professional level, if there still were professional tap dancers

Their marriage held together because of such qualities, and all the usual banal, valid, historic and mysterious pressures, plus a few extra. Just the same, Esther recognized he would always be liable to slip into one of those spells as a deeply egomaniac, posturing nuisance who could play, or *had* played, first bassoon to top concert level, and thought he could speed through all hazards on account of his divine and divinely given talent. So, he'd probably go in for provocative, arrogant, persistent, mouthy behaviour in the wrong places. If she'd tried to warn him, he would have said there *were* no wrong places for

Gerald Davidson; he owed his presence wherever he could get to.

A TV arts show wanted him to appear in a panel. This would boost his self-regard a notch or two higher. Experts on first bassoon playing assured her of Gerald's genius. 'Fluid, guileful, dexterous, one-off, magisterial, impish,' a *Guardian* reviewer said about a Gerald performance at the Barbican. Esther found she remembered word-perfect such crap, though possibly meaningful crap if you were familiar with that sort of crap.

Two

Just ahead of Larry Edgehill, as he walked to the Tube station, a large, very noticeably undamaged silver BMW pulled in, alongside three boarded-up, fly-postered ex-shops. It seemed to wait for him. The posters touted a tattoo parlour, bargain hairstyling for men and women, guitar tuition, two used furniture auctions. Edgehill recognized the sparkling car, and its registration, ADP 12. Most local people would. In any case, the brilliantly preserved condition marked it out as the toy of someone extremely magnificent on this, the Whitsun Festival municipal housing estate; 'extremely magnificent' signifying the car could be left in the street, or anywhere else on Whitsun, and nobody would have the inane cheek to hurt, filch from, or even touch any part of it, let alone take it.

The vehicle and its gaudily intact exhaust system, tyres and mirrors etc must belong to a leader in special commerce, and of at least brigadier level in the eternal Great War against neighbouring Temperate Park Acres estate. Actually, of course, as Edgehill knew from the famed reg, the owner's rank would turn out to be much higher than brigadier: say, Chief of the General Staff – his. Edgehill kept walking along Gideon Road. He had to get his morning train for work. Yes, work. Not long ago, he had been switched from Sport programmes at N.D.L.tv to produce a regular arts, or Arts, show for the company. That was fine, or even better than fine. But, as he saw it, there were the arts, or Arts, and there was life, or Life. Not the same. Not even sodding similar. For him, the Arts meant these culture sessions weekly, in series of thirteen over a three-month period twice this year, and going on similarly into 1999, then even beyond. Whereas Life he regarded as the Whitsun housing estate, its vandalism and general thuggery; the cash complexities detaining him as a resident there; the heavy mortgage that got him the Whitsun flat a few years ago; the incessant territorial drugs trade savagery between Whitsun and Temperate Park Acres, including deaths, like the young, nosy journalist's lately, plus, of course, turf fight casualties. Admittedly, people said the arts, or Arts, and life, or Life, should be properly linked. If not, the arts, Arts, would appear phoney, elitist, irrelevant, effete.

And, yes, Edgehill would admit a connection between the two did sometimes happen.

Now.

Although he might, and did, try to avoid all contact with Whitsun's gang lads, it wouldn't necessarily stop *them* seeking contact with *him*. He saw that Adrian Pellotte had the front passenger seat in the BMW, next to his chauffeur/ *aide-de-camp*/ bodyguard/secretary/hit man/poison taster/gatekeeper/adviser on the novels of Anthony Powell/enforcer/valet/counsellor/echo/pal. Edgehill favoured walking on, possibly upping his pace, though unnoticeably, if he could do it: best avoid seeming rude or offhand to Adrian Pellotte. This was *one* reason for not turning your back on him. Off*hand*? That might be only the start. There were lots of other bits Adrian could take off you, or have taken off you. A couple of toes, for instance. A couple of balls. Edgehill tried to believe the car's arrival had nothing to do with him, tried very hard to believe it. How *could* the car have anything to do with him?

The car had something to do with him.

'May we offer a word of very sincere congratulation on your television show week after week, Mr Edgehill?' Pellotte said through the open window, his voice and eyes angled up towards Edgehill's throat/face in an almost credibly friendly way, most likely not at all foreshadowing a rip. 'Or Larry, if you'll permit, this being informal. A high, maintained standard. Remarkable. Dean and I have long wished to pass on our thanks. Your programme's a staple for us.'

'Plus we have a fairly vital topic Adrian would like to discuss with you,' Dean Feston said.

'Which?' Edgehill said.

'Vital,' Dean replied.

Edgehill halted and crouched. He had never spoken to, or been spoken to by Pellotte before, just seen him and the BMW on its regular, cash-harvesting or disciplining trips about Whitsun, civically respecting the speed limit, slowing even further for hang-about pigeons, direction-signalling top notch, like a good deed in a much worse than naughty world: they'd had clips from a new production of *The Merchant of Venice* on the programme lately, and some lines stuck in Edgehill's head.

'Yes, a staple for us, the programme, isn't it, Dean?' Pellotte said.

'Oh, great,' Edgehill said. 'Thanks. We're always delighted to hear from—'

'It has what could be described as range,' Dean Feston replied. 'This is what gets our response – Adrian's and mine.'

He would be about 185 pounds, a lot of it bone and sinew, dark suit, white shirt open at the neck and three buttons down, no medallion. A whisper said he had been pulled in by the police lately, then released, uncharged. The reporter's death? Feston's missing medallion could not be more renowned. Its absence set a tone, indicated a particular, very muted, Whitsun-racketeer style. *Vogue* might pick up on it soon for one of its *milieu* features.

'Thank you again,' Edgehill said. 'Which other vital topic do you—?'

'Consistency,' Dean said. 'We can rely on *A Week in Review* for continual perceptiveness, yet not jargon or pedantry. Adrian's averse to jargon.'

'We deeply liked that item you screened last week on the Tate Retrospective, didn't we, Dean?' Pellotte said.

Edgehill felt conspicuous chatting on long, straight Gideon Road, very visible from ahead and behind. Nobody would think the car had pulled in to ask him directions. Pellotte and Dean didn't need directions around Whitsun. They directed.

Edgehill said: 'The programme tries to—'

'We'd already been up town to enjoy the Retrospective, you know,' Pellotte said. 'We do like to keep on top of things. How else to pull one's weight in conversation otherwise?'

'Yes, how fucking else?' Dean said.

'A Retrospective gives that sequential aspect,' Pellotte said. 'Dean's got such an appetite for learning. It's an inspiration.'

He would be seven or eight pounds heavier than Dean and a couple of years older, about forty-five. Pellotte had on a grey, pinstriped suit, his dark hair brushed smooth, not spiky or tinted. His face was entirely unscarred and free from cell pallor, his tie burgundy and in a modest knot, no flashy, imperious bulge. He didn't do hand jewellery of any kind. Whitsun gossip said pushers and wholesalers as far off as Carlisle and Linton-upon-Ouse spoke wonderingly of this principled dearth of rings, despite magnificent commercial, unprosecutable success on and around the estate, regardless of a new clean-up, top woman detective. Yes, tone. Obviously, in view of Pellotte's non-decorativeness, it would have jarred if Dean wore a medallion. Unflashiness and Pellotte were synonymous, understatement his statement.

'It's good we could intercept you like this today, Larry,' Dean said. 'We didn't want to come ringing your front doorbell – disturbing you and giving the street cause for talk first thing in the morning.

When Adrian calls on some people at home, especially when it's early, there can be neighbourhood interest. Rumour. Gossip, etcetera. If we conduct visits of that sort they will often have, well . . . to be frank . . . often have a sorting-out purpose.'

'Sorting out?' Edgehill said.

'In a special sense,' Dean said.

'Which?' Edgehill said.

'Someone in the house needing to be sorted out,' Dean said. 'This wouldn't have been decided hastily by Adrian and me, but it would have been decided on.'

'The sorting out?' Edgehill replied.

Dean said: 'If we arrived at your place, 19a Bell Close, pre-breakfast, folk on the estate could imagine you were in some sort of difficulty – could think you'd foolishly, disgustingly, crossed Adrian – been skimming from deals, say, and doing tetramisole or hydroxyzine mixes. *Undue* tetramisole or hydroxyzine, damaging the firm's reputation for notable quality. In fact, of course, we wouldn't have had that kind of ticklish, reprimand purpose in calling on you, but people form ideas of their own. It's what's known as their "perception".'

Edgehill wondered whether to people in Gideon he'd look like a Pellotte associate, though a lowly one, who could be required to stoop and take a kerbside briefing which wasn't brief. He'd prefer not to have that sort of reputation, thanks. If Edgehill had owned a car himself and used it to drive to work, unwanted encounters like this would be impossible. But almost as soon as he bought his Whitsun flat he'd realized – been made to realize – that vehicle ownership here didn't really serve, unless you were Pellotte or one of his staff, and – crucially – *known* to be one of his staff. Otherwise, if you kept a car in the street, pieces of it, or it itself, would disappear some nights, or days, and, in fact, as to pieces of it, *most* nights or days: anything removable. You might keep it elsewhere, out of the district, and go to pick it up by Tube train or bus or hike or folding bike, but you still had to pay insurance postcode related, and the postcode of *your* address, not the car's, with bulky weighting for likely vandalism and, almost just as likely, taking, driving away and torching.

'An informal encounter like this is better,' Pellotte said. 'I'm more comfortable with that. Doorstepping – so crude and potentially . . . potentially unpleasant.'

'An Englishman's home is his piss-hole,' Dean said. 'I guessed you'd probably be walking to the Tube at about this spot – the former fruit and vegery – around now, you see.' He glanced sadly at the planked window. 'We were fond of this shop. But the owner, Greymatter Charles, decided he needed no protection, and look what happened.'

'What did?' Edgehill said. 'I was never clear on that. Nor about the other two shops.'

'They thought if they banded together, formed a kind of cooperative, they'd be able to look after themselves,' Dean said. 'You'd imagine someone called "Greymatter" would have better judgement than that, wouldn't you? But "Greymatter" – the name might have been a joke, meaning the reverse, like "Slim" for some fatso.'

'We have a note showing your routine, Larry,' Pellotte said. 'That kind of very rudimentary information. Address and so on. Kept entirely confidential, believe me. You've heard of data security? Meet Dean, its greatest fan.'

'Just a basic fact store,' Dean said. 'Nothing worrying in the least. Adrian would hate to be thought of as some Big Brother figure, wouldn't he, watching everyone on Whitsun, creating dossiers? Again, not at all his way.'

'My timetable is pretty simple and easy to chart,' Edgehill said.

'We've observed that,' Dean said. 'I don't say this is unwise. You're in a non-hazardous occupation. Why should you fear interference?'

'Well, I should be moving on,' Edgehill said.

'And possibly a mention of some other factors,' Dean said.

'Which other factors?' Edgehill said.

'That Tate item on your show, certainly a triumph,' Pellotte replied. 'Most of the panel people had it so right in their discussion of the Retrospective, Larry. On the whole, very well-selected contributors.'

'Which other factors?' Edgehill said.

'Several of the people you get on there are quite knowledgeable, and all credit to you, Larry,' Pellotte said. 'I gather you'll offer an occasional panel place to Detective Chief Superintendent Esther Davidson's husband, Gerald. Fine idea. Distinguished bassoonist.'

'The data shows he gets around a bit too much, but, still, an undoubted artist,' Dean said.

'Often these actual practitioners can talk so forcefully, are so down-to-earth and precise,' Pellotte said.

'Mind, we were glad you didn't have that slimy fucker, Rex Ince, on the panel last time,' Dean said. 'He's the sort who just *has* to snipe and niggle, doesn't he? So predictably negative. Hardly what we might call aesthetic. No decorum. Talks like he's the only fucker in the fucking world who ever heard the fucking words "perspective" and fucking "ambience".'

Dean, behind the wheel, had to lean forward to get these insights past Pellotte and to Larry through the window.

Edgehill said: 'We try to vary our—'

'Ince is sad,' Pellotte said. He gave a small wave of his right hand to scatter tolerance towards Rex Ince.

'To quite a degree, Adrian believes in that famous adage,' Dean said.

'Which?' Edgehill said.

'"Live and let live",' Dean said.

'Fine principle,' Edgehill said.

'Yes, to quite a degree,' Dean said, 'except when some totally unreasonable, sneaky, insolent fucker has to be countered, obviously.'

'Which unreasonable, sneaky, insolent fucker?' Edgehill asked.

'Obviously, "live and let live" doesn't necessarily mean someone like, for example, Ince. He's Cambridge, isn't he? A fellow of one of the colleges. A don, as they're termed,' Dean said. 'Mind, I'm not necessarily against Oxford and Cambridge – or "Oxbridge" as they're called together – though we've run across someone else from Oxbridge lately who didn't really suit. Is this coincidence, or is it Oxbridge?'

'Didn't suit in which way?' Edgehill said.

'Yes, in his undergrad days he was at Oxford, this one,' Dean replied.

'Who?' Edgehill said. 'Did something happen?'

'We had an eye on him, as you'd expect, but then, suddenly, unnecessary.'

'The murdered journalist?' Edgehill asked.

'I've got a note somewhere about Ince and the college.'

'And you've done surveillance on *me*, too?' Edgehill said. 'You have a note?'

'Big, ugly, official word – "surveillance",' Dean said. 'Not at all one Adrian would be happy with. We've familiarized ourselves in a general, practical and I trust helpful fashion, that's all. What else are neighbours for?'

'In strictly germane aspects only,' Pellotte said.

'Germane how?' Edgehill said. Hell, he must get a car and vary his routes. After all, you could rent a lock-up garage on the estate and not leave your vehicle unprotected in the street. But the awkward thing about 'lock-up' as a term on Whitsun was it didn't really mean 'lock-up', not in a lasting sense of lock-up. It expressed a hope only. 'Lock-up' definitely indicated you could lock up the garage when you first took it over, and the lock had been checked and replaced after a previous tenant. But, soon, the lock to the lock-up would be re-wrecked by visitors one night or day, drawn to it, naturally, because it *was* locked up and could therefore be assumed to have something inside *worth* locking up, such as a car, and/or items too hot to be kept at home or offered to a fence at a decent price yet, or a stack of crack, skunk, H and other commodities. So, the garage wasn't a lock-up except historically, and the car previously securely locked up in the lock-up was then in as bad or worse situation than parked on the street, where it would at least be in sight; if they left it there, that is.

Also, the lock-ups tended to be in secluded, cul-de-sac corners of Whitsun Festival – and the same, probably, on Temperate Park Acres – locations where at dusk or later, or virtually any fucking time at all, group numbers could be unfavourable to you, and non-Festive and non-Temperate matters might happen when you walked to or from the vehicle, regardless of closed-circuit television surveillance, which, in any case, had usually been fucked up. On the whole, Edgehill knew the suburbs would have more comfortable conditions, including garages that were actually part of a house – i.e., integral – as with his parents' avenue in Petts Wood, Kent, but, so far, Edgehill considered the burbs too distant – and, of course, pathetically . . . suburban. Larry had the awkward half-conviction that in his kind of work he should stay close to ordinary London lives. And this possibly meant where he was, for the present. A sort of rickety logic came into play – the only sort available to Edgehill currently. This said, forget car ownership and the very fluid meaning of that word, 'ownership', when applied to Whitsun cars, Larry, boy. Take public transport.

'You speak of surveillance, Larry,' Dean said. 'No, no, no. Intrusiveness is simply not Adrian's style. Clearly, that would hardly be live and let live. Why would we *need* to do surveillance on you, for heaven's sake, Larry?'

'Yes, we must let you get along,' Pellotte said. 'You'll doubtless have a full day ahead, in preparation for the next *A Week in Review*. Simply, we wanted to touch base and express our approval. We are groupies of your show! But perhaps we'll make contact again in due course. There are certain continuing matters. Substantive.'

'Oh?' Edgehill said. He disliked the sudden 'but'.

'Personal matters,' Pellotte said.

'Notable matters of a troublesome kind, extremely personal to Adrian individually – as a person,' Dean said.

'Personal? In what way?' Edgehill asked.

'Sensitive,' Pellotte said.'Possibly you know something of it already?'

Something of what, for fuck's sake? Edgehill did not actually say this. People on Whitsun never talked to Pellotte like that. Nor people anywhere else, most probably. Although Edgehill wanted to answer Pellotte confidently, he decided it would be a kind of dangerous impudence to stick his head too far into the BMW through the window and direct his voice right at Pellotte, he wearing such a tie, and simply *being* Adrian Pellotte anyway.Yet, replying from the pavement, with a small gap between him and the car, Edgehill felt some of his words could get lost or mangled in traffic din. They might be key words. Edgehill realized that *any* words you spoke to Pellotte on notable personal matters – personal to him as an individual – certainly, *any* words might be key words. Altogether, this setting on Gideon seemed a dodgy way to hold a three-sided conversation. His back ached and, off and on, his eyes swam, from the effort of keeping arched. But no choice.

'I'm uncertain what you mean,' he replied.

'Truly sensitive this matter, and fundamentally personal in a personal context, believe me,' Dean replied.

'We're not talking trade, Larry,' Pellotte said. 'This goes beyond the commodities.'

'Well beyond. Personal,' Dean said.

'I can't tell how much you know of this exceptionally special matter,' Pellotte said.

'In what respect, Mr Pellotte?' Edgehill said. He didn't feel like risking 'Adrian'.

'This is what I mean by personal,' Pellotte replied.

Edgehill still didn't see how anything personal to Adrian Pellotte as an individual could possibly involve *him*. And Edgehill longed to make sure that nothing personal to Adrian Pellotte as an individual ever did involve *him*.

'Yes, perhaps we can talk more substantively later, Larry,' Pellotte said. 'I have a notion this would be advantageous.'

'Advantageous to almost everyone,' Dean said. 'It's part of that live and let live policy.'

'This has been splendidly constructive,' Pellotte said.

Edgehill pulled back and straightened. Dean took the car away from the pavement and into the traffic. Edgehill resumed his walk. Occasionally, someone who'd grown used to seeing him on his morning trek would wave and smile, and he'd respond to the friendliness. Was he too harsh about Whitsun? Couldn't it sometimes show worthwhile comradeship? Possibly the waves and smiles seem a little more deferential today because the BMW conference had been observed and much mobile-mentioned?

'And did I see you up the road in a long chinwag with our Mr Pellotte?' Udolpho Wentloog-Jones said.

He ran the newsagent booth at the end of Gideon, not far from the station, did some minor pushing – so the word went – and knew pretty well everything about Whitsun. He lived in what was known as *Old* Whitsun, the original village-like district, and considered classier than the estate, as if *Old* Whitsun went back to Pentecost. Edgehill bought his *Guardian* and *Sun* from Udo every working day. 'That car – it always tells a tale though, doesn't it, Larry? Yet, what tale? The new lady chief of detectives, Mrs Davidson, might be interested to know you chat with Adrian Pellotte in a friendly manner.'

Edgehill tried to work out what the 'our' meant in 'our Mr Pellotte'. 'Our' geographically – because he lived on Whitsun? 'Our' because he had a sort of eminence, and therefore gave distinction to the community, as, say, '*our* gracious Queen' did in the national anthem? 'Our' because Udolpho knew him and assumed Edgehill must also?

'They're into the arts,' Larry said. 'We had a word or two about the programme I work for.'

'A word or two or a couple of thou. *A Week in Review?* Well, yes, I know he's interested. Books. Art. Dean, also. That kind of area. I bump into some of Adrian's people now and then, you know, on a business footing, and they speak of these habits. Plus, his daughter – a worry. Did he mention that? I expect he mentioned that. This would be his purpose in talking with you?'

'Pellotte's daughter? Never met her. Never heard of her,' Edgehill said. Might this be the 'personal' topic? Oh God, involvement with Pellotte's family.

'It's to do with the programme, in a way,' Udolpho explained.

'Which way?'

'He's got *two* daughters. But Dione. Doing something with that guy you use plenty as chairman on *A Week in Review* discussions.'

'Rupert Bale? Doing what with him?'

'*Doing* something.'

'A relationship?'

'You know, like a would-be couple. Did he want to talk about that? I don't think he likes it. Well, you wouldn't expect him to. Nor Dean. Bale – he lives on Temperate, doesn't he?'

'So?'

Other customers required serving. Udolpho turned away.

After a couple of minutes, when they were alone again, Edgehill said: 'No, I've never heard any of this.'

'It's private – not a general buzz. But in the way of trade I talk to some of his staff now and then. It's been referred to. Not always as satisfactory. No, not satisfactory. I thought he must have been . . . well, describing things for you. It seemed some considerable conversation you had. Like important.'

'No, not about that.' Or possibly, yes. Had the later part of it been about that, but kept muffled, coded, delayed?

'No? Really? Well, forget I spoke, will you?' Wentloog-Jones said. 'Maybe I shouldn't have. He's subtle – Adrian. He'd probably arrange a street rendezvous just to touch base, as he might say. Then, later, the crunch.'

'Touch base?'

'Make contact. A preliminary. Did he say "touch base"? That's a phrase of his. It's often his way in negotiations, and so on. Then a follow-up . . . follows. Did he say he might look you out again – for something "substantive"? Another of his terms. They're not necessarily threatening. Not necessarily at all.'

Edgehill went on towards the station. Was he getting pulled into something on Whit, something *special*, something exceptionally fucking special, and exceptionally fucking dicey? Petts Wood, or a spot suburbanly similar – did he suddenly hear them calling him, like glib sirens? He wouldn't say his wish to up-camp from Whit, and from contact with people like Pellotte and Dean, a matter of snobbery and/or gutlessness, not totally. For him, at least until the Gideon seminar today, it had consisted almost entirely of the slightly laughable, unquenchable, relentless desire for off-street parking, or – not an impossible aim – a garage actually attached to the property. He'd come to revere the term 'integral' to describe a garage, the way some could be thrilled by a religious or erotic or fiscal word. His Whitsun flat itself was only just off-street, and, on the whole, not a pleasant street in any of the standard meanings of 'pleasant'.

Ten years ago – certainly twenty – people in his kind of executive post would probably have set themselves up in a place considerably different from Whitsun. However, when he bought the flat, London prices were still preposterous, and getting more so. And he had been a print subeditor then and not earning so well. In standard style at the time, he'd planned to get what he could afford under the post-Thatcher buy-not-rent policy for estates – i.e., the Whitsun flat – wait for it to appreciate, and use the increase to set himself up after a couple of years in a non-estate area, say Ealing, Camden Town, Battersea. But values there – in Ealing, Camden Town, Battersea – went ahead vastly faster than the worth of his Whitsun place. He stayed stuck.

Of course, Whitsun Festival was a lovely, spiritual title, with its oblique reference to the Holy Ghost and the gift of tongues, so relevant to a mixed race population. But quite a lot of non-spiritual stuff undeniably went on. And a mile or two up the road lay Temperate Park Acres, that other municipal estate; it, too, with a name full of similar happy, soothing overtones, which must have taken council officials weeks and imagination to create. Between Whitsun and Temperate the vicious, continuous, drugs-centred, territorial battle went on, taking in all the substances, but mainly crack. As a matter of fact, Rupert Bale, regular chairman of the programme, did live on Temperate. Udo had that right. As with Larry in Whitsun, Temperate must be the best Rupe had been able to afford. Although Bale amounted to more or less a culture programme *star* through presenting *A Week in Review* so frequently, the kind of contract *he* had would be shorter still than Edgehill's as a producer, possibly covering only the current series. People like Rupe could disappear overnight from the box for ever. Who remembered Vernon Escott or Maud Bass? Rupe would recognize this precariousness and not overspend on accommodation. And Larry knew Bale had been hit by an expensive divorce not long ago, and there'd be maintenance to pay. For now, he still had to put up with Temperate, though he'd told Edgehill a while back that one day he hoped to sell and go to somewhere like Wandsworth, or even St John's Wood. Dream, dream, dream. What the Temperate householder, Rupert Bale, hadn't told Edgehill about was an involvement with a daughter of the Whitsun householder, Adrian Pellotte. Nightmare, nightmare, nightmare? Actually, Pellotte was a double householder. Edgehill heard he'd had two properties knocked together in Hawthorn Close.

Three

Gnomes, elves, pergolas, bowers, gazebos, pine sheds of many
sizes, gates, fencing, bird baths, conservatories, turf, sundials, statuary human and animal, including Romulus and Remus-type
titted wolves. Appears entirely legit, busy operation. Three or
four vans with company name on, Happy Gardening Solutions.
Plus lorry for heavy stuff.

Her people had downloaded from Tasker's laptop what looked to
Esther like research notes for the article, articles, he'd planned to
write about the Whitsun and Temperate drugs firms. They had not
found much else of use in his Chiswick flat. He lived alone and
didn't seem to be in a relationship. To have a peep at Pellotte's
cover business, Tasker must have been out to the big horticultural
supplies site at Lesser Davit in Hertfordshire. Customers there
wandered around examining what was on offer, and he wouldn't
stand out as he barometered the place. It seemed he'd wanted some
background colour – as well as evidence to tell him that more
went on here than the advertised happy gardening solutions. Esther
thought she scented disappointment in his phrase 'appears entirely
legit, busy operation'. That 'entirely' was a scream of frustration.
So, what had he hoped to see – skunk wheelbarrowed?

Statuary: classical-type robed female figures; plus the animals –
those wolves, then horse pairs, seals, otters, hounds; birds – eagles,
wingspread, as-if-sunning cormorants, swans, gulls. Admin
block/showroom, new, brick built. Ground floor for plate glass
window display of lawn mowers, strimmers, branch-mincers etc.
First floor – what??

Esther could sympathize with the 'what' and double question marks.
He obviously considered this amount of first-floor office space – if
that's what it was – too lavish for the scale of the garden business.
Esther had often wondered about it, too. The whole impenetrable
Pellotte enterprise was controlled from here, was it – the headquarters
out in the countryside at Lesser Davit, the selling ground Whitsun

Festival estate and as much of Temperate Acres as could be won and held?

> Pellotte on site today – perhaps every day. I arrived 9.03 a.m. and his car, BMW, ADP 12, already alongside the main doors to admin block/showroom. Parking spot marked 'Chairman' in gold lettering on a small blue board fixed to a metal post. Necessary? Plenty of room for cars on the site. Does he do his major deals here – deals unconnected with gardens, happy or not? Maybe wants to impress suppliers or rave organizers or street festival promoters. Went into showroom and pretended to examine mowers. Stairs and lift to first floor through turnstile requiring code card. Two healthy-looking members of staff on what looks like watchman duty at turnstile. Dark suits, very white shirts, unmedallioned, jackets buttoned: weapon concealment?

Yes, watchman duty. Esther knew that the two, or another two, were constants. If it ever came to a police raid at Happy Gardening Solutions, those sentries could probably get an alarm signal to Pellotte in time for him to flush away anything incriminating, whatever the cost, and spread illustrated booklets about patios on his desk. But would there ever be a raid?

> Possible tail on me for the latter part of the visit. Maybe I loitered too long among display room machinery. The watchmen watched, and perhaps reported upstairs about the uncommitted, gaze-about lawnmower man. When I leave the show room I sense someone behind me, following over towards the sheds, gazebos and bower section.
> Conversation (undisclosed recorder):
>   Him: 'Looking for anything special, sir?'
>   Me: 'Just enjoying the general spread and feel of the place.'
>   Him: 'But something in particular?'
>   Me: 'I can forget it all when I spend an hour here.'
>   Him: 'Sure, but what in particular?'
>   Me: 'I can shut off from all the rest of it for a while. An interlude of therapy.'
>   Him: 'The rest of it?'
>   Me: 'The usual run of things.'

Him: 'What's the usual run of things for you then, sir, if I
      may?'
Me: 'General.'
Him: 'Which aspect?'
Me: 'Urban.'
Him: 'Where exactly?'
Me: 'Yes, urban.'
Him: 'Been before? It interests you?'
Me: 'This place, quite famous in its way.'
Him: 'Which way would you say that is, sir?'
Me: 'If you're staff I quite envy you your working
      conditions.'
Him: 'Yes, I'm staff.'
Me: 'Which side do you specialize in? The sheds and so on?'
Him: 'Are you a shed person?'

Might be (must be?) Dean Feston. I've heard of him and Pellotte
in general chatter around Whitsun and Temperate Acres. Pellotte's
multitasking assistant. Early forties? Build about right for description of him – 180 to 190 pounds? Fair to reddish hair, in
retreat. Also his clothes: dark suit, white shirt open to three
buttons, again, no medallion. Plentiful muscle and sinew. Suit
jacket buttoned.

Me: 'I thought you were probably staff. Security?'
Him: 'The mowers? Have you got a big lawn where you
      live?'
Me: 'I've always fancied charging around on one of those
      buggy models.'
Him: 'Have you got a big lawn where you live? Are you
      local?'
Me: 'Urban. That's why I need to come out occasionally
      to this sort of setting.'
Him: 'A bit of a trek, is it?'
Me: 'Worth it.'
Him: 'Where from exactly?'
Me: 'It's certainly my aim to get a place one day with a
      good expanse of lawn. If looked after well, it can
      become one of the main attractions of a property.
      That's widely recognized, by estate agents, and so on.
      "Maintained, mature gardens to rear."'
Him: 'When you said "Security" – why did you say
      "Security?"'

Me: 'A lot of valuable machinery here. And the sundials
       – beautifully made. They called you down, did they?'

Him: 'Who?'

Me: 'The two sentries on the gate, like the cherubim in
       Genesis, keeping Adam out of Eden after the Fall.'

Him: 'You go to church? Where would that be?'

Me: 'Most know that tale.'

Him: 'Called me down from where?'

Me: 'Upstairs. Offices?'

Him: 'Why would they call me down?'

Me: 'As Security. Maybe I hung about the expensive
       mowers too long, without buying. They might think
       I was casing. I'm sorry if I caused a scare.'

Him: 'Casing what?'

Me: 'The showroom and the machines in it.'

Him: 'I wondered if we should have a name and address,
       so we could send you brochures re special offers, that
       kind of thing.'

Me: 'Do you mean about garden stuff?'

Him: 'Naturally, garden stuff. What else from a Gardens
       Solutions centre? Your details to be added to our
       records, and treated as totally confidential data.
       Without obligation.'

Me: 'I'm very much on the move these days.'

Him: 'From where to where?'

Me: 'Indeterminate. Some wouldn't like these continual
       changes. But they seem to suit me.'

Him: 'Why *is* that?'

Me: 'Oh, yes, people say to me, "How can you put up
       with all these constant upheavals?" But I reply: "I
       don't see them as such. I see them as progress. We'll
       be lying still a long time eventually."'

Him: 'Do they say a name?'

Me: 'Who?'

Him: 'The people who ask "How can you put up with all
       these constant upheavals?"'

Me: 'Which name?'

Him: 'When they ask, "How can you put up with all these
       constant upheavals?" Do they say . . . "all these
       constant upheavals", and then your name, such as "all
       these constant upheavals, Frank or Len?"'

Me: 'I don't think I know anyone called Frank or Len.'

Him: 'No, that's not the point, is it, I meant . . . oh, let's move on? Which people say that to you?'

Me: 'What?'

Him: 'About the upheavals.'

Me: 'Friends and so on.'

Him: 'Which friends and so on? Are they local?'

Me: 'Local in which sense?'

Him: 'What do you mean, "in which sense?"'

Me: 'Local to here or local to where I live.'

Him: 'You don't live locally then – locally to here?'

Me: 'Various.'

Him: 'Various what?'

Me: 'Various friends who say "How can you put up—?"'

Him: 'But they all say, "How can you put up with these constant upheavals?" do they?'

Me: 'Many.'

Him: 'These are obviously people with your well-being at heart.'

Me: 'Oh, certainly.'

Him: 'Where do you meet with them?'

Me: 'Bump into them in the street, that sort of thing.'

Him: 'Which street?'

Me: 'Vary various.'

Him: 'And as soon as you bump into one of them, he or she says: "How can you put up with these constant upheavals?" Does he or she?'

Me: 'Not as soon as, because at that point they wouldn't know. Only when I've told them I'm living somewhere different now.'

Him: 'Different from what?'

Me: 'Different from where I was last time.'

Him: 'Where was that?'

Me: 'It would depend.'

Him: 'Depend on what?'

Me: 'On when I bumped into him or her. Things could have changed more than once if I hadn't seen them for quite a while.'

Him: 'Someone was telling me the other day about an old television series called *What's My Line?*'

Me: 'A lot of those early programme had quality, perhaps
       to some degree lost now.'

Him: 'A panel had to guess someone's job. They could ask
       certain questions, but not come straight out with,
       "What's your job?"'

Me: 'That would have killed the show because there'd be
       nothing left to wonder about.'

Him: 'If I had to guess your job I'd say Press.'

Me: 'And I suppose I was guessing *your* job, when I said
       "Security". The executives who created that *What's
       My Line?* programme must have cleverly realized how
       much folk liked puzzling about others' occupations.'

Him: 'The press can be very intrusive sometimes.'

Me: 'I've heard that. They did for President Nixon, didn't
       they? Doorstepping people. There's a film about it
       on the movie channel now and then. Robert
       Redford.'

Him: 'The press – always after the sensational. Their
       reporters will lurk and spy. We, ordinary members of
       the public, need protection from that, I think you'll
       agree. And if the protection is not offered by the
       authorities, we have to protect ourselves.'

Me: 'People say "No comment", I believe. That's quite a
       rejection.'

Him: 'I don't suggest the press should be banned.'

Me: 'Most would agree it has a role. It goes right back
       in our history. Dispatches from the Crimean War in
       the *Times*. William Russell.'

Him: 'The press can give useful reviews of books and music
       – that kind of thing.'

Me: 'You're into the arts and literature, are you?'

Him: 'I don't always agree with what they say.'

Me: 'You're entitled to differ.'

Him: 'It would be a dull lookout if we all thought the
       same.'

Me: 'An element of debate brings vigour.'

Him: '"Live and let live" is one of my guiding rules, within
       reason'

Me: 'Plus, colour pictures more and more now.'

Him: 'Where?'

Me: 'The press. Sport, for instance.'

Him: 'Or the finance columns can be useful.'

Me: 'True.'

Him: 'You have an undoubted right to walk about here between the hours of nine a.m. and five thirty p.m. That can't be gainsaid.'

Me: 'This would be part of the "Live and let live" theme.'

Him: 'An open door.'

Me: 'Not to upstairs in the showroom and admin block.'

Him: 'I've really enjoyed this conversation.'

Me: 'Yes.'

Him: 'I'll keep an eye open for you.'

Me: 'Where?'

Him: 'I feel I owe you that.'

I left.

The mad indirection and gibber of most of this demoralized Esther. It matched too bloody exactly the general tone of the Tasker case: brickwall resistance to understanding. They'd found the recorder and tapes in his flat. Detectives familiar with Whitsun said the 'Him' voice was almost certainly Dean Feston. Would any of it really have been of use in an article? Much of it sounded like a parody of a Pinter play.

She needed something plain, factual, definite, to restore her mind to clarity. Esther drove over again to the big public park where his body had been found. Talking of madness – Esther knew this to be not a particularly sane trip. She wouldn't be finding anything new. Not the objective. She hoped for escape from the silly deviousness of the recorded chit-chat at Happy Gardening Solutions, and to look at a solid reminder of what had happened soon after the chit-chat to one of those taking part. In any case, she didn't want to go home yet. Gerald would be there, and not at his sweetest. Two reasons:

First, *Orchestra*, the professional magazine for musicians, had listed those considered the greatest living players on each classical instrument, and Gerald did not figure under 'bassoonists'. Two others were named. If they'd picked only one he might have been reasonably all right. But to be pushed to third really got to him. And, of course, he couldn't be certain that *Orchestra* regarded him as third, or twenty-third. They'd named two. This did not mean that if they'd chosen three, he would have been it.

She left her Ford in the car park at the edge of Martin's Fields and walked over the grass towards the children's adventure playground. It had been a cold late autumnal day and now, mid-afternoon, only a few people were about, walking the dog, or jogging, or practising place kicks at the rugby posts. Of course, the playground had been closed for a week after the discovery of Tasker's body on the youngsters' curly chute there and, although it reopened a few days ago, no children played in the enclosure now. It might be on account of the weather. More likely, for a while the Fields and amusements would be regarded by parents as jinxed and they'd keep their kids away.

Suppose Esther told Gerald he should certainly have been placed first or second in the bassoonist tally, he would see that for what it was – the would-be soothing verdict of someone naturally biased in her hubbie's favour, and more or less ignorant of bassoons and of bassoon world league tables. The knee-jerk, worthless words might inflame him further. And suppose instead she argued that if three were named, he must have been included, he would take this as a declaration that, yes, she considered him third rate. Gerald could get rough-house when offended on such a scale, and Esther didn't fancy any of that just now. She had a tricky job on needing concentration and a brain not dulled by recent blows or distracted by widespread pain.

Luckily, Tasker's smashed body had been found early by one of the park keepers opening up the playground for the day. The slide was quickly tented and the area taped off as a crime site before any youngsters and their parents arrived. A notice near the gate said: 'This playground is intended for children between the ages six to fourteen.'

But adaptable, obviously.

'The nearest public phone booth is in Stanton Road. The nearest Accident and Emergency Hospital is the Fildew General in Lent Street.'

Unneeded, both, in this case. Her mind slipped back to Gerald. The second reason for his present unpredictabilities centred on that TV invitation. At times he seemed thrilled. At others he regarded it as 'piffling' and 'footling' – or *said* he did. She knew he would accept. It was the panellist status that riled. He thought there should be a programme, or possibly programmes, devoted only to him. He believed he deserved this, or he *had* believed it until that list of great bassoonists ignored him. Gerald considered he was being treated not quite as a musical nobody, but only not quite. He could be used to make up the numbers – either as third or worse in the magazine list, or on a panel of four or five where his personal voice could get only a share of attention, despite his flair.

Tasker had not been killed in the playground. That happened somewhere else and the body arranged on the slide at night after the gate lock to the playground was picked. Did this location, this careful, grotesque placement have any special meaning? Did it say something about why Tasker had been beaten before the bullets? Was the message that Tasker had childishly imagined he could do an exposure piece on the firms and should therefore be presented, slaughtered and bruised, in a juvenile, six to fourteen, playground? And the slide? A devious drop down and down to elimination from his cocky reporter's nosiness?

Gerald quite often had decent moments. Immediately after the discovery of Tasker's body, he'd seen that Esther was exceptionally shaken by the circumstances of this death, and monstrously flippant disposal of the body, and for a time shelved his egomania and grew considerate, kindly, tender. Yes, she'd admit he could be like that now and then. Hardly ever did he fail Esther when he judged her to be genuinely needy. And, occasionally, he could maintain such warm thoughtfulness for quite an impressive while. Hours.

This afternoon, Esther stayed outside the playground, her eyes directed at the slide. Uselessly directed. All she'd see was the empty chute, no late pointers. On the morning he was discovered she'd had the call at seven forty a.m. and arrived just after the Scenes of Crime team and before the tenting. She could still call up the sight of Tasker, flat on his back about halfway down, each arm over the side, perhaps to anchor him and stop the body slipping further, possibly off the chute altogether. The people who brought him here wanted a better show than a crumpled body on the ground at the end of the slide. Did they intend Tasker to look like a delighted and excited child as the slope took charge? But, in fact, because of what had happened to his face elsewhere, there could be no semblance of little-boy excitement and delight on it.

Now, as Esther zombie-stared, a park keeper came to end-of-day lock the playground gate. He didn't seem to recognize Esther. Maybe he'd been off when the body was found, and hadn't seen her around here then.

'It's perfectly all right in there now, you know, lady, if you want to bring your children along to the rides and so on. I can understand the . . . the, well, queasiness, but it's all been thoroughly spruced up. Not a trace of . . . of anything.'

'Thanks.' She went back to the car.

At home, Gerald was accentuating the negative: 'I don't know about this TV thing, Esther. I've seen the programme once or twice, haven't I? It has that Rex Ince on it often. Cambridge – a don. He behaves as if he thinks the whole damn thing should be about him, not the topic they're discussing.'

A rival. 'Does he, dear?' She'd like to keep matters still mild this evening, no knockabout. Perhaps he'd prefer that, too. If he was going on television he wouldn't want old scars evident. And she'd seen enough scars lately.

Gerald imitated a quibbling donnish voice: ' "Oh, yes, William Boyd can describe room interiors well enough in his novels, but let me recount what happened to me one day in Tasmania." That's fucking Ince. Do I want to line myself up on the screen with such people?' Yes. But Esther didn't say so. 'And then the chairman,' Gerald added. 'The usual chairman. Bale? Rupert Bale? One of the people who drinks with us works in television, though for a different company, and says this Bale is in a somewhat stressful situation involving Adrian Pellotte – Baron Pellotte of the Snorts. Bale and Pellotte's daughter have something going, apparently. Possible difficulties there. Bale's from the wrong estate.'

'Temperate not Whitsun?'

'Like that. What bothers me is that if this Bale has such worries he's likely to be a bit all over the place as chairman of a programme. No control, I mean. So, panellists screaming at one another. A noise competition.'

'You could hold your own, Gerald.'

'Unwise, inappropriate, for me to be seen in something chaotic and shambolic like that. I'm a name, Esther, a reputation. I have to guard these. I can't allow myself to be yelled at by a twerp like Ince. It would confuse and upset those who see me, know me, for what I am.'

'Many of those.'

'We'll watch the next damn programme in the series before I decide anything. That is mere good sense, isn't it? And how was *your* day?'

'Admin chores.'

'Tasker?'

'Of course, I have people looking at that.'

'I gave my own mind to it for a while.'

'Did you, Gerald?'

'I wonder if you've thought about the significance of the playground.'

'In what sense?'

'It's a place for children, isn't it?'

'Certainly.'

'Tasker gets arranged there, like a child. Are they telling the world he was stupidly, childishly naive? Perhaps this is not the kind of insight that would come to police officers. It's a revelation from a different kind of mind. Not necessarily a *better* kind of mind. One doesn't claim that. No, indeed. Different. An artist's mind. A mind that is used to dealing with the thematic, the intrinsic, rather than the obvious – a mind that can hear the unspoken – the unspoken but very present. Look, I don't mind if you present this idea as your own to colleagues, Esther.'

'That's a true kindness, Gerald.'

Four

Larry Edgehill thought things could get worse – *knew* things *would* get worse, had already started to get worse. On-screen – on-screen! – on-screen Priscilla Sandine, a panellist, say twenty-six or -seven, puts all her big, insistent and vibrant charms towards Rupert Bale, chairman for the night, and, God, does he respond!

Well, fine in different circumstances and with different people. But . . . But! But Rupert Bale is apparently promised, or something like that, to Dione Pellotte. Here, in view of millions, on Larry's programme, *A Week in Review*, Sandine and Bale ferociously sparkle and brilliantly, almost rampantly, interlock. Adrian Pellotte will not care for this, and, of course, he'll be watching. Isn't the programme a favourite of his and Dean Feston's – their staple? And probably even more so now, because of Dione's link with Rupe. Link? Would tonight's show make Pellotte wonder how reliable that link was, and how reliable was Rupe? It could be very bad when Pellotte didn't care for something and when he began to wonder. Think of the journalist, Gervaise Manciple Tasker, who'd probably offended Pellotte by poking into his life – possibly including Dione's life – now dead in undetermined circumstances. Some of the circumstances. Not the playground slide.

A Week in Review always went out live. Tom Marland usually directed, with Edgehill in overall charge. In the hospitality suite, pre-programme, Edgehill had noticed Rupert Bale on the other side of the room, alone and with a glass of what might be orange juice. He looked troubled. If difficulties with Adrian Pellotte hovered anyone might look troubled.

Pellotte had been a frightener for years. Since the death of Tasker his name commandeered even stronger scare elements. True, the death, as far as Edgehill knew, had never been officially connected with Pellotte, although gossip said two of his people – Dean Feston and a woman called Cornish – were hauled in, then released. Official connections were not the only ones. How about *un*official? How about guesswork? How about wise suspicion?

So, *did* Pellotte difficulties hover over Rupe? Perhaps, after all, Pellotte would grow to like the notion of his daughter partnered by a television star, even a television star who looked like Rupe and lived on Temperate. Perhaps, yes. Perhaps. There'd better be no messing with Dione by Rupe, though. And Pellotte and Rupe might take different views on what amounted to messing.

Would Pellotte and Dean have a 'note' on Bale? This would probably be a big priority when a man started something with Pellotte's daughter: one of Dean's top-grade fact trawls. Edgehill wondered whether he, himself, looked troubled, following the Gideon ambush. It was frightening that they had a 'note' on him, though from 'just a basic fact store'. For Bale there must also be the usual anxieties and tensions about running the show. A couple of the newspaper critics had savaged him lately. That wouldn't do his nerves or his mortgage chances any good either.

Even before the broadcast it had worried Edgehill to think of Pellotte and Dean Feston watching *A.W.I.R.* together tonight. Pellotte's house? Dean's? Would anyone else be present? The daughter, proud of her alleged beau? Pellotte's wife? Members of Dean's family? Edgehill had a notion he'd heard Dean was divorced. There'd be big attention on Rupe if Udolpho had things correct, and Udolpho generally did. At moments during the Gideon confrontation Edgehill had felt Pellotte and Dean Feston spoke as if they *owned* the programme, the way they owned Whitsun.

In Hospitality before the show, Edgehill had glanced back towards Bale and the orange juice. Priscilla Sandine was talking to him. It would be her first appearance on *A Week in Review*. She was smartly got up in what looked to Edgehill like some kind of white jump suit to low calf length, and a black blazer. Her short fair hair had been given a sort of close, spiky, zigzag cut. Her shoes looked pricey – black, high-heeled but not absurdly. Although panellists had to dress their top halves all right, shoes didn't normally get much camera, and those who spent big on them just the same must be financially all right. That sort could be a fucking pain. They weren't desperate for money, so they might act maverick.

He didn't know her very well. Naturally, he'd done the greetings when she arrived, and during those few moments was aware of a very strong Sandine sexual force, though not necessarily meant for him in particular: more general, more scattergun. As he'd watched her and Bale later, he saw that Rupe, also, felt this power play fiercely and promisingly on him. He perked up notably, smiled, shifted about on his feet, obviously trying to respond, though Edgehill couldn't hear what was said, because of distance and the

all-round talky-talky din. At that stage, pre-studio, Edgehill could
hope that this apparent instant steaming rapport would not get
carried over *too* damn hot to the actual broadcast, and to the screen,
watched in whichever venue by Pellotte, Dean and kin.

This hope died. The actual steaming rapport between them in
the broadcast . . . steamed. And the trouble was that, obviously, it
would look to anyone impartial, or partial in the way Pellotte and
Dean would be partial – yes, it could look as though Rupe might
not keep himself exclusively for Dione Pellotte. Her father would
not like this, and nor would Dean. Based on that Gideon exchange,
Edgehill thought Dean could be very dutiful and slaughterous in
the interests of Pellotte's daughter. For Dean, the words 'Pellotte's
daughter' might have holiness, and he'd be ready to wipe out anyone
who failed to show them proper reverence, or seemed to: for instance,
Rupe Bale doing lust exchanges with Priscilla on fucking TV – well,
not quite fucking, but in the vicinity.

Early drinks in Hospitality had to be the right amount to loosen
performers up, without making them rat-arsed and incoherent. Too
little meant the panellist stayed pedantic, dull, mealy-mouthed,
clichéd, *idée fixée*. Too much . . . Oh God, too much could bring
blather even woollier than the standard blather of an arts programme.
There might be physical threats; cursing; walkouts; the disintegration
of basic grammar, syntax and word forms; spittle. Edgehill had
wondered whether Priscilla Sandine was alcohol-powered now and,
if so, would top-ups make her more vividly and engulfingly hormonal
later?

The company had brought Edgehill over from Sport to give to
arts what they called 'an emphatic yet wise popularity'. After all, TV
soccer kept its hold on supporters. Now, very, very now, he wanted
Sandine at the right tipple level to help keep a wise hold on *A.W.I.R.*'s
bit of audience, 'right' meaning chirpy, but not hungrily homing in
on Rupe's zipped bulge.

This evening, they'd discuss an exhibition of Far Eastern floral
art at the Whitechapel Gallery; *The Royle Family*, a BBC satirical
TV programme; a new Abel Vagrain novel, *The Insignia of Postponement*;
and a revival of an Auden-Isherwood play, *On the Frontier*. Heavyish?
So, before the On Air light glowed, trickle the correct number of
liveners into the panel gaggle. A live show got liveners. Until the
Sandine treatment, Bale had looked as if he *needed* a livener. But
Rupe never did touch alcohol before a programme. Even a mouthful
made him slurred.

Nellie Poignard, the burly, energetic, intuitive, cheery head of News and Current Affairs, had looked in to Hospitality before the programme on a brief visit. She held a glass of gin and bitters.

'How are things in the homeland, Larry?' she asked.

'Whitsun? Serene.'

'Something terrible is going to break on the estates, I know it. Oh, we get news stories all right from Whit and Temperate Acres, but I constantly feel we're only nibbling the edge.' She sipped.

People from other departments often appeared for a free drink or two before the programme, and sometimes Edgehill also invited prospective panellists to come and acclimatize themselves. 'What am I missing, Larry?' she said. 'You'd know things from the inside.'

'What things?'

'Things.'

'I commute from and to, and that's about it,' Edgehill said. Or this was how he wanted it. The kerbside meeting with Pellotte and Dean didn't add up to news – the kind Nellie understood. Nor did rumours from Udolpho.

'Occasionally, I just drive about on both estates, no real objective, no purpose, Larry, but trying to absorb a bit of the atmos, the undercurrents, the omens. *Something's* hatching. *Something's* going to happen. We've seen turf battles, like the one where dear Gladstone Milo Naunton died, leaving poor Bert Marsh widowed. There'll be more. Ordinary people might get caught up.'

'Apocalypse not quite now?'

'Bad. Yes, it looks calm on both estates, I admit. Horribly, falsely calm. I might see the famous BMW going about its happy, time-honoured business, reg ADP 12, celebrating Adrian David Pellotte's ownership, but also his fandom of the twelve Anthony Dymoke Powell novels in *A Dance to the Music of Time*. Dean Feston will usually be at the wheel. He's had a long out of clink spell.'

'Disappointed? No news interest?'

'They follow their undiminished, undiminishable, dirty trade: delivering, collecting, punishing. In a different era these people would have been bank robbers. Drugs is safer, more profitable. Stuff goes up by a factor of what – 150, 160 by the time it's on the street in Britain from Colombia? Margins so huge it doesn't matter when they lose a stash through raids and seizure. If the police hit the luxury side, the trade goes downmarket for a while to the cheap, bulked-up additive stuff – more boric acid or hydroxyzine or tetramisole. And vice versa. Importers and wholesalers respond to

fluctuations like any good entrepreneur. The traffic's unstoppable.
They simply collect. Their minions do most of the risky stuff.'

'The barons have time to pop up to London Retrospectives.'

'They do that? Of course, they can occasionally turn brutal themselves. Think of Tasker. Self-protective.'

'Nothing's proved there, I hear.'

'Nor will be. They know how to arrange that.'

'Arrange?'

'Fix. And, listen, Larry, last time I saw Pellotte and Dean they
were near your place,' she said.

'Yes?' He thought he kept this sounding reasonably unruffled,
despite feeling reasonably ruffled. 'Bell Close – that's you, isn't it?'
she asked. 'The car sort of dawdling, surveying, casing.'

'They get about.'

'Do they bother you?'

'They probably don't know me, or anything about me.'

'No? Really?' Perhaps she'd heard about the Gideon road
encounter. Wasn't it her job to hear interesting points from Whit,
and from everywhere? 'And then this murder – the reporter.'

'He didn't live on one of the estates, did he?'

'No, but he was sniffing about on both, so it's said. Provocative,
Larry.'

'Don't your people sniff about on both, too?'

'*We* know the protocols. It looks as though *he* didn't.'

Nellie edged away. A girl from make-up had taken Rupe Bale
back to their room for some adjustment to his get-up, hair or
complexion. Priscilla Sandine, journalist, would-be film-maker, was
suddenly alone. Edgehill had gone across to her. When she spoke it
scared him. 'What do *you* think, Larry? I was just asking Rupert –
why don't we hear what happened *afterwards* to the Italian waiter
in *The Godfather*.'

'*The Godfather*? A waiter? Afterwards?' Larry said. God, was she
sozzled already? He might not want talk here in Hospitality about
topics due on the programme later in case they grew stale, but *The
fucking Godfather*, a twenty-five-year-old film and discussed over the
decades inside out and back again?

'Yes, afterwards,' she said. 'Michael Corleone shoots the police
chief and the Turk while they're in a restaurant. A waiter served
them. What happened to him later? We demand a continuance.'

Her glass was not completely empty, but more empty than full.
Enough? As to waiters, Edgehill knew he must get an immediate

signal to Sacheverell Biggs. Sachev, from catering, had been doing arts hospitality for years, and Larry counted on him to judge when a refill for a guest's glass would be OK. Also, though, to judge when it might be catastrophic for a performer.

Sachev sometimes stood behind the small hospitality suite bar near the wall telephone, and sometimes circulated with bottles on a tray. He was moving about now on the other side of the room. Larry must get a clear, downright eye message to him: '*Dodge* Priscilla Sandine.' A feeling of responsibility for others was very strong in Edgehill. It would be neglectful and cruel to expect Rupe Bale and the others to cope with Sandine drunk on a live show. Keep her from the drink – from any further drink.

But Sachev had finished with the people over near the door and stepped towards Priscilla and Larry, the Glenlivet in pale, ample, friendly readiness on his tray, plus companion supplies. He turned his head aside for a second to pour for someone else, and broke eye contact with Larry. Then Sach came on. Larry sent him the NO BLOODY MORE FOR HER look. Too late. Much too damn late. Sachev certainly did finally note and totally understand Larry's order. By now, though, for Sach *not* to replenish Sandine's almost empty glass would be blatantly rude, an anti-hospitable snub, particularly as the almost empty glass got shoved towards Sacheverell in Mohammed-Ali-style, powerful, short-arm jabs; like what-the-fuck-fucking-well-kept-you-sonny-boy? She wanted what she wanted also from *The Godfather* – a continuance.

Priscilla had taken the full glass unhurriedly to her lips and let it stay there an unhurried while, though Larry thought she had certainly passed the unhurried, savouring, small sip, connoisseur stage. The movement came from her sex depository. It was intended to show she had lips, in case this hadn't been sufficiently noticed, and that the lips exercised discrimination and persistence, and always knew to a t what they were sucking on. She spilled none of her drink. So, maybe not entirely pissed? Not yet.

A little way off from Sandine and Edgehill, Tom Marland, who would direct the programme tonight, must have caught bits of *The Godfather* conversation, or monologue, and looked terrified. How would she react on camera? Sandine wrote a books column in one of the broadsheets – good, sensible articles. Marland and he had agreed she deserved a run-out on the show. Mistake? Priscilla was an unpredictability. *Some* unpredictability could be good for a TV show. Too much might sink it. At least that know-all prick Rex Ince

wasn't on tonight's panel and liable to increase the hazards: Ince
with his dud impishness and ludicrous jacket. Sharp-chinned Selina
Mysan and those massive Bedlam chuckles didn't feature this evening,
either.

Bale had just returned from his supplementary visit to make-up,
and Edgehill recrossed the room to him. 'I saw you and Priscilla
enjoying each other's company. Full of vim and so on, isn't she?'
Larry said.

'Sandine? Oh, yes. She's great. Intuitive. And so on, as you say.
We sat in the stalls together at *On the Frontier.*' He sipped the safe
drink. His mood seemed to sink again. 'What do you make of those
fucking slaggings off, Larry?'

'Which?'

'You know. Me pilloried,' Rupert said.

'Where?'

'The heavies.'

'*Have* they pilloried you, then?'

'You've seen the stuff. You get a clippings service.'

'I don't recall it, and I wouldn't give weight to that sort of thing,
anyway.'

'What about upstairs?'

'The boardroom? Nobody's mentioned bad reviews to me.'

'If I get drubbed in the papers, it reflects on you, Larry. Ultimately,
Flo Tait, as Head of Programmes, is going to ask what you think
you're doing.'

Get him off this theme. He has to be confident in the studio. Bale had
a youthful face under brown curly hair kept short and, yes, could
usually go into instant likeability when the cameras came on. Nothing
must endanger that.

He went for a final pre-programme pee. Nerves. Natural enough.
Priscilla Sandine may have been watching him and Edgehill from
elsewhere in the room, and approached Larry now. She had finished
with *The Godfather.* She took another good sip of her drink. 'You've
been trying to comfort Rupe, have you?' she said. 'He's had a bit
of a critical bashing lately, poor duck. And perhaps there are other
worries, too. He'll have a life of some sort off screen.'

'Yes, we all have that.'

'His might be . . . well, stressful.'

'Is it?' Had she heard something?

'I'm asking – is it?' she said.

'I wouldn't know.'

'As producer of the show, shouldn't you? Didn't I read he lives on Temperate?'

'So?'

'Probably not entirely restful.'

'Where is? It's not significant.' No? But he said: 'As producer of the show I produce it. That's the lot.' He might have said to her, instead: *'Yes, he does have a life outside the studio and you could easily add to its threats and stresses tonight, if on-screen you look as though you're about to flash cleft at him and, incidentally, at viewers, of whom there are one or two – three, actually – who might dangerously resent this – your flashing at Rupe, that is.'*

Edgehill didn't, couldn't, say it.

'I've always thought Rupert a terrific chairman,' she said. 'He helps make *A Week in Review* so consistently brilliant.'

'Well, yes,' Larry said.

'But he needs someone to bring him out of himself a bit more on air, don't you agree? Tap his potentiality. Sex him up. Unencumber him.' She drank some more.

Oh God, she drank some more.

'I think we should let Rupert set his own pace,' Edgehill had said hurriedly, though he hoped without obvious panic. 'People have come to expect a certain, very recognizable style from him. We mustn't interfere.'

Meaning, *you* mustn't interfere with it, you hazardous, presumptuous, well-shod, nicely barbered, piece of arse. Edgehill had to ask himself, whom would Pellotte and Dean blame if Sandine did try to sex Rupert up on-screen? Who picked the people and shaped the show? Who oversaw the drinks supply? Answer: the programme's producer, L. Edgehill, known familiarly to Pellotte as Larry, but this did not guarantee everlasting mateyness or safety.

'Style?' Sandine said. 'Well, yes, he has a style. And to a degree it works. But we could up it a notch or two, I feel. We need to get his blood moving, don't we, Larry?'

We? She spoke as if they had a partnership task to transform Rupe. 'Oh, I don't see it like that.'

'Are you . . . are you, well, *scared* of something?' she asked.

'Scared?' *Wouldn't most people be scared to hear Pellotte and Dean had been data delving in the BMW around Bell Close, and specifically 19a there?*

'Does Rupert have special pressures?'

'Just the usual. We want a good show. A lot of good shows.'

'And I'm sure you will get one, get a lot.'

So fucking well behave yourself. 'I know you'll contribute effectively and memorably to the programme's reputation.'

'Honoured,' she said. No hiccup.

It had been time for the studio. All taking part went downstairs then. Edgehill left Sachev to tidy up the Suite and prepare for their return, post gig.

Five

Bumped into that group of slumming drinkers again, this time
in the Dragon on Temperate Acres. They're friendly, treat me as
if I'm one of them, but I don't like it, and if I ever write them
up must do it cool. They talk too loud, draw attention, possibly
antagonize. They're middle-class, professional/artistic/media, I
think. I try to avoid. But they do occasionally come up with
good information – good enough to dig further into. NB –
non-attributable information, of course. Very. And NB further
– some of what they relay as fact is rumour, buzz, gossip that
they've picked up on their jaunts. Starting points only for real
investigation.

This opened another set of the journalist, Tasker's, laptop notes.
Esther reread them. Later, she'd get on to the summarizing transcripts of the interviews with Pellotte's Dean Feston and Gabrielle
Barter Cornish, when they were pulled in on suspicion of the
murder.

    (1) League-tabling: I hear Harold Perth Amesbury, present head
    of the Temperate Acres firm, and Adrian Pellotte are among
    the 2,500 –3,000 major drugs wholesalers in Britain. (Would
    have guessed something like this, though without actual
    numbers. To have figures is confirmation of a sort.) Minor
    pushers on salary or percentage – compare *affiliati* in Naples
    Camorra drugs firm.

Esther knew her husband would watch *A Week in Review* tonight.
She'd have to watch *with* him. The programme was almost sure to
put Gerald into a loud, farcical, possibly violent rage. Most likely
this would begin before the show actually came on. She decided
to stay for a while, peaceful in her office, dawdling through the
notes.

(2) Cover firm for the Temperate Acres operation is Abracadabra
Leisure Facilities based in Uxbridge, Middlesex.

Of course, Gerald's rages could be fun, but when defending herself
and/or retaliating she had to be careful she didn't hurt his hands or
mouth in case this messed up his bassoon playing.

(3) Harold Perth Amesbury: caretaker chief only. Succeeded to
leadership six months ago on retirement to his estate in
County Wexford of Percival Acton Verity (aka Incremental)
through illness (kidneys) and recurrent trouble with old
gunshot wound (thigh). Two deputy-chairmen, perhaps
angling for Supremo job. See below. Amesbury seeking
chance to secure his position (i.e., via successful campaign(s)
against Whitsun).

There might be a big concert due with Gerald soloing. Betty
Grable insured her legs, and Esther often told him to do the same
for his lips because her left lacked the absolute accuracy to avoid
them always. Her right, better. Her right usually chinned. From
somewhere in his genes, Gerald had an ironish chin, and rarely
went down, although he might stagger about dazed and bleating
for a while. She'd get him into a chair and fan him with a music
score while humming some Bach, to make sure he stayed evil, so
they could continue it. A fat lip, or lips, caused by knuckles slackened
grip on the bassoon mouthpiece and Gerald wind that should have
produced accurate music got wastefully blown into the open air.
Some notes would sound dodgy – frail.

(4) Pellotte's daughter, Dione, involved, so far non-cohabit, with
TV personality, Rupert Bale, a Temperate resident.
(5) Possible skimming off the top by operative(s) and/or over-
mixing on Whitsun. Pellotte aware and displeased.

Gerald was certain to regard *A Week in Review* as intellectually
decrepit, pretentious: lightweight but deadweight. His notion that
getting invited to take part constituted an insult would be strength-
ened. Of course, he meant to accept the invitation if it came and
knew he did. His fury arose from the tumult inside him: contempt
for the show, and frenzied determination to get on to it. Esther
would never accuse Gerald of being uncomplex or rational. He could

hold one position and its opposite at the same time. Gerald gloried in the contrariness of this, thought it proved freedom of spirit, but also knew it was mad; and the two-way tug caused his twitchy, idiotic anger. Above all, Esther hated to see froth-spit on one of his already loathsome bow ties. She thought she'd go home just in time for the programme, so she wouldn't have to witness Gerald working himself up into a pathetic, all-round passion ready for it. He'd expect her to be with him for the actual show, and she did occasionally feel obligations to Gerald. If you'd often nearly felled someone with old one-two punches, and been eye-gouged and nearly felled yourself, it set up quite a little helpmeet bond, a sort of mutuality.

(6) I hear that about half of British wholesalers live on their main trading ground, rather than in bigger, more lavish, and therefore more conspicuous, properties elsewhere. Pellotte, Verity and now Amesbury fall into this category. (Dubious? Can't see how any of these slumming tipplers could know this.)

(7) Management structure of Temperate firm:
 (a) Chairman: Amesbury
 (b) Joint deputies: Jake Ilton Underhill Camby
  Piers Watmough (known as Tame)
 (c) Head of buying: Wilma Renee Charteris
 (d) Personnel director: Joel Jeremy North
 (e) Collector: Vernon Rice-Laidlaw (known as E.R. – Equity Release)
 (f) Legal liaison: Maud Lucy Field
 (g) Security: Philip Gain

(Argument among group about North and Gain. Several say Gain is Personnel, North Security, not vice versa. NB again, CHECK INDEPENDENTLY. Unwise to persist with queries to group. Liquored, these people semi-shout their views, regardless of bar staff and other customers – possible jungle drums to Amesbury etc.)

Definitions as given to me:
 (a) Chairman: Overall control, biggest earner.
 (b) Joint deputies: Split duties: Camby, street and rave trade, Watmough high quality clientele. Amicable arrangement???
 (c) Head of buying: bulk deals with importers. Much travel.

(d) Personnel director: recruitment, discipline.

(e) Collector: responsible for company income from pushers.

(f) Legal liaison: organizes defence lawyers and general support when staff charged with supplying and/or violence.

(g) Security: armourer and press relations. Protection of firm's leadership and maintenance of battle readiness in case of Whitsun or other attack. Suppression of inconvenient publicity.

(8) Management structure of Happy Gardening Solutions, Whitsun firm:

(a) Chairman: Adrian Pellotte

(b) Multi-role assistant: Dean Feston

(c) Live on Whitsun in adjoining houses 21, 22 and 23 Hawthorn close. Pellotte has had 21 and 22 knocked into one.

(d) Tone of firm unflamboyant and super-muted. No further information available.

Sat

Tribe – a Temperate club. Disco. Queue at eleven p.m., about twenty minutes. Bouncers: dark suits, white shirts, silver ties, earpieces. No bother getting in. Converted furniture depository? Burgundy walls, false ceiling, stainless-steel bar, biggish dance space, low lighting. Music by Say Again, Stones, Aptitude, Causeway's Cause and others I can't pick. Took a while to spot dealers. Jacketed. Pockets. Undrinking. Invitational. They hang back to be approached. Obviously, many people are regulars and know them. I make it four. And an overseer? Gets to the four in turn, dumpy, jeans, dark hair rubber banded behind, training shoes, maroon shirt, crimson jacket overlong, pockets. Restocks pushers? Done discreetly. A slob but dexterous and a lovely mover. I see no packets. Harvests their deal money? Done discreetly. I see no notes. Might be Vernon Rice Laidlaw – E.R., the firm Collector, or possibly Jake Ilton Underhill Camby, deputy chairman who does discos.

I ask a girl, three-quarters cut and/or high: 'Is that Camby?' Then conversation (undisclosed recorder) – NB might be useful to (a) lighten article and (b) indicate condition of typical clientele:

'Is it what?' she says.

'Camby?'

'Is what Camby?'

'Him.'

'Which?'

'Roll-top maroon shirt.'

'Who's Camby?'

'You know – *Camby.*'

'What's he look like?'

'Roll-top maroon shirt. Ponytail.'

'I don't mind ponytails. Some hate them. My friend Delia says ponytails make her sick, just the sight, except on ponies.'

'Or he could be Laidlaw. Also called E.R.'

'You'll do my head in, all the names. E.R.? Like on TV as used to be? I'm with someone. He's in the toilet.'

'Might he know?'

'What?'

'Camby. Or E.R.'

'He won't like it.'

'What?'

'Talking – you with the names and things, such as "maroon shirt".'

'It's only names.'

'I don't believe in bunking off with someone else while a boyfriend's in the toilet for whatever reason. I've only been out with him once before, though. He's crude as snot.'

'No, I'm not asking you to do a flit.'

'So why fucking not? What's wrong with me?'

'I'm interested in these names.'

'Fuck the names. All men. You gay? You want to lift his roll-top maroon shirt?'

Enough.

Sun

Went to the ten a.m. morning service at St John's on Temperate for background/atmos. Pretty, quite big, Norman church, probably from the days when Temperate Acres was temperate acres and a country village. Roofing lead looks intact. Crowded. People in their best gear. Lots of families. Youngish sidesman sees me looking for a seat and comes forward helpfully. Dark, good suit, darkish tie, black lace-ups, head slightly bowed in general reverence but face visible and radiant with Sunday Christian joy, neat, multi-spike, fair hair, unobtrusive ears.

'Come,' he invites warmly. As we walk up the long aisle to where he knows of spaces, he says gently, inaudible except to him and me (no recorder) something along the lines of: 'We guessed you'd turn up for a gawp here, you fucking fuck.' ('Gawp' definitely the term and 'fucking fuck' also verbatim.)

'Who did?'

'We did. We think you ought to fuck off out of it now, love.'

'Who do?'

'Us.'

'But which?'

'There's only one us.'

'You Philip Gain of the Temperate firm? Or Joel Jeremy North?'

'I don't want my name put about, especially not in church.' He steepled his hands before his chest for a moment to empha- size the undoubted church qualities of churches, evident inside a church.

'Sorry.'

'A board decision.'

I ask along the lines of: 'Fuck off out of what?'

'The whole fucking shebang. Nosing at the Tribe. Trawling with the pub crawl mob at the Dragon. And so on. They're harmless, but are you? What is it the Psalm says?'

I reply: '"Behold, these are the ungodly, who prosper in the world; they increase in riches. Their eyes stand out with fatness. They have more than heart could wish."' (Think that's right – sticks from school Relig. Educ. BUT CHECK.)

He replies: '"Let the lying lips be put to silence." That means you, arsehole, and what you're going to write in the paper. *Were* going to write in the paper. "Let the lying lips be put to silence; which speak grievous things proudly and contemptu- ously." Here, sir.' With a big, gracious wave of the arm he indicates a free seat.

'Thank you.'

'You're very welcome, if you can believe that.'

'*I* think fat eyes suit you.'

Lady vicar. Good sermonette. Title: God's graffiti. Summary:

generally graffiti a pain, but God used it to warn Belshazzar with those words on the palace wall during a feast. 'Mene. Mene. Tekel. Upharsin' – meaning 'You have been weighed in the balance and found wanting.' Daniel interpreted it for the king and was promoted to Number Three. But, that night, Belshazzar, king of the Chaldeans, got killed, his kingdom taken by the enemy. God will always look after those on his side, like Daniel, who came out fine from the den of lions later. But the writing is on the wall for those who defy God. We should all 'dare to be a Daniel'. These were the words of the last hymn of the service: 'Dare to be a Daniel, dare to stand alone.'

Vicar goes to door during this to be ready to shake hands with those leaving and say a word or two. As we heartily clasp, and I mutter thanks for her pulpitting, she sculpts a true smile and I get from her in a wonderfully considerate, pastorly tone: 'They don't like outsiders poking about, you know – a kind of impiety. Ever thought of golf reporting instead?'

'Dangerous.' I'm walking to the car. The sidesman catches up, passes me. He says: 'Mene. Mene. Tekel. Upharsin. Ufucker.'

I say: 'By golly, you've got the gift of tongues. Pity about the rest of you, though.'

Sun – later
Possible tail? Old, small, navy, nearly unnoticeable Volvo behind me often, and perhaps oftener than I realize. Never too close, but always close enough. Also in the street near the flat. Not the probable Dean Feston figure from Happy Gardening Solutions. A woman, late twenties maybe, fair/blonde, looks tall behind the wheel. Sits very straight, as if on a horse. Wrap-around sunglasses. But perhaps she did follow from Happy Gardening Solutions. I've an impression now that such a Volvo appeared in the mirror on my way home then. Hindsight imagination? Reg. E117WP. Have to talk to her. She's another point of contact. This could be important stuff.

Over the past couple of days, Esther had read Tasker's notes five or six times, but whenever she reached this point in them – the decision to go and confront Volvo woman – she felt startled by the bland stupidity of it, wanted to groan. In fact, the first time she read it, she *did* gulp and groan in disbelief. Oh God, this ludicrous impulse in reporters to unearth, to discover. They behaved as if they had (1) a licence and,

above all, (2) a duty, to go barging into any closed, perilous area that
interested them and ask their manic questions. 'This could be important stuff.' The cheerful idiocy of it! It could also be lethal stuff. Perhaps
it *had* been lethal stuff. The registration was held by Happy Gardening
Solutions. Did the fact that Volvo woman *was* a woman make him
discount the dangers? Did Dean Feston anticipate Tasker would discount
the danger if Feston sent a woman?

I exit the flat by the back lane and nip around to the street.
She's parked against the traffic flow, driver's side to the pave-
ment. I'm approaching from behind the car and tap the closed
window. She opens. Tries to look unsurprised. Isn't. She gets a
smile going, but it takes a while. Cared-for teeth. Squarish face,
small nose, pout mouth, eyes not assessable behind the shades.
Is a looker, though, no question.
I say: 'Can I help you in any way?'
'Not that I know of.'
'Why are you here?'
'Why are you asking why I am here?'
'Why *are* you here?'
'Is it your concern?' The smile gets into place here, takes the
edge off her answer.
'Is it?'
'Hardly,' she said.
'You're waiting, are you?'
'Well, I do seem to be waiting.'
'What for?'
'Yes, as you can see, I'm waiting.'
'Who sent you? You've been behind me.'
'I've been *what*?'
'Tailing. What's it about? You're Pellotte's?'
'I'm what?'
'Pellotte's.'
She started the engine. 'Goodbye.'
'I thought you were waiting.'
'I've waited.' She saw a gap and moved out across the oncoming
traffic and joined the line of cars going the other way.
Yes, about twenty-eight, estuarial accent, denim waistcoat over
beige striped shirt/blouse, jeans. No jewellery.
Not much of use, except proof she can brickwall. And force
her way into a traffic lane.

Not much of use to Tasker, Esther thought. Perhaps to others though. She decided she'd better get home now and share *A Week in Review* with Gerald. She could look at the interrogation transcripts tomorrow – re-look.

Six

Oh, but wasn't this something? Alone in the hospitality room now, Sacheverell Biggs gloried. He watched *A Week in Review* on the big monitor and felt like a kingmaker. Or, actually, queenmaker. Either way, not just a waiter. More than catering. Look, yes, look at the Sandine woman! He, Sacheverell, had fixed her up with the astonishing, vivid sparkle she gave the programme, and the inspiring confidence, wit and energy. He and the Glenlivet. And especially the almost disallowed *bonus* Glenlivet. The *crux* Glenlivet.

In addition to the sparkle, confidence, wit and energy, note the sex. Oh, yes! Like a sweetly flung lariat noose, it dropped irresistibly and extremely unresisted on Rupe. Sacheverell wouldn't claim to have started all that up from nothing with the whisky. He'd admit she seemed this way as soon as she arrived in Hospitality. And after a while, it had turned very precisely towards Rupe Bale. Perhaps she was permanently this way. Perhaps she'd always find a Rupe Bale. But, now, her on-screen display made the hospitality suite behaviour seem half cock, so to speak. And Sachev felt entitled to think the drinks helped her campaign, made her bolder – *even* bolder. Oh, yes.

For a second, while savouring this marvellous, blatant screen steaminess, Sachev did suffer a moment of worry on Rupe's account. If he already had a love life, somebody watching this show might now be feeling foam-at-the-mouth jealous and very, very fucking vengeful. Hadn't Sachev heard a kitchen whisper that Bale was seriously romancing the daughter of a big crook on the Whitsun estate? No, not *a* big crook, but Adrian Pellotte himself, known of everywhere, far beyond Whitsun? The biggest. God, dicey. However, Rupert, a gifted, surviving star of TV and radio, must have enough sense to know the risks around this kind of Sandine situation, mustn't he? Mustn't he?

At home, Gerald, in front of the screen, said: 'Look at Bale. This is courage, Est.'

'In which respect?'

'I mentioned him to you. He's discussed by people in my group – knocking off Pellotte's daughter.'

'You were afraid the stress would upset his chairmanship.'

'He has triumphed over such stress. This is what I mean by courage.'

'Courageous to have a relationship with Pellotte's daughter?'

'Courageous to behave the way he is behaving with this other piece. He will follow his instincts, dauntless, unconstrained. He is the true artist. As you'd expect, I know, I wish to be associated with someone of such strong selfhood and integrity. I'll be honoured to join this programme.'

The panel were discussing a play, *On the Frontier.*

'This woman might not be included next time,' Esther said.

'It's not to do with the woman.'

'No?'

'It's to do with him – with robustness of his spirit, the elegance of his spirit.'

'Perhaps it will get up Pellotte's nose.'

'Of course it will get up Pellotte's nose. It is the function of the artist to get up people's noses when necessary.'

'Bale might be punished.'

'Of course he might be punished. It is the role of the artist to suffer for his beliefs and impulses.'

Once they'd all gone off to the studio, Sacheverell always gave the hospitality suite a quick clear-up for when they returned, and then settled down before the screen in an armchair, with a coffee from the machine. Although the programme lasted only forty minutes, they had to do voice levels and so on before the actual broadcast began, and remained away for an hour and a half. Generally, Sacheverell would watch soccer or cookery until *A Week in Review's* start time, switch to that for, say, ten minutes, then go back to soccer or cookery. Or anything but *A.W.I.R.*

The point was, these panellists, and Rupe Bale, and Larry Edgehill and Tom Marland, sincerely, even fervently, thought their programme mattered, and Sacheverell considered he should give it a bit of a glimpse, out of . . . well, politeness. He aimed to have a small but sincere, admiring smile of congratulations in place when the team reappeared after the broadcast in Hospitality for their second stage bevies and reciprocal smarming, and he believed it would be disgustingly false if, in fact, he had seen no fragment of the show. Of course, nobody among this crew present tonight would ask him what he thought of the programme. In their eyes, he was still and only the bottles bloke. They did not go along with Priscilla Sandine's splendid, demented theory on the importance of waiters.

Invariably, he switched back to *A.W.I.R.* from one of the other channels a couple of minutes pre end. If there had been any serious mishap during the forty minutes, such as someone throwing up or dying from a heart attack, he reckoned he would be able to sense it from the final sequence, no matter how cleverly Tom Marland might manage the cameras to avoid anything unsightly. Suppose Biggs were ignorant of the catastrophe because he'd watched a different channel, it would be an unforgivable error to greet them on return with his standard smile of congratulation for their studio brilliance. They'd realize he'd missed not just the vomiting or death but the whole show. This could be damn hurtful.

In any case, tonight, once he saw how Priscilla Sandine immediately steam-heated the programme, he did not *want* to move on. She was as good as soccer, better than TV cookery. And, the truly marvellous thing – she made Rupert, in the chair, seem great and fully human, also. It mattered. Sach knew that one or two press critics had given him a mighty pounding lately. Sacheverell resented this. Surely, it should be recognized that Rupe kept the studio verbiage flowing pretty well, and managed to look fascinated by what panellists said, although mostly frog spawn.

They had been to see the West End revival of a play that originally came out just before the Second World War, *On the Frontier*, and Sach wondered whether Rupe and Priscilla had sat together in the stalls and possibly established a special closeness. This might explain the screen zing now, flesh-to-flesh intensity, like Taylor and Burton in *Cleopatra*.

Sach thought Rupe Bale's job was to be the connection for this culture show with ordinary folk. Larry Edgehill, and those above him in N.D.L.tv, hoped a scattering of average viewers glimpsed the programme for long enough to note Rupe, and decide that, if *he* ran the thing, it couldn't be above *any* fucker's head. But Sacheverell knew that, despite this good gift, Rupe generally displayed what Sach called no fizz, a catering term for dud champagne.

Now, Sandine magnificently altered this. And, tonight, Sach stayed with *A Week in Review.* Horny: they both came over horny – dangerously horny for Rupe. Suddenly, he sounded strong, cheerful, in command. Aroused? Sacheverell decided Rupe *must* have been banging her already, or must be about to, after the show, if the pair could wait. Yes, 'dangerous' was the word.

Gerald said: 'A chairman like Bale would entice the absolute best from me. I am someone who needs a foil, a Boswell. Bale could be it. I'm going to get in touch with Edgehill, the producer, and say I'm available.'

'Are you sure Bale's brilliance tonight isn't entirely thanks to Sandine?'

'Bale would sense immediately what I, uniquely, can offer the programme, and he would have the skill to draw it forth. I don't wish to sound arrogant, Esther. I don't say I can bring *everything* required for such a show, but I can bring *something,* and that something, is special to me, is unmistakably Gerald Davidson.'

Another ritual on these nights when *A Week in Review* went on air was that Flo Tait, N.D.L.tv's Head of Programmes and a main board member, rang at the end of the show from home, or wherever she might be, to give Larry Edgehill her verdict. For democratic reasons, Flo liked to be called Flo, never Florence, never Mrs Tait. N.D.L.tv went in for first names. After the programme, she would come through on the wall phone just behind Sacheverell's bottle table, and he often took the call first. She was suspicious of mobiles.

Although people in the hospitality parties never asked Sacheverell what he thought of the programme, Flo sometimes would – sort of *vox pop* him. More democracy. And a management ploy. Tonight, the phone went off while the show's final credits had only just started rolling, and nobody from the studio was yet back at hospitality. He left his chair and answered.

'That you, Sacheverell?'

'Hi, Flo.'

'Did you see it?'

'*Did* I?'

'Fantastic?'

'No other word,' Sacheverell said.

'Well, yes, *one* other.'

'Which?'

'Voracious.'

'Oh.'

'For each other. Those two! Rupert, Sandine – the making of the show.'

'I wouldn't argue.'

'They gleamed on-screen. Near-porn. And yet depth, too. Terrific on Vagrain's novel, *The Insignia of Postponement*. Jointly terrific.'

'Right.'

'Pinpointing the shifting symbolism of the old-fashioned diving suit and the lead boots,' she said. 'Captivating and thrilling viewers. People will long to read the book.'

'Well, yes.'

'Ever seen anything like it – short of Taylor and Burton?'

'I thought the same, Flo.'

'Rapport.'

'That exactly, Flo.'

'I suppose Rupe's shagging it?'

'This is something I—'

'If not yet, soon. Like tonight.'

'Here's Larry now,' Sacheverell replied. 'I must get around with the drinks, Flo. After a session like that they'll be so dry.' He handed Larry the phone. The rest of the studio contingent filled the room. Sach gave them a richer smile than usual. Most people headed for the bar-table. At this stage, Sacheverell stayed behind it to serve. He'd move around with top-ups later. He could hear Larry's part of the conversation.

'Yes, I thought it went quite nicely, Flo . . . Thanks . . . Well, thanks. I'll tell them . . . Just somehow they seemed to hit it off . . . An affinity . . . Yes, . . . Yes, powerful, tangible . . . Sorry, Flo, I missed that. Is he . . .? Oh, I get you. I wouldn't know . . . But it's not really something I can ask either of them, is it? . . . Like in *Cleopatra*, you mean? . . . Oh, a lot of noise here. People all around now. It's awkward . . . Well, *he's* on a contract, of course. Probably six months. *She* – this was a one-off for her. A trial, really . . . Oh, I agree . . . A natural . . . Sorry . . . Did I hear that right? A totally new series for just the two of them? *Did* I hear that right? . . . You propose it? . . . Rex Ince and Selina will be cross. They've been nagging me to do something like that for *them* . . . I agree, Rupert and Sandine are probably better . . . It's the din here – I didn't get that . . . Drink? Oh, she had just a couple of looseners . . . Glenlivet, I think . . . Sach and I try to keep it to exactly the right level . . . An art . . . If it's too much, panellists are liable to start talking out of their backsides . . . What was that? . . . Oh, *in vino veritarsehole*. Right. Well, yes, they'd have met at the gallery and the theatre for *On the Frontier* . . . Possibly . . . No, I don't remember who sat with whom at the theatre.

Yes, they might have, I suppose, if only to relieve the dreariness of the play . . . Sort of cinema back-row, you mean? . . . Tom realized at once how watchable they were in the show tonight and gave them plenty of camera . . . I'll tell him, yes. He'll be very pleased.'

And Edgehill knew it to be all true, this magical metamorphosis of Rupert. Sandine did what she half promised Larry she would do. She'd ditched *The Godfather*, switched to Rupe and his blood, and so on. A bellyful of booze made her zoom, not nosedive. Grand! Edgehill had watched her performance, half thrilled, half appalled, thinking of Adrian and Dean. Pellotte's daughter wouldn't have enjoyed it either. She'd watch because her man appeared. *Her* man? Her man and who else's? And Flo wanted the two of them, Ralph and Sandine, to put on reruns of this crotch concurrence in a series! Hell, marvellous!

Larry saw Sachev Biggs was gazing at him, probably trying to read his reactions to Flo's call. He gave Sachev a thumbs up. He didn't deserve any blame. Or not too much, anyway. He was only a waiter, the bottles bloke. He hadn't intended hanging a notice around Rupe's neck, and possibly Sandine's, saying 'Dump me dead in a playground'. Possibly around Larry's, too.

Sachev offered Edgehill a small, solemn nod in acknowledgement. Teamwork.

'This has been a seminal experience for me,' Gerald said.

'I hope Sandine and Bale dodge that.'

Seven

There were no more notes from Tasker's laptop and the next day Esther turned to the transcripts of the Dean Feston and Gabrielle Barter Cornish interrogations, done separately, of course. Feston had been questioned by Detective Sergeant Abner Cule, one of Esther's best interviewers. He would have seen the Tasker laptop recovered notes. Esther skipped some preliminaries. Then:

Cule: 'Did you know the deceased, Gervaise Manciple Tasker?'
Feston: 'Not really *know*. Had met, as I realized later.'
Cule: 'Later being?'
Feston: 'After his death.'
Cule: 'How did you meet him?'
Feston: 'He visited Happy Gardening Solutions at Lesser Davit.'
Cule: 'You were present at Happy Gardening Solutions and saw him there?'
Feston: 'My place of work.'
Cule: 'Many people must visit Happy Gardening Solutions.'
Feston: 'Many, indeed, seeking solutions to their gardening problems, which is why the firm is called what it is, obviously.'
Cule: 'But you remember Gervaise Manciple Tasker?'
Feston: 'Of course, I didn't know at the time his name was Gervaise Manciple Tasker.'
Cule: 'How did you discover that?'
Feston: 'The media.'
Cule: 'In what sense?'
Feston: 'I read in the papers and saw on TV News that a man had been found dead. There were pictures of him taken before this terrible event – the children's playground, all of it.'
Cule: 'And you recognized him?'
Feston: 'Right.'
Cule: 'That would seem to indicate he'd made quite an

impression on you – given that you would see great
numbers of customers there.'

Feston: 'I've a memory for faces. Oh, yes. It's quite an asset
because people met at a certain part of our time here
below may float back in later, and it helps if we can
place them, as it were. You will, I'm sure, have read
the novels of Anthony Powell – spelt P O W E L L
but pronounced *Pole* – where characters drift in and
out of one another's lives over twelve volumes. Think
of his one-time girlfriend, Jean Templer, turning up
all those years later married to a South American
colonel. That's why I'm so interested in his books –
called *A Dance to the Music of Time*. Mr Pellotte too,
of course.'

Cule: 'Gervaise Manciple Tasker won't be dancing back into
your life.'

Feston: 'There will be losses, gaps.'

Esther had watched some of the interview via the one-way glass.
Feston looked at ease, as Esther would have expected. He'd been
through a lot of interrogations before. He knew what signs Cule
would be alert for, as symptoms of lying and guilt. Feston didn't
give any, not in what he said, nor in body language. The manuals
taught that guilty liars were inclined to answer the interviewer's
questions in brief, terse terms and offer no additional comment.
That is, if they answered at all. Feston's reveries about the writer –
Powell, Pole? Who he? – such wanderings would be regarded by
some interrogation experts as evidence of untroubled innocence. So
would other reactions. For instance, Esther saw no hesitations in
Feston's replies. In fact, he seemed to be enjoying the chance of a
chinwag. His voice sounded comfortable and assured, his grammar
stayed OK, and his breathing. All sorts of research had been done
on breathing as an indicator of truth/falsehood.

Cule: 'Even though you have this exceptional memory for
faces, was Tasker's visit special in some way, so that
you recalled it on seeing his pictures?'

Feston: 'Mr Adrian Pellotte, chairman of Happy Gardening
Solutions, is very keen to build a good, warm, personal
contact with customers. Above all, personal. Staff,
including myself, willingly follow that practice. In this

day and age when so much buying and selling is done remotely – by phone, for instance – the personal aspect in our kind of business becomes even more important. There is a kind of brotherhood formed by a shared interest in things of the soil.'

Cule: 'Soul?'

Feston: 'Soil. But soul as well.'

Cule: 'What is your role at Happy Gardening Solutions?'

Feston: 'I am Mr Pellotte's driver.'

Cule: 'But do you also have a role specific to Happy Gardening Solutions?'

Feston: 'I try to busy myself, when we're not in the car.'

Cule: 'In what ways?'

Feston: 'General. As it comes. I like to think of myself as an all-rounder, in the best sense of that term.'

Cule: 'Which is the best?'

Feston: 'Not a dilettante, knowing tiny bits about a lot. Able to turn my hand to many a task.'

Cule: 'What drew your notice to Gervaise Manciple Tasker?'

Feston: 'He seemed to be wandering about, a little lost.'

Cule: 'You asked him what he was interested in, did you?'

Feston: 'I think he wanted to look at sheds. He seemed to have an inclination towards sheds. People do get inclinations. It might be sheds, it might be flagstones, or bird baths.'

Cule: 'And, given his inclination, did you take him to see the sheds? Which kind of shed did he seem inclined towards – for instance, a gazebo-type shed, or just a shed for keeping garden tools in?'

Feston: 'There is, indeed, a wide choice of sheds, varying very considerably in price, as you'd expect. Some people inclined towards sheds are subconsciously looking for a bolt-hole, a private nest, a den, four walls and a roof, though in miniature when viewed against more substantial property.'

Cule: 'Did he buy a shed?'

Feston: 'No, not that day.'

Cule: 'Did he come back and buy a shed another day?'

Feston: 'I don't know. I didn't see him again.'

Cule: 'Did he buy anything at all on the day you did see him?'

Feston: 'Not while I was with him.'

Cule: 'Did that seem odd to you?'
Feston: 'In which way?'
Cule: 'Did it make you wonder why he was there at all?'
Feston: 'People do come to sightsee. It's a spot that frees them
          for a time from their urban surroundings, yet reason-
          ably accessible to London. They can follow those
          inclinations I mentioned, in a relaxed style. Mr Pellotte
          is happy to provide the ground for that.'

Cule liked to operate in a room with no table between him and
the suspect. He believed a table not only imposed distance, but acted
as a kind of protective barrier for the subject, a rampart. Also, with
no table to hide the lower body any uncontrolled, spasmodic movement there would be on show. Some interviewees could regulate
their facial expressions well enough and keep their features deadpan
or relaxed or even jolly. They concentrated on this, because they
believed the interviewer would watch the face for giveaway symptoms of confusion or fright or concealment. Their anxieties might
register in their feet and legs, though. And in their bladder and/or
bowels, of course: this would be evident whether the room had a
table or not. But Feston stayed composed throughout his entire body.
He didn't smile non-stop, like a frozen, taunting, defensive pose, but
when he did smile it was a happy testament to mateyness and
contentment. Esther had the idea he knew there would be an invis-
ible audience behind the window, and he behaved as though he
wanted to convey that mateyness and share that contentment not
just with Cule but with her and anyone else taking a peep. You'd
think Feston was the host and all the rest guests to be considerately
cared for and entertained. No wonder he'd risen to be chief bottle
washer and top dogsbody in the Pellotte outfit.

Cule: 'You talked to him for some while, did you?'
Feston: 'I wanted to find what he was focused on.'
Cule: 'As to happy solutions for his garden?'
Feston: 'Exactly. This seemed very much in line with Mr
          Pellotte's ideas about the personal.'
Cule: 'Do you have a security function with Pellotte's firm?'
Feston: '"Security" in what sense?'
Cule: 'In the sense that this non-purchasing visitor might
          be some kind of spy.'
Feston: '"Spy"?'

Cule:	'On reconnaissance.'
Feston:	'What would there be to spy on at Happy Gardening Solutions?'
Cule:	'You talked. What about?'
Feston:	'I've said, I tried to get him focused.'
Cule:	'On sheds?'
Feston:	'On whatever.'
Cule:	'Did someone call you down because they thought this customer might not *be* a customer, but someone loitering, casing the place?'
Feston:	'Call me down from where?'
Cule:	'From the firm's headquarters upstairs.'
Feston:	'I try to get around the grounds quite a bit, to see things are OK, and offer that personal contact when needed. Although Mr Pellotte is keen on this, he hasn't always got time to see to it himself. I'm glad to circulate on his behalf.'
Cule:	'The offices are above a showroom, aren't they? He'd been looking at big mowers in there. But not buying.'
Feston:	'With those big mowers, people often come in two or three times, or even more. They are expensive.'
Cule:	'Would the people who called you down suspect he was using an apparent interest in the mowers to cover his real interest – the way up to the firm's offices on the first floor, and how that entrance was guarded? Perhaps with the intention of describing these arrangements somewhere, and raising queries about why such exceptional vigilance was needed?'
Feston:	'Oh, you'd be surprised how many people see themselves as like a tank commander when sitting on one of the biggest mowers! Brmmm, brmmm! They're thrilled. Amusing in its way. That doesn't mean they'll rush to buy, though. Their lawn must be extensive enough to justify it.'
Cule:	'The people who called you down would probably wonder, wouldn't they, whether this was some journalist, ferreting about for a story about your firm. Or someone from Temperate preparing plans of your headquarters. Either way, they're going to be worried and they'll call security. That's you, isn't it?'
Feston:	'Unless you've got a manor house and acres, one of

> the big mowers is an extravagance, a bit of conspic-
> uous consumption – boasting, in fact.'

Cule: 'You had him marked as a reporter, I expect. You'd know the shed and/or big mower didn't really matter.'

Feston: 'We get all sorts there. That's the thing about gardening – it's classless.'

Cule: 'You say you didn't know his identity at this stage. Did you try to get it, and, say, an address?'

Fenton: 'We discussed many a topic, I can assure you.'

Cule: 'Did you get a name and address finally?'

Fenton: 'Happy Gardening Solutions would like to maintain a link with our customers, by brochures delivered to the house. That kind of practice. It's part of the personal approach established by Mr Pellotte which I believe I spoke about just now. But there would be no forcing of ourselves on people. It can be counterproductive. Think of the hostility to timeshare projects because of hard-sell methods.'

Cule: 'I was talked into timeshare by some persistent woman in the Seychelles. One of my biggest errors ever, believe me.'

Esther didn't. A lie. Watching, she felt sure of that. Esther knew it to be the kind of trick tactic most interrogators used, though not one recommended in any manual. There could be no official endorsement of deception. Of course, Dean Feston might recognize a tactic, anyway. He had all that experience. Cule would risk it, just the same, because so far the interview had produced next to nothing.

Feston: 'Oh'.

And Esther saw his right leg quiver for a second. Not more than quiver – much less than a twitch. But Cule, also, would see it. He had crafted it. The purpose of such a lie broke into seven easily defined parts:

(1) For the moment it reversed power arrangements in the room. The interviewer, until now controlling from the catbird seat, suddenly looked weak, and possibly weaker than the interviewee. Feston had said without saying it that he would never get taken in by a timeshare sales woman.

(2) This apparent weakness might please the interviewee. 'I've

knocked the bugger off his perch.' The leg tremor signalled joy at a little victory, and perhaps more to come.

(3) The interviewee might think he should consolidate his one-upness by sympathizing with the interviewer, offering condolences and condescension.

Feston: 'I'm sorry. But that's what I mean, isn't it? These people are trained to break down even the strongest, most clued-up buyer?'

(4) The interviewee relaxes more, gets smug. 'This cop's not just human, he's dim.'

(5) The interviewer notes the fall into self-confidence – shocks him, hits him hard with the real, businesslike questions.

(6) He's confused by the latest change.

(7) His answers become less controlled, even careless.

Cule: 'I'm interested in a Pellotte staffer called Gabrielle Barter Cornish.'

Feston: 'Ah, Gabrielle.'

Cule: 'We have someone else talking to her.'

Feston: 'A valued employee of Happy Gardening Solutions.'

Cule: 'What duties?'

Feston: 'General. But mainly on the customer relations side.'

Cule: 'Meaning?'

Feston: 'That essentially personal approach favoured by Mr Pellotte.'

Cule: 'Would it involve tailing someone?'

Feston: 'Tailing?'

Cule: 'You like full background data on people, don't you? Famous for it.'

Feston: 'This can be helpful in our dealings with customers. We like to record what interests them, so they are informed of new products they might wish to avail themselves of.'

Cule: 'Did you put Gabrielle Barter Cornish on to Tasker to find where he lived and chart his movements?'

Feston: '"Put on"? In which sense?'

Cule: 'A company car, bumper-to-bumpering.'

Feston: 'Gabrielle might have sought some information on him for her own purposes.'

Cule: 'Which?'

Feston: 'Which what?'

Cule: 'Purposes.'

Feston: 'The customer relations area that I've spoken of. Mr Pellotte encourages staff to follow their own initiatives.'

Cule: 'Something about him and your conversation at Happy Gardening Solutions disturbed you, yes?'

Feston: 'Why would I get "disturbed" by a visitor to Happy Gardening Solutions? A chat of that kind is so normal.'

Cule: 'You asked Gabrielle Barter Cornish to do some checks on him, did you? Mobiled her, so she could be ready to pick him up when he left? Did you tell Adrian Pellotte you felt troubled about this "customer" – Tasker.'

Feston: 'I didn't know his name was Tasker.'

Cule: 'But you wanted to discover it, and anything else you could, or that Gabrielle Barter Cornish could. Would you have authority alone to send her after Tasker? Did Pellotte suggest it, or, perhaps, confirm your decision as security to have him tailed? Do you hold in a data bank somewhere his name, address and daily routines?'

Feston: 'All of the "data" – i.e., ordinary information – all of such "data" I have on him comes from media reports of his death – single, a journalist, as you've suggested – freelance, flat in Chiswick, late twenties.'

Cule: 'We know when he was killed and, of course, where he was found.'

Feston: 'Awful.'

Cule: 'But not *where* he was killed.'

Feston: 'That would be crucial.'

Cule: 'We're told death occurred sometime in the evening of Saturday, September nineteenth. Can you recall how you spent that day? It's not very long ago.'

Feston: 'I would certainly have gone in to Happy Gardening Solutions in the morning. Saturday is a major trading day for us, of course.'

Cule: 'No, take things backwards, from the evening, will you?'

Feston: 'Backwards?'

Cule: Begin with the evening and then go step by step over
          your activities during the afternoon and morning.'

There was a theory around that if a suspect were told to give his/her
account of events in reverse order he/she would be more likely to trip
up. Lying took plenty of effort and care, even when presented as a
straightforward version of things: much more effort and care than telling
the truth. To lie in an anti-sequence way brought big extra strain, and
possible errors. University researchers somewhere claimed to have
proved the effectiveness of this type of interrogation and had given
it a name – 'cognitive load interviews'. All interrogations involved
applying a load to the interviewee's brain. Back-to-front interrogation
aimed to apply an *over*load.

But, of course, Dean Feston had heard of this ploy, and knew
how to cope. Just as he had known how to cope with Cule's earlier
attempt to throw him by momentarily upending the status positions
and making himself look stupid. That tiny leg jerk might have signalled
a minor triumph, but Feston had never slipped into complacency.
The transcript didn't bother to follow any more questions and
answers, merely summarized Feston's description of his activities on
September 19 which, naturally, said there'd been no contact with
Gervaise Manciple Tasker, nor even a sighting of him. And for a lot
of the time there were references to witnesses who would support
Feston.

The transcript of the interview with Gabrielle Barter Cornish
was similarly useless. Probably under advice, she refused to answer
all questions. Feston would never do that. He enjoyed conversation
too much.

Eight

Dean Feston said: 'The newspaper critics seemed to have liked what some others might regard as an extremely unfortunate development on the latest *A Week in Review* programme, Larry. Massively unfortunate. I call it unfortunate – massively unfortunate – but I can assure you that Adrian in no way feels you, as producer, were to blame. Not entirely at all. He does not see intent there. Hardly any intent to injure him personally.'

'This is a live show and one must expect . . . well, life and all its unpredictabilities,' Pellotte said. He laced his voice with patience, reasonableness, conditional mercy.

'It's what Adrian means by "live and let live" as quoted previously,' Dean said. 'Up to a certain point, live and let live, his mantra. Up to a certain generously arrived at point. He believes that many have an absolute right to life. Yes, many.'

'A pleasant place you have here, Larry,' Pellotte replied.

'It suits me,' Larry Edgehill said. This time, Pellotte and Dean *had* doorstepped him. But they came by taxi, so there should be no neighbourhood speculation about the BMW parked outside 19a. They both wore fine, dark, double-breasted suits, Pellotte's grey, Dean's navy, to show respect for Edgehill and his property, though he knew they would probably have dressed with the same care if here to take him apart.

'Adrian's thinking was that another interception in the street, as occurred in Gideon Road, previously, wouldn't be quite right for a more . . . more *substantive* talk,' Dean said. 'I concurred readily, very readily. We did mention in Gideon the likelihood of something more substantive probably being necessary later, didn't we? Adrian saw the Gideon meeting as valuable and, indeed, timely, but only what the diplomats call "talk about talks", meaning the more substantive get-together would follow.'

'Along those lines, yes,' Pellotte said.

'And then, on top of those, as it were, *general, prevailing* issues covered at that time in Gideon comes this additional, unexpected grossly gaudy lech factor in the latest of your programmes, Larry – your name across the screen in large, proud letters, "Produced by

Larry Edgehill". Adrian felt we needed a more settled environment for such a multifaceted discussion.'

'Yes,' Pellotte said. 'Probably better like this.'

'Yet we still did not want to cause misguided and possibly detrimental comment from neighbours, and so, the cab.'

'A surprise – the visit, I mean,' Edgehill replied.

'I always say that Adrian and discretion are true blood brothers. His first thought always – discretion. Almost always. Plus empathy.'

'Basic,' Pellotte said.

'If that fucking taxi driver starts blabbing around he knows what he'll get,' Dean Feston said.

'What?' Edgehill said.

'Oh, yes,' Dean replied.

'What?' Edgehill said.

'Don't tell me taxi drivers are too stupid to realize how liable they are to garrotting, perched there, imprisoned behind the wheel, looking ahead, a passenger directly behind them,' Dean said. 'This passenger could be carrying a nice little length of cord or chain. All right, there might be a sliding panel behind them, but it's standard, not reinforced, glass, you know.'

'No, I've never asked,' Edgehill said.

'Forgive us for arriving unannounced,' Pellotte said.

'It's fine,' Edgehill said. 'I'll make some tea.'

Pellotte gazed about. 'Just right for someone at the moment on his own,' he said.

'You *were* partnered, weren't you, Larry, your fourth relationship, but a decision to split twenty-nine weeks ago?' Dean said. 'Amy Wright. She's with a snooker hall manager now Preston way – Graham Clatworthy. A 2.1 honours degree in Leisure and Entertainment from somewhere. These new courses! But they do say the classics are making a comeback.'

'A useful spot, this,' Pellotte remarked. 'The shops, the pub and Tube walkable.'

'As we, of course, know,' Dean said, chuckling.

'Our profile shows you don't run a car at present,' Pellotte said. 'Not since the silver Ford, 1995.'

'Not needed, as you say,' Edgehill replied.

'Give Adrian the word if you do get wheels,' Dean said. 'He can help in that respect. Instantly. This is not the kind of thing he'd speak to you directly about. Adrian would hate to sound intrusive and managing. But, yes, we *can* arrange immunity. We put a word around in the vehicle's favour. The reg is fed into our Data Resource Pool and reaches everyone fast. Sometimes cars get damaged on Whitsun, or even stolen.'

'Is that right?' Edgehill replied.

'But not if it's a car people know Adrian is, as it were, interested in personally, although it isn't his. Sort of proxy.'

Edgehill went into the kitchen and made tea. They sat in the living room. Dean had an easy chair, Edgehill and Pellotte on the settee.

Dean said: 'When I refer to a "grossly gaudy lech factor" relating to the programme, I imagine you can make a guess at what it is, Larry, even though unexpected.'

'I have a daughter,' Pellotte said.

'Dione,' Feston said.

'Lovely name,' Edgehill said.

'Why I stressed "personal" in Gideon,' Dean said. 'Anxieties of a father about his daughter or daughters must inevitably be categorized personal. What could be more so? I'm bound to think of King Lear.'

'Well, I have two daughters, but it's Dione I'm concerned about now,' Pellotte said. 'I don't know whether anyone has mentioned Dione to you, Larry.'

'I've heard of her, naturally,' Edgehill said.

'In which respect?' Dean said.

'Or to be more precise, I wondered if Rupert Bale had spoken of her,' Pellotte said.

'In a personal manner,' Dean said.

'On an intimate basis,' Pellotte said.

'Rupert?' Edgehill said. 'No, I don't think so.'

'Leaving aside temporarily that "grossly gaudy lech factor" during the latest programme – the actual, or seeming, lasciviousness right off the Richter scale – I have to explain, we're into a kind of *Romeo and Juliet* situation here,' Dean said, 'though with age adjustments. Or *West Side Story*.'

'Oh?' Edgehill replied. *Take it gently.*

'Love crossing frontiers – not so much family frontiers as local geography,' Dean said.

'A worry,' Pellotte said.

Edgehill said: 'Do I gather your daughter and Rupert are—?'

'Oh, you're considerate, tactful, but I think you've probably heard something of this,' Feston said. 'Rumour. At least one outside bastard sniffing around the situation – or would have, if he'd continued.'

Edgehill said: 'I—'

'This relationship puts Adrian in a predicament, doesn't it, Larry?' Dean said.

'Predicament?' Edgehill replied.

Dean set his cup down, stood up, and did some limited pacing in the fairly small room, as though so agitated by his thoughts now that he needed to work some of them off in physical movement. Probably he had often paced a cell like this, just a few steps possible each way. 'I mean, on account of his status – that's Adrian's – his status on Whitsun, a status by no means easily achieved, and always under . . . under, I won't say subversive, disgusting threat, but always liable to challenge and to dirty schemes by a welter of grasping, envious, swinish dear friends and colleagues, who have to be controlled, kept under, or they'll start planning a takeover, the treacherous, insurgent louts. For instance, to illustrate status, I mentioned Adrian could put an edict out that any vehicle of yours should be properly respected on Whitsun, and respected it would be – paintwork, windscreen, even aerial. "Touch me fucking not." But this power has not arrived like an entitlement, gift-wrapped, unworked for. Divine right doesn't run on Whit. Adrian's position must be guarded and nurtured.'

'You can take care of all that, I imagine,' Edgehill said. 'Par for the course.'

'Rupert's a bit of a star, although it's culture, so he's well known to some in Whitsun – and also known as coming from Temperate,' Dean replied. 'Kilimanjaro Terrace.'

'They met at a concert in Smith Square up town,' Pellotte said.

'Haydn, Mozart,' Dean said. 'That kind of area.'

'Dione's a sucker for both,' Pellotte said. 'She's a mature woman. I don't intervene. In fact I don't mind them. Haydn's got a lot of body. Mozart fussyish, can be. "Filthy Mozart" didn't someone call him? I'd obviously exclude Symphony Twenty-Nine from this judgement, though. He really gets into the majestic with that one.'

'Rupert likes to keep in touch with the arts scene generally,' Edgehill replied. 'Part to do with the job. Width of experience. Concerts would be in his normal itinerary. As chairman, he has to speak from an established cultural background. He's dealing with experts.'

'Adrian certainly doesn't criticize him for that, wherever he may live,' Dean said. 'I expect the programme gets a lot of complimentary tickets to concerts and so on.'

'I gather Bale's divorced,' Pellotte said.

'Yes,' Edgehill said.

'Adrian's not making a moral statement,' Dean said. 'Merely factual. Divorce need carry no stigma these days. It can come to any of us, can't it, self included? And I think of royalty. Some reckon there's a positive ratio between the scale, general bullshit and showmanship of a royal marriage and the speed of its collapse, only the Queen and Philip excluded.'

'My daughter has just ended a long relationship,' Pellotte said. 'She knows her own mind. Very much so.'

'Yet friendly, tolerant and mild,' Dean said. 'Larry, how often do you suppose she's heard that supposed joke, "Dione! How's your saucy daughter?" from people she bumps into around the shops and so on? Dione being the mother of Aphrodite, goddess of love, as everyone knows? *Our* Dione will always smile, though, as if genuinely amused by the crass fuckers. This is a kindly, balanced person – as one might expect of any child of Adrian.'

'A new friendship based on shared musical tastes sounds good for both of them, Dione and Bale, then,' Edgehill said. 'It would give depth.' But naturally he sensed very rough perils. Music had a lot going for it, but also limitations when considered alongside the troublesome realities of Whitsun and Temperate.

'Well, yes it might be good,' Pellotte said. 'I want her happy. If Bale's the one who can do it, Bale it has to be, phoney and gauche though he is. Some of that might wear off eventually.'

'This is a fatherly thing with Adrian,' Dean said. 'Priority.'

'Certainly,' Edgehill replied. 'Understandable.'

'Understandable, indeed, Larry,' Dean said. 'You have no children yourself, according to our researchers, but I can see you sympathize – can see it in your body language – the way you hold your cup.'

'Certainly,' Edgehill said. He glanced down to see how he was holding the cup, but could read nothing unusual. He had it by the handle with thumb and first finger. Did that show a wholesome esteem for family relationships? Dean might have special insights.

He sat down again. He seemed calmer. Perhaps he had considerable stress to deal with, and not just the problem of Dione. A rumour said he and another Pellotte employee were taken in for questioning about the murder of a journalist who had possibly shown too much interest in the firm. The sniffer? But for now at least the pacing had been effective.

'Two people on the rebound from what appear to be unsatisfactory partnerships,' Dean said. 'It's a familiar kind of situation in our day and age. But this doesn't cheapen things in the least. I mean, not a matter of desperately grabbing whichever pair of trousers comes along first. Partly what I was getting at in remarks about divorce and the absence of taint now. We're not back to all those marriage break-up difficulties covered in Charles Dickens' *Hard Times*.'

'The shared musical tastes show real affinities,' Edgehill replied.

'Yet complex, you see that, do you, Larry?' Dean said.

'In what respect?' Edgehill asked.

'Several of my people don't like the idea of a daughter of Adrian Pellotte bound up with someone from Temperate,' Pellotte said. 'The information's around and spreading.'

'Why I refer to *Romeo and Juliet* and *West Side Story*,' Dean said. 'Obstacles.'

'But this is so narrow, Adrian,' Edgehill said. He wished to sound like an ally, ready with some of that empathy Pellotte prized, and so the first name seemed more right, now.

'True, but several of our crew *are* narrow,' Dean said.

'Narrow and dangerous. I have to take due notice of their views,' Pellotte said. 'I must not provoke mutiny.'

'That's an aspect of leadership. Why I said complex. The fact is, Larry, very few of our folk are into the arts on a compulsive basis,' Dean remarked. He leaned forward, obviously wanting to give Edgehill a longish statement. 'To them it wouldn't signify that here you had two emotionally bruised and possibly lonely people luckily brought together by Haydn and Mozart, unquestionably genuine composers. This is outside the range of comprehension for some in the firm. I don't say they've never even fucking *heard* of Haydn and Mozart. They're not zombies. We've got people in Mensa and one who sailed through all tests for the Foreign Office, then decided no, he didn't want to be our man in the Democratic Republic of Congo, thanks. He took a ground-level post with us instead, though he's moved up a few steps now and runs Home Delivery, which probably brings in more than he'd have got as an ambassador.

'But few of our folk would regard that kind of concert, however well played, as excuse for a romance with someone from Temperate. They can street deal all right, and sell at raves like galloping magic. This is their bent, but it's a very specific, limited bent. You're right – narrowness. Talk to some of them about Conrad's *Shadow Line* and they think you mean snorting coke at dusk. They're the same type who'd ask – and ask in quite a stern manner – they'd ask if you, Larry, living on Whitsun, should be using someone from Temperate, such as Bale. And more or less as a fixture. Well, no, they wouldn't ask, because they wouldn't have any doubts. They see this as a kind of . . . well, cool disregard for long-established custom and practice, Larry. And stronger – even disloyalty. That flagrant way your name hugs the screen after a show featuring Bale.'

Edgehill said: 'But, to my knowledge Rupert isn't in any way concerned with . . . well, gardening products or—'

'He *lives* on Temperate. For them, nothing else matters,' Dean said.

Edgehill said: 'We wouldn't employ him if—'

'They don't do subtlety. Maybe nothing else would have mattered for *me* not long ago,' Pellotte said. 'I abhor melodrama, but we're in a war setting, Larry. Temperate's the enemy. Them and us, and nothing seemed too bad for *them* in my view then – "them" being the business hierarchy mainly, yes, but the whole estate, too, for accommodating them, conniving with them. Frankly, I, myself, didn't like you using Bale so persistently. It seemed . . . it seemed unnecessary.'

'Gratuitous. Like giving Adrian the finger. Tactless,' Dean said. 'Arrogant. Adrian can't abide arrogance.'

Pellotte's tone switched, grew less assured. Did Edgehill hear a tremor? 'But now – now, there's Dione, my daughter.'

'Adrian's had to rethink,' Dean said. 'He has the courage to admit it.'

'Inevitable,' Pellotte said.

'He has the *bravery* to rethink,' Dean said. 'What I referred to as complex, you see. Extremely so. The fatherly aspect. Priorities.'

'Some of these people – the people who object – can grow wild, Larry,' Pellotte said. 'They get themselves high and go berserk. They could decide to start a cleansing spree. This is how they see it – cleansing.'

'That word from the Balkans strife,' Dean said.

'But these are only your tribesmen,' Edgehill said. 'They're not going to disrespect you, Adrian, surely.'

'Normally we can manage them,' Pellotte said. 'You're right and they're basic street pushers and contract heavies. But occasionally they become unreasonable, maverick. There are some on head pills they don't always take, and some the head pills don't get through to because the size of dose they need would kill a rhino.'

'This is the sort who'd soup themselves up to the quiff and then

drive to Temperate and blast people on the street just because they
are on the street in Temperate,' Dean said. 'Being there in Temperate
makes them guilty, like Sodom and Gomorrah. Or like that team
who shot up girls on an estate in Nottingham. It's rudimentary, mad
hate. *In*temperate. All right, there can be a case for it, if part of a
strategy. I think of Bomber Harris in the Second World War, hitting
German cities, to break general morale. Ditto here? We don't sympathize with that kind of operation every time, though. Attacks have
to make operational sense.'

'You mean Rupert's threatened by these people running mad?'
Edgehill said.

'Who knows who's threatened?' Pellotte said.

'It's wider,' Dean said. 'For instance, Adrian mentioned about Bale
chairing your show – mentioned how we've always considered that
unfortunate, much as we like the programme itself – Doel's trans-
lation of the Corneille play, *Medea*, so intelligently discussed, and
extremely enlightened commentary on the Martine Quase-Yungle
exhibition, to take recent memorable examples. Maybe we have to
adjust now, because of Dione. But several of these other people in
our firm – they loathe the idea of anyone from Whitsun – *anyone*
– yes, anyone from Whitsun speaking to anyone from Temperate –
anyone – *anyone* from Whitsun – such as you, Larry – anyone speaking
to *anyone* from Temperate through an earpiece microphone, which
I suppose you have to with Bale – you as overall producer. They
consider it foully close. So one-to-one. I've heard people in our firm
describe it as such – "foully close".'

'Marland, the director, would do most of that,' Edgehill said. He
felt almost insane himself, answering this charge, as if it needed
answering; but it *did* need answering because the conversation was
with Pellotte and Dean. RSVP, and quick.

'At crisis moments it would be you as you, you in person, speaking
from the Control Room,' Dean said. 'That's their perception, anyway.
And it's their perception we're talking about now.' Dean had a long,
lean, sorrowful, reputedly much clinked, face, and perhaps the problem
of Pellotte's daughter really took that sorrowfulness a lot further, gave
it a quota of despair. His eyes were bright blue but could do true
sadness, and regret on a nationwide scale. Most likely he'd managed
plenty of education, art appreciation and all-round reading while locked
up, including psychology and the subtleties of body language.

'I can look after Adrian,' Dean said. 'My role. But then there's
Dione and so on.'

'Yes, Dione,' Pellotte said.

'My God,' Edgehill said. 'They'd go for *her*?'

'And possibly you, Larry,' Dean said. 'We're talking about crazed, unlogical, *anti*-logical, implacable elements in our firm. Excellent, winsome lads and girls in ordinary circs, who'd stand by one another and us almost to the end, but they'd see you and Dione alike – both unforgivably mired by Temperate contacts.'

Pellotte gave another small, explanatory wave. 'It's simple, Larry. I want Rupert Bale off that estate and living somewhere else. Anywhere. It doesn't have to be in Whitsun. No. It would be unreasonable to insist on that. Just get him off Temperate. Then the difficulty's gone. For everyone.'

'Location, vital,' Dean said.

'That's all right,' Edgehill said, relieved. 'He's aiming to move to Wandsworth or even St John's Wood. He's sure Wandsworth or St John's Wood will suit and help define the real Rupert Bale. He thinks his image is more Wandsworth or St John's Wood than Temperate Park Acres, especially since his boost with Sandine via *The Insignia Of Postponement* and so on.' He felt an obligation to do what he could to protect Rupe Bale – felt a sort of responsibility for him. This kind of slightly absurd dutifulness towards someone could hit him occasionally, as though he were captain of a ship and had to look after the crew. He tried to escape it. He *wasn't* captain of a ship, and he didn't have a crew. But the urge to shelter somebody in trouble would often come back.

'I know Bale wants to up sticks,' Pellotte said. 'Dione's told me. He's *aiming* for those districts. But can he do it, as the housing market stands? We've run a lot of inquiries around Bale.'

'As you'd expect, Larry, because of Dione,' Feston said. 'This would be like vetting Diana for Prince Charles, although the other way about as to gender. We'd have to background a lad like Bale, given the situation. An ex-wife, children, if any, armament preferences, if any, furniture, dentistry, schooling, his residence – these are matters we must quite legitimately be privy to.'

'Not easy to sell property on Temperate now,' Pellotte said. 'And then he has to stack up a heap as deposit somewhere sweeter. Top London areas cost a real packet. That's the nub of it.'

'For a while Adrian worried Bale might get fired from the programme,' Dean said. 'Meaning he couldn't anywhere near afford a move.'

'Dione won't let me help him, them, with money,' Pellotte said.

He half sobbed and turned his dark-haired, neat head away from Edgehill for a couple of seconds, possibly to hide tears. 'There'd be no difficulty, but she refuses. I have to abide by that. She's adamant.'

'Dione's always been a bit haughty about where the cash comes from,' Dean said. 'It's delicate, embarrassing, but Adrian won't mind my mentioning this. Simply, it's the way some kids are, my own the same when we were all together. In a way it's admirable – shows values. And also idiotic, because, obviously, as children and young grown-ups they've lived in homes paid for by the money, and have been fed, nicely clothed, top of the range training shoes, privately educated, privately medicalized, by the money, gone business class on holidays paid for by the money. They seem able to shut their eyes to that. But then something like this housing matter comes along, and – wham! – they discover fiscal purity all of a fucking sudden.'

'Headstrong,' Pellotte said.

He'd brought his face back around now, composed once more and benefiting to quite an extent from its scarlessness. Edgehill thought that if he were televising an interview with Pellotte, it would be possible to arrange camera shots to make him look unegomaniac, principled and good-natured. Strong cheek bones would often suggest something very like integrity and/or brain power. Photographing soccer managers had taught Larry many humanizing skills.

'Yes, headstrong. This can be a fine quality, indeed, a necessary quality, but also awkward,' Dean said. 'Another word for it is bolshiness.'

'Bale has to keep earning and earning plenty,' Pellotte said.

'He does OK, Adrian,' Edgehill said. 'He has a radio series with the BBC as well as his work for us.'

'But how steady is it all?' Pellotte said. 'Is there security?' He spoke as though his own career among the Ecstasy and crack and coke and H were wonderfully stable and guaranteed.

'Until the other day, Adrian felt concerned about bad reviews Rupert's had recently from some of these eternally snide, know-all telly critics,' Dean said.

'Only one or two,' Edgehill said.

'Unkind. Sharp,' Dean said. 'They come out with entirely in-appropriate phrases. These are phrases they work on and keep in a drawer until they see a chance, and then, wham! Maybe some truth in them, but called for? That's the point, isn't it? Are they called for? Anyway, those kind of onslaughts could have got Rupe dropped. We don't say you, personally, would have sacked him, Larry, but there are people above you – Florence Tait, for instance, Head of Programmes – and, of course, she'd read the critics. She can't have shit poured week after week over work that's ultimately her bag. So she might have spoken a few words to you about Rupe, the words being, "Fucking fire him." And, if sacked, he'd stay on Temperate because he'd be so hard up. Our firm would have been in for dire internal trouble. Likewise, *you* as producer might have had trouble, Larry. Adrian wondered if we should look out some of these critics.'

'Look them out?' Edgehill said.

'Look them out and have a constructive, intelligent chat,' Dean said. 'They're traceable. Home addresses. But we decided it was too late. The damage had been done. Probably in that quiet style he has, Adrian could have persuaded them not to snipe at Rupert ever again, the sods, and even to give him big, well-documented praise in their next articles, but it's the slurs that stick, isn't it, Larry?'

'However, then came this newest *A.W.I.R.*,' Pellotte said.

'This is what we mean by a complex state of things,' Dean said. 'One peril seems to disappear – possible loss of Rupert's job – to be replaced by another just as messy and formidable. Priscilla Sandine. I spoke of a factor. In fact, two factors. And very much related.'

'Priscilla Sandine a peril?' Edgehill replied. *Yes, Priscilla Sandine a horrific peril.*

'I'm referring mainly to *The Insignia of Postponement* item, naturally, but the topics generally in that show,' Dean said.

'Suddenly, a sort of . . . well, a sort of *emergence* of Rupe Bale,' Pellotte said.

'And how!' Dean said. 'Like some bit of larva from under a stone becomes a butterfly.'

'Yes, the critics thought he did quite well,' Edgehill replied.

'Oh, "quite well"!' Dean replied. 'This is what would be regarded as understatement, I suppose! Or litotes, as it's known. But, anyway, now we have a developing situation.'

'Bale – notable on that programme,' Pellotte said. 'I can see why Dione might be attracted, despite his lips and so on.'

'And we pick up fine rumours – not of the possible heave-ho for Rupert, as seemed on the cards for a time. The opposite! A future pairing of him and the pray-fuck-me-do woman, Sandine, in their own show,' Dean said. 'To capitalize.'

'Oh?' Edgehill said.

'Yes, indeed. Now, don't pretend you haven't heard,' Dean said. 'I should think you're working on the proposal.'

'We know you have to be discreet in what you make public at this stage, Larry,' Pellotte said.

'There are many plans about for new programmes. But that's entirely usual,' Edgehill said.

'Certainly,' Pellotte said.

'And one of them – the chief one – is Rupert and Sandine,' Dean said. 'We've done some soundings. Part of our Rupert dossier. As you'd expect, I'm sure, Larry.'

'You can see my pleasure, and yet my anxiety, over this, can't you, Larry?' Pellotte asked.

'The two factors previously mentioned,' Dean explained. 'One, preservation of Rupert's job: we're all for it. Two, the Sandine appetite: we're not.' Dean seemed to think he'd better continue in simple form for Edgehill. 'Adrian wants Rupe to stay in work, perhaps earning more in the new set-up. And this seems likely. All at once, Rupert Bale is seller's market, and will stay seller's market for a while, at least. Rupert has turned icon, has been *turned* icon. He can demand an increase. This would help him get off Temperate. And then one of our problems has gone. Dione and Rupert buy a nice home in, say, Wandsworth or St John's Wood, and none of our work force will feel angry about it henceforward, because he has left Temperate. And so Dione Pellotte is no longer fratting with the enemy, as it was known in, say, France during the Second World War. Women got their heads shaved in 1945 as punishment.'

'Such a move, fine, fine, fine,' Pellotte said, though not with full satisfaction. To Edgehill the words sounded damn provisional. *So* provisional. 'Look, Larry, I might not have to worry any longer about Bale staying in work, but now I do have to worry, on my daughter's behalf, as to what's between him and this Sandine, don't I?' Pellotte said.

'Factors, you see, Larry,' Dean said.

'They're moving on together, very together, Rupert and Sandine,' Pellotte said. 'We've switched from concern for Rupe's job to something else, possibly more difficult and grave. I'm talking of a very disturbing, very body-based, blood-based closeness between those two, Larry. That's what made *The Insignia of Postponement* item above all . . . resonate.'

Right. Oh God, yes, right. The critics said so. Flo Tait said so. Sach said so. Everyone said so. But Edgehill replied at once: 'Oh, suppose there *were* such plans for them and a duo programme did result – suppose, *only* suppose – this would be an entirely professional arrangement, an on-screen relationship, nothing more, not in any way a sexual matter, if that's what bothers you. Many of these man-woman work pairings exist in television – work pairings which are that and that alone, no matter how linked the two may seem.'

'It troubles me. It troubles Dione,' Pellotte said. 'She's had enough distress of that kind. I want her happy.'

Edgehill said: 'I can assure you, Adrian, that—'

'He looked as if he hoped to bang Sandine right away as part of the programme,' Dean said. '"And now, viewers, we come to our next item – me giving one to a panellist in situ." That fantasy is what made the show crackle. This was a book made flesh in front of us, or nearly. Rare.'

'Just flair,' Edgehill said.

Dean said: 'You don't get that kind of heat from the Melvyn Bragg Sunday nighter *South Bank Show*. All right, we see Marilyn Monroe's knickers over an updraught in the programme's opening captions, yes, but playful only.'

'In its childish way, innocent,' Pellotte said.

'You appreciate Adrian's dilemma now, do you, Larry?' Dean said.

'I want you to make sure Rupe gets the new position, the new show,' Pellotte said. 'And I do realize it has to be a pairing with Sandine. To deny this would be stupid. As performers, they depend on each other. But I also want you – you, personally, as a favour, which I'm sure you won't withhold—'

'Adrian's *very* certain of that,' Dean said.

'I want you to make sure it stays from now on like you describe, Larry, just to do with books, and paintings and plays.'

Edgehill said: 'Really, Adrian, that's exactly how—'

Pellotte stretched his left hand forward to reach Edgehill and gave his arm a slight squeeze. It might have been intended to proclaim everlasting friendship and trust. Certainly it might. Or, then again, it . . . 'You and I – we share a Whitsun background, Larry,' Pellotte said.

'Adrian sees that as a kind of brotherliness, with all the privileges and responsibilities it brings,' Dean said.

Edgehill said: 'Yes, but—'

'Adrian is famed as one who recognizes help from a friend, Larry. What he's saying is, all right, *The Insignia of Postponement* talk produced an impact. As long as this was confined for Rupe Bale and the Sandine woman to the discussion on your programme – possibly spreading to other items on the night – OK. It looks as if it will

get him a juicier job. So far so grand. We know sex sells, and this
was an element. However, we don't want the special quality of their
first encounter to get built in to the series, if they jointly run a
show. It should be cultural, intellectual, *not* pube-based – i.e., not a
threat to the Rupert-Dione relationship, a flaunted mockery of the
Rupert-Dione relationship.'

Pellotte nodded.

Dean said: 'Adrian is devoted to his daughters and desires Dione
to be lastingly happy with Rupert Bale in Wandsworth or St John's
Wood, or any equivalently non-Temperate part of London. And we
know – absolutely know – we can rely on you, Larry, to see that a
father's hopes for his dear daughter are not trampled.' Dean's voice
softened, took on a vast, spiritual solemnity. 'Larry, consider: might
there one day be children for Dione and Bale, a dearly cherished
family? Adrian, in his position, is accustomed to thinking beyond
the immediate to the long-term. What I would unashamedly call
the dynastic, in this case. He must protect the future.' Dean paused,
making sure Edgehill appreciated the immensity.

Then, with congratulation in his tone, Dean said, 'Adrian remarked
to me, before we set out today: "This is one for Larry Edgehill.
Only he can assist us. He will earn our regard – will be eager to
earn it, despite recent unseemliness." Adrian never misjudges. How
would he be where he is otherwise? How would he be so esteemed,
so revered?'

Nine

Esther had a call on her office phone.

'I'm Belinda.'

'Right.'

'Most likely you know he was at Tribe, this dead one – the one on the kids' slide, but not sliding anywhere, Gervaise Etcetera – oops, that's cruel! It might take a while going through the tapes, but you're going to find me, aren't you? I'll be on club CCTV talking to him when my boyfriend was in the toilet, and after that. So, look, I don't want your people tracking me down and a platoon coming around my house with questions, or where I work, or at the club. Ask anyone on Temperate – you've got to be careful who's knocking your door. The same on Whit, I expect. This is very visible, while they're knocking and waiting and looking friendly, not smashing the door down today, and like they expect info. Anyone can tell it's police whatever clothes. So, I decided to ring. Sort of get in first? He wouldn't like it – your people at my house, and he'd be sure to hear. He didn't like it at Tribe, talking to him, to Gervaise Etcetera.'

'The boyfriend?'

'It wasn't a long-time thing, him and me, but he thought he had like ownership. I played along, for a while.'

Crude as snot, was he? Esther left it unspoken.

'Nor my parents wouldn't want it – heavies at the house, asking things,' Belinda said.

'You live on Temperate?'

'Even if your lot came in a plain car – it's not good. This would be a topic. Man or woman cop, it wouldn't matter. And I don't want to come in there, to the nick. This also could be seen. Or you've got officers in the building who might put a word to where I wouldn't like to have a word put – Harold Perth Amesbury.'

'No, no, it wouldn't happen.'

'Which you've got to say. But it might. I fancy living a bit more of the future, you know. It's not guaranteed though.'

'Well, I'll meet you somewhere away from here and from Temperate. Give me a place and time.'

'Just you?'

'Just me. Belinda what? I'm Esther Davidson.'

'Yes.' Belinda said a friend ran a hairdressing saloon, Scissors Movement, off the estates, but not far. There was a back room for tea-making and stores. Iris didn't mind if they used it. Belinda had told her that Esther worked in debt management, and that her parents would worry if they thought she had problems. 'Iris doesn't know much about police, but put on something a bit gaudy so you don't seem plain clothes.' Belinda might get something done to her hair before or afterwards to make the visit look ordinary and reward her friend. That would be only decent. 'You could, too, if you like. She's pretty good. Customers of all ages.'

'Well, perhaps,' Esther said.

'Better than spilling it all on the phone.'

'Much.'

'As long as it's one-to-one.'

'It will be.'

'Making poke-about visits to my house and work and Tribe definitely unnecessary?'

'Definitely.'

Esther arrived a couple of minutes before Belinda at Scissors Movement. She must have decided to have her hair done after the meeting, not before. Leatherette, tubular armchairs. They sat opposite each other near the gas ring. Esther wore a purple T-shirt with 'Pamplona' in silver letters across the front. Iris made them tea. The shelving behind Belinda had a scatter of fresh towels, bottles of shampoo and dye, a green first-aid box, spare bits of equipment, a tattered *Hello!* magazine. That sweet, slightly acrid hairdresser smell.

'This Gervaise — cool name, yes? — this Gervaise, he was asking questions and coming out with names, just like they were just ordinary names. Casual? You don't go around speaking names in Tribe, not the sort of names he was speaking,' Belinda said. 'Men. *Their* names. They're not gay, but I asked him if he was, because of an interest in men, but I guessed he wasn't. I knew he must either be pissed or media. When I asked him if he was gay, it was really to shut him up, spouting these names, spouting these names to me, like I'm going to help him with them. I mean, he's only just met me, or hadn't really met me properly at all, just bumped into me. It's dangerous. People don't like it.'

'Which people?'

'The people whose names he was asking about.'

'These would be people from the Temperate firm, would they?'

'You know the names. You're chief of detectives. You must know these names, even though you can't . . . even though they . . . even though they and the firm keep going all right.'

'Camby. Laidlaw.'

She stared at Esther for a couple of seconds but didn't speak or give any sign in her face.

'You'd recognize these people?' Esther said.

'Of course I'd recognize them. Any regular at Tribe would recognize them – what they looked like, why they're there. But I didn't let on to him I knew. That could have made it look like I was helping him. I wouldn't want that, would I?'

No, you wouldn't, Belinda. Again, unspoken, though.

'At Tribe, you should be careful not to get tied in with people you don't know.'

'Obviously.'

She stopped, sat back hard in her chair and pointed a finger at Esther. 'Hey – you don't ask what we talked about,' she said. 'You know already, do you? He left notes? That's what they do, his sort. Reporters. They write stuff down, or on a laptop. In the press and on TV they said he was a reporter.'

'But afterwards,' Esther replied, 'when you'd finished talking, what did he do then?'

'My boyfriend returned from the toilet. He'd been buying. He'd snorted some off the back of his hand. It's a skill. You need a wide hand and it's got to be steady or you're wasting half of it on the toilet floor. I didn't know him very well, but when he'd had a snort it usually made him cheery for a while, but you can't be sure on something like that, can you, so I had moved away from that Gervaise Etcetera? It seemed safest. Quite a crowd there, and the lights dimmed down, so I couldn't see him for a while. I think he must have left. And then we get this development.'

'Which?'

'A situation.'

'Which?'

'Someone comes over.'

'Camby? Laidlaw?'

'This is me, standing with the boyfriend, and someone comes over and is asking who was the guy I was talking to not long ago when the boyfriend was not there.'

'Which of them?'

'You get how awkward it is, do you?' she replied.

'Because you hadn't told the boyfriend?'

'"Who was the guy you were talking to for quite a while previously?" Most likely it'll be on the CCTV and you'll see who came over and asked this question. I don't want to say who it was. I'm not a grass. I just want to stop you coming around my place and so on. Why I'm talking. Only that.'

'Nobody's going to say you told us.'

'Nobody's going to say I told you, because I haven't told you and I won't. So, Vernon hears this question about the other guy.'

'Vernon's the boyfriend?'

'Was. It folded.'

'I'm sorry.'

She gave a small wave with her right hand, perhaps meaning their break-up didn't matter much – not to her. She'd be about twenty with a round, mobile, clever face, her hair dark and short and in need of a bit of shaping from Iris. She wore a knee-length denim skirt, cerise blouse and battered looking trainers. Whatever drinking and doping she did, it hadn't dulled her grey-green eyes. She watched Esther as though she needed watching, in case she tried some ploy, even on away ground picked by Belinda.

'If it's on CCTV, you'll see how Vern's really shocked and angry because some other guy has been mentioned. He says: "Which guy, Belinda? You never told me about a guy." And this is *so* correct. This other guy – not Gervaise Etcetera, but the one who came over and asked the question—'

'Camby. Or Laidlaw.'

'He doesn't give a monkey's that he's bringing me trouble. A bit of delicacy is not his game, is it? All he cares about is finding out about this guy I talked to when Vernon was in the toilet. "Who was he?" he says.'

'Of course, I don't know who he was, not at that time I didn't, not even his name. So, that's what I tell them.'

'"Some guy just comes up and talks to you?" Vernon said. He's doing his "You looking at my bird?" act. "Where is he now?" Eyes gone narrow, mouth so tight, breathing ferocious. Nice blurring from the snort all gone.'

'They don't believe you?' Esther said.

'Don't believe what?'

'That you didn't know him,' she replied.

'Vern thinks I've been fratting with some stranger who tried his luck because I looked solo. That's going to niggle. He's been in the toilet, faithfully doing nostrils duty, and I'm among the crowd, making myself available. He'd consider it . . . well, indelicate. And the other guy, the one with the questions—'

'Laidlaw? Or Camby?'

'He thinks the guy – that's the one who turns out to be Gervaise Etcetera – he thinks this guy's been dredging for stuff about Tribe and some of the people there because he's on a big dig mission.'

'Which was true,' Esther said.

'So, I say he's a cruising gay who wants to know can I show him any others in Tribe. I tell Vernon this was why I never mentioned it – because it didn't seem important, a gay searching for gays. But is he going to believe that – a gay asking a woman about other gay men? Maybe not, but I had to try *something*. The questions keep coming, like, What did we talk about? And I say I told him I couldn't help because I didn't have a clue who was gay, except I knew Vernon wasn't. And then he says – I mean, not Vernon, but the one who'd come over – he says I seemed to talk to him for a long time. Was it only to say I didn't know if there were gays about? He asks do I have a name for him, or an address, especially an address. And, of course, I haven't. But Vern says, "Did he want you to meet him somewhere else some time? That what it was about?" I say, "No," but does he believe this, either? He keeps on with it, even in bed later, and, afterwards, he's going through my clothes and bag in case I wrote down a number or something for the one I was talking to while he was in the toilet. In a way, jealousy like that is nice – it shows he cares, but it's also insulting. So I get rid. He was common as underarms anyway.'

'Did anyone tail Tasker from Tribe?'

'Wouldn't know. I lost him. I didn't see him leave.'

'He might have still been in the club when Camby came over to talk to you. Or Laidlaw?'

'Yes, he might have been there when someone came over. Like I said – crowded, lights down.'

'So, Camby could have tailed him after speaking to you and Vernon? That's Camby or Laidlaw.'

'You're stuck on those two names, aren't you?' Belinda said.

'They're wrong?

'Somebody could have tailed him, if Gervaise Etcetera was still in the club.'

'Or one of their staffers?'

'Whose staffers?'

'Camby's. Or Laidlaw's. They'd have had people there, wouldn't they – pushing stuff? But are you saying those names are wrong?'

'I'm not saying anything as to names of personnel,' she said.

'At least tell me if it's neither of the two.'

'Gervaise Etcetera did leave some notes, then, did he? An account of the scene? The CCTV might tell you if he was still in the club.'

'It's important for us to know what happened afterwards.'

'That right?'

'Absolutely.'

'Someone gets beaten up and murdered and put on show in a kids' playground – yes, I can see this might be regarded as important.' She stood. 'I've got an appointment with Iris. I can't help with afterwards. I've told you everything I know.'

'I ought to have your surname and address. And Vernon's.'

'Not on. I know you can find them if you want to, but I'm not giving them. It wasn't that kind of meeting.'

'Which kind was it?'

She took the magazine off the shelf and held it up. 'Hello. Goodbye. This kind,' she said.

'The club CCTV missed you entirely,' Esther said.

Belinda frowned. 'Couldn't you have told me earlier?'

'Of course I could have.'

That evening, Esther went to hear Gerald playing in a concert at the Silurian Hall off Oxford Street in the West End. He really loved her to be in the audience. She knew he regarded it as bringing her to heel. As he'd see it, the prime prat, she was there because of him. Only because of him. And, of course, this couldn't be more true. He and the bassoon controlled her leisure for anything up to five hours, taking into account the travelling and an interval. In addition, being a wife, she would have to clap the performance sincerely for a good while, which meant he also controlled her hands during this spell of loyal applause, not like when they were belting each other and he might get a sudden, very startling set of knuckles over the heart or in his throat.

One of the most useful things about Esther was, although she could have done without all classical music, she didn't detest any particular work or composer more than the rest – certainly not the embittered way Gerald detested JS Bach and Copland. For instance, she would sit right through this concert and maintain a look of perfect interest, even appreciation: no bored-as-buggery shifting about on her chair, no get-lost-for-God's-sake coughing. And Vivaldi – she could spot a bit of almost tune in the piece of his they did. And then Elgar. Taking into account what composers could be like, she considered he kept things reasonably sane and genial in his stuff.

Gerald's main exposure came in a Paul Hindemith sonata. Esther did not find this intolerable, or even close to intolerable. She shouted 'More!' at the end, although he hadn't pre-asked her to. He wouldn't, because that would empower her, as though calling the sommelier for another bottle. 'More!' she yelled, and they replayed a bit of the Hindemith. Esther decided she could get used to Hindemith eventually if she stuck at it, which she might not, though.

At the end of the concert, Esther made her way down the hall to speak to Gerald and give him her production-line congratulations. 'Precise, meticulous, yet by no means unimpassioned, Ger,' she said.

'This is a balance I always seek.'

'And find.'

'Yet I ask myself, is music about mere balance?'

'What answer do you get?'

A man and woman approached. Esther recognized Rupert Bale from television. 'Mr Davidson,' he said, 'you have just guided us along such a spiritual journey. Hindemith – an enigma, yet brilliantly decoded by you. Oh, forgive: I'm Rupert Bale. I do some arts TV, you know. And I hear from the producer that you'll be joining one of our panels soon. Marvellous. This is Dione Pellotte. We're both nuts about Hindemith.'

'I'm Esther Davidson,' Esther said.

'Are you a Hindemith fan, too?' Bale asked.

Esther spun her word hoard and let whatever wanted to come out come out in whichever order it wanted to: 'He's full of semblancing yet also of sublime interaction and tact,' she said.

'Exactly,' Bale said.

'What's it mean?' Dione said.

'We come to many concerts,' Bale said.

'You're police, aren't you?' Dione asked Esther.

'This evening is not about me but about Gerald and his wonderfully accomplished colleagues,' Esther said.

'I was impressed by the last *A Week in Review*,' Gerald said. He sat hunched and resting, before packing his bassoon. Did he look deficient without the instrument actually in his mouth? Other players called au revoirs as they left.

'You don't mean the gig with that fucking Sandine tart sere-
nading Rupe's crotch, do you?' Dione said. 'They discussed a novel
– *The Insignia of Postponement*, or some such daft title – the *Royle
Family* and a couple of other things.'

'This was a programme with pace and focus,' Gerald replied.

'Yes, well the only pace I wanted to see was Sandine flung out
fast on her high-slung tits,' Dione said.

She was about twenty-seven, twenty-eight, slim, not too tall, with
good skin, and a tidy profile. A near-beauty, no question. She wore her
fairish hair brilliantly rough-cut, probably not at Scissors Movement.
Although addressing Gerald, she kept an unbroken stare on Esther, as
if amazed anyone could actually *choose* to be a police officer, and therefore should be studied for the explanation. Belinda had done some
staring, too. Perhaps Dione's face was slipping into chubbiness. She'd
have to watch herself. Crook barons shouldn't have chubby daughters.
They ought to be elegant and at a good fighting weight. She wore an
excellent dark blue woollen suit, possibly her Hindemith gear, and
moderate heels. 'You had some of Dad's people taken in as suspects
for the death of that sneaky journalist, didn't you?' she said. 'My father's
mentioned you. He mentioned a bassoonist husband.'

'It's something that does happen to me,' Esther said.

'What?' Dione said.

'Getting mentioned by people's fathers – if their fathers are of a
certain kind,' Esther said.

'Which kind?' Dione said.

'The kind that mentions me,' Esther said.

Bale said: 'My view is that, though somebody's skills might lie in
one art only – say music – he or she will probably be able to speak
intelligently and in no-nonsense terms about other arts, too. This is
why we look forward to your participation in *A Week in Review*.'

'Of course, you had to let them go,' Dione said. 'It's just a regular
tic by police. Some crime beats you – you can't crack it, so let's
blame Happy Gardening Solutions. But not the main man, my dad,
because you're scared of him and his influence. You pick underlings.'

'Your dad does have influence,' Esther said. 'So does cyanide.'

Gerald said: 'I feel it would be a narrowing of . . . of, yes, a
narrowing of the very soul for someone who excels in one art, such
as music, to believe only this art really counts. It is a kind of blas-
phemy against the general, precious creative impulse.'

'Are you a tit man?' Dione asked Gerald. 'Is that why you've
agreed to take part? She's not in every show, you know.'

'Does that disappoint Rupert?' Esther replied.

'Width of outlook – so crucial in a panellist,' Bale said.

'Did you ever run across him?' Esther said.

'Who?' Dione said.

'The sneaky journalist,' Esther said.

'I feel that with Hindemith we certainly hear the call of a certain period – say Europe in the thirties,' Bale said, 'and yet this is also music that bridges so many time zones, so many areas of the world, even the cosmos. Listening to your playing, Gerald – if I may – I could feel both these qualities of the composer. It has been a privilege.'

'So, where do you go next?' Dione asked Esther. 'Who will you terrorize tomorrow?'

'Journalists can stir – can make tense situations worse,' Esther replied.

'Which tense situation?' Dione said.

Ten

Naturally, Abel Vagrain, author of *The Insignia of Postponement* and other works, realized he could be pulled into something a little dangerous, a little terrifying. Although his new book had been given such an extraordinary boost on television, with all kinds of sweet results, he came to see after a while that it might also bring bad trouble.

But one of the early sweet results was this girl, Karen Tyne. Lithe, conversational, cheerful, straddling him now with a commitedness that surely went beyond mere fandom and hero worship. They had met at a publicity and signing session devoted to him and *The Insignia of Postponement* earlier this evening in a massive Hampstead book shop, Voluminous. Another good by-product of the brilliant, famous/notorious TV coverage was bookshops like Voluminous wanted to cash in, and had organized sales events for Vagrain and *Insignia*. It didn't happen last time: one of his previous books had been featured on *A Week in Review*, but vividly slaughtered then by a panellist called Rex Ince. No bookshops wooed him after that. Things were so magnificently different now.

Karen had bought a copy for him to autograph, and engineered happy chats with Vagrain in his role as a hot, sought-after author. 'I adored the television item,' she'd said. 'As a matter of fact, I sort of know Rupert Bale, chairman that night.'

'Really? How? Wasn't he wonderful?' Vagrain said.

'Good old Rupert.' The shared interest in Bale had given her and Vagrain a quick, useful route into a kind of familiarity, then closeness. And, eventually, they'd drifted back to her place.

He'd never previously had a one-night stand. He'd *written* about one-night stands, and notably, as a matter of fact, in *The Insignia of Postponement*, although he realized one-night stands might, on the face of it, suggest the total, blood-rush opposite of postponement. He felt especially glad that in the book he had always given his treatment of one-night stands a lot of tenderness, shared joy, sincerity – a fleeting sincerity, true, but perhaps more touching and attractive as a result.

Early on in Voluminous he had asked her what she meant by

'sort of' knowing Rupert Bale. Explanation: a friend of hers had a relationship going with him – a 'significant' relationship. This friend was *not* the woman, Priscilla Sandine, who'd appeared with Bale on the show the other night and helped him make the programme fizz. No, but a chum of Karen called Dione Pellotte. Dione, she said, had the significant love affair under way with Rupert Bale, significant and what she termed 'touched by grievous peril'. Some of the vocabulary sounded quaint to Vagrain, yet exciting – not just *peril* but *grievous* peril.

In Voluminous, after he'd done a reading from one chapter, some short speechifying and many signings, one of the younger women from the audience had re-approached him, holding a copy of *Insignia*. Karen. She was lovely, and, of course, he'd noticed her when she queued earlier for his signature. She said how much she'd enjoyed the TV discussion of his book and mentioned the link with Bale. 'So I usually look in at the show. Also, a one-time history tutor of mine appears sometimes as a panellist. Ince.'

'Rex Ince? I've come across him.'

'Done you damage?'

'Done *you* damage?'

'An unfadingly odious jerk. I watch, hoping he'll die on-screen or get hit by double incontinence. But, anyway, that night he wasn't there to taint things. I realized at once that I must have *Insignia*. Absolutely must! I've been reading Anthony Powell, but I'll put that aside.'

Later, when he lay unstraddled by Karen, revelation came suddenly to him. With an *actual* one-night stand, as against an imagined episode for a book, you could not always know while it was taking place that, in fact, it *would* be a one-night stand. A one-night stand earned its breezy, clear label not simply because two people made love more or less immediately they met. The words also clearly meant that the two people never made love again, and possibly never even saw each other again. Vagrain could not be certain he and Karen would never meet again. He might not want such a split.

At the signings, some other people from the bookshop audience had crowded around for a personal word with Vagrain, and Karen declared she must not hog him. *Hog me, hog me! Get your gorgeous questing snout wherever in my confines you like! Snort and grunt over me! Gulp me, chew me, nibble me, swallow me!* But he did not yell or even say this. 'I'm interested in your reactions to the TV treatment of the book,' he told her. 'Perhaps a word or two more in a minute, if you wouldn't mind hanging on? I'll just say hello to these kind folk.' As tactfully as he could he closed down his conversation with the other customers and joined Karen near the three-for-two counter. She looked up from the book, smiling.

'Oh, they're so right,' she said.

'Who?'

'On *A Week in Review.* That woman and Rupe Bale.'

'Right how?'

'Spot on about the tastefulness and bold burn of the love scenes.'

'I didn't want to win *Literary Review*'s Bad Sex Award.'

'You couldn't – couldn't ever. Vivid, vigorous, so very credible, never clumsy or gross, always meaningful and unrushed. Even the one-night stands. *Especially* the one-night stands.'

'You read fast.'

'Well, yes. *Not* unrushed. I was carried along.'

They talked some more. Then he said: 'Look, I'm afraid we have to move on. They want to close up.'

'Oh, dear, yes. Rabbiting away like this, I lost track. I live not so very far from here. It's a fine night.'

'Well, yes.'

Getting straddled in her single bed had been excellent, and with no problems because, of course, only enough width for one body was called for – his. She, being on top of him, did not demand any of the latitude for herself. In this bed, Vagrain's arse and back required a good mattress foundation, and that would almost do; possibly, plus a little extra on each side of him to give leverage and purchase spots on the sheet for her knees during busy and ultimately very effective thrusts and pullbacks.

Now, though, afterwards, as they lay alongside each other, things became a little cramped. He'd have to remember that for when he wrote again about one-night stands. She put her head on his chest to save space. 'I expect you wonder what I mean when I call their relationship "significant",' she said. 'Probably you'd argue all relationships are significant. Your books are so good on relationships.'

'The essence of much storytelling.'

'Do you know the name Pellotte?' she asked.

'You said it's your pal Dione's name.'

'And, naturally, her father's.'

'No, I've not come across it.'

'He's very big on Whitsun Festival.'

'I *have* heard of the estate,' he said.

'Not always good things, I expect.'

'Drug empire wars with another estate? A journalist murdered, trying to investigate things – found on a kiddies' playground slide? Terrible.'

'Temperate Park Acres – the other one. And so, this big, bloody, continuous tension affects their romance.'

'In which sense?'

'Dione equals Whitsun, Rupert, Temperate. The journalist might have been prying into that, or attempting to.'

'Ah! Like *Romeo and Juliet*. Classic,' Vagrain said. 'I can see this is a real situation.'

And, yes, God, it was potentially a brilliant topic for fiction. Classic, yet modernized and taken down a social level or two or ten. Another *West Side Story*, but sufficiently different not to seem like repro/copycat/pastiche. Dangerous, certainly. The journalist's death probably proved it. Wouldn't it be craven to let that deter him, though? In any case, he would be turning the set-up into a story, into fiction, not attempting to expose it in the press. He felt excited by the notion and wanted to sit up. But her head on his chest kept him flat.

'Dione – scared in so many ways,' she said.

'Scared how?' he said.

'Scared for her father, to start with.'

'*For* her father?'

'Yes, for.'

'Not of?'

'For.'

'But you said he has a powerful standing on one of the estates.'

'He does. He does . . . for now.'

'He's in danger?'

'Staffers in the firm might object to his daughter dating someone from Temperate – maybe even going to live with someone from Temperate, possibly marrying him. An ordinary girl on Whitsun might – would – get away with having a boyfriend on Temperate. Of course. I imagine it happens all the time. A Whitsun boy and Temperate Acres girl. There's no great gulf fixed between the estates. Not everybody is part of the drugs strife. But Dione is *not* an ordinary Whitsun girl. Really, she couldn't be less ordinary. She is Adrian Pellotte's daughter. He is, to date, the undisputed Number One on Whitsun. And Dione's behaviour and choices have a bearing on Daddy's position and security. Her love affair insults him and all belonging to his firm – that's how some of those members would regard it. This is the crux: all of them feel tainted, except possibly his chauffeur and odd-job man, Dean Feston. Result? Hatred and contempt of Pellotte for permitting it. Perhaps Tasker, the journalist, had sensed this, meant to make something of it. He'd know what ambitious, wild, envious, recriminating people work for these outfits.'

The pile of adjectives delighted Vagrain. He loved the extremism of what she described. He could provide more adjectives: the extremism was dark, daft, sickening, credible. It would rightly guarantee a right-on page-turner, if he could write it right, but not a *cheap* right-on page-turner: there'd be a theme here, a message, insights, oodles of *zeitgeist* and social commentary. He would thoroughly research both estates, regardless of personal hazard, build a milieu. The point was, there couldn't *be* an estates story without personal risk. If you wanted to write accurately about war, you had to be there, suffer what Karen might call 'the perils'. His behaviour would not be stupidly irresponsible, but calculated, thorough, honest. He'd get the total picture, then develop it to, say, 100,000 words, something to be really reckoned with in hardback on bookshop shelves – at least as reckonable as *Insignia*.

'You said Dione is scared in several ways,' he said.

'This woman.'

'Which?'

'The programme woman.'

'Priscilla Sandine?'

'Dione likes how she brought Rupert on in the show – sort of transformed him. He'd been having a bad time with the critics, was depressed. She restores him, resurrects his star factor.'

'Well, yes, great.'

'Great but also worrying. Something between those two, Abel? Was that how the magic worked? Dione's half in favour, half ferociously jealous. Her father frets, too – half in favour, half ferociously suspicious. Half a dose of suspicion from Adrian Pellotte is a very nasty fraction.'

Stupendous, epic, thrilling, Vagrain thought – this vast tangle of hope, contentment, pain and anxiety. It would take a real, unflinching novelist to show the intricacies of what she described, chart the passions, get convincingly to the resolution, whatever it might be. He felt brilliantly excited, stirred. He gently drew Karen's head up on to the pillow alongside his.

'What would you call it?' she said.

'What?'

'The book.'

'The book?'

'About all this.'

'Who said I might do a book?'

'You're fascinated, aren't you? But be careful. What would you call it – *Daddy's Girl*?' she asked.

He eased her over on to her back. This way, too, only one body width had to be accommodated in the narrow bed.

Eleven

Tasker's murder turned symbolic – meaning, of course, extra trouble. Fuck! Always this danger with any unsolved case, and above all a violent unsolved case. Yes, Esther thought, fuck! Thought only. She would have liked to at least mutter this, possibly shout/scream it, give it substance and clamour, but there were people about, people of an influential kind. They had chairs in front of her at the conference table, and their name was Insolence, or should have been.

Naturally, she'd seen from near the start that Tasker's death might take on a meaning beyond itself, might come to typify a general, poor state of things, especially if nobody had been nailed for it, or looked like getting nailed. Almost always, an arrest, followed by a charge/charges could restore tidiness, encouraged a belief in the inevitable, good victory of virtue and order. This was the supreme aim of policing – to prove the inevitable good victory of virtue and order. Or at least to encourage a belief in the inevitable good victory of virtue and order, even if, in fact, a victory for virtue and order might not be inevitable or even fucking likely.

To date, though, the Tasker investigation had produced nothing to bring comfort. The reverse. There'd been the couple of arrests, but no charges. Arrests without charges were deeply worse than no arrests. They made the police look panicky, desperate to get someone locked up and headlined, regardless – regardless of evidence fit for a court.

So, the death became a symbol. Of what? The media would highlight it as another sign, yes, symbol of a national/international/universal, cosmic catastrophic decline. Obediently, the media's readers, viewers, listeners would think the same. Causes of the catastrophic decline? A list:

(1) Police failure.
(2) Abject police failure.
(3) Customary police failure.
(4) Eternal police failure.
(5) Bred-in-the-bone police failure.
(6) Possible police dab-in-the-hand connivance/involvement/corruption.

(7) Ungovernable major city areas on account of (1)–(5), and maybe (6).

(8) Gang wars unchecked by police in ungovernable city areas because of (1)–(5) and maybe (6).

(9) Brutally effective gang resistance to scrutiny, exposure (by an investigative reporter).

(10) Brutally effective gang terror ploys to deter scrutiny, exposure (the playground display).

(11) Effective defeat of interrogation helped by (1)–(5) and maybe (6): (that is, arrests but no charges.)

(12) All this had a wider significance, yes? That's what symbolic meant. Assume the savage, unpunished crime and the incompetence or complicity of the police mirrored something national, international, universal, cosmic. Then, the gangsters and their cleverness and ruthlessness would triumph countrywide, and possibly worldwide, perhaps already had.

Bad. But these people across the table stopped Esther from mouthing in some form – howling? Screaming? Yelling? A surely justified curse out of horror/disgust/fear/rage/helplessness at these 1–12 elements.

Commander Bernard Chawse, one of Esther's bosses, had called a meeting. When she arrived, somebody from the Mayor of London's empire was with him and somebody from the Home Office. Esther would guess from a glance at how they were dressed, smiled, sat and radiated chicanery that they had important jobs on the spin, publicity or press relations side, though their posts were described by Chawse in introductions as, Executive Head of Projects (London Mayor's office) and Deputy Administrator Major Future Enterprises (Home Office). Chawse said he couldn't actually *stay* for the meeting himself, unfortunately – *very* unfortunately – on account of some other meeting he'd just been unfortunately asked to chair, because the Chief, who should have chaired it, had unfortunately been suddenly required to chair another meeting to do with security for a Royal visit, and therefore an irresistible priority, unfortunately. Perhaps. Chawse was known to hate discussions with Executive Heads of Projects and Deputy Administrators of Major Future Enterprises or similar, particularly if he foresaw recriminations. Esther had heard and believed that his quick climb up the ranks was mainly due to an unmatched flair for foreseeing recriminations and being required elsewhere as an irresistible priority.

'I'm sure Chief Superintendent Davidson – Esther – will be able to deal with your queries, Veronica, Maldwyn,' he said, leaving.

Esther sat down opposite them.

Veronica, the Deputy Administrator, spoke first. She had a voice rich in sales skills and power-talk. An obvious flair at alchemizing bullshit attended each word. She radiated a kind of logic, her kind. 'Let me tell you how the thinking goes, will you, Esther? It's long-term, but in such a scheme – admittedly only a "concept-for-development matter" at this stage – such thinking *has* to be long-term.'

'Thinking as to what, please, Veronica?' Esther asked. 'Which, as it were, ballpark are we in?' She felt that in a meeting with Executive Heads of Projects and Deputy Administrators of Major Future Enterprises or similar, she must get her jargon in first.

'A splendid metaphor, if I may say,' Veronica replied. 'You intuit brilliantly! But I suppose intuition is a cardinal ability in a senior officer. Yes, we are, in fact, talking about sport, Esther – and, oh, very incidentally, yet truly importantly – how good to be on first name terms so soon! Maldwyn and I don't always meet with such ready familiarity in our work.'

'Indeed not,' Maldwyn said.

'What one could term the very acme of sport,' Veronica said, 'and in the widest sense.'

'I'm intrigued,' Esther said.

'Sport as a virtually all-embracing term,' Maldwyn said. 'Its parameters extensive. Table tennis, sculling – you name it.'

'These really are extensive parameters,' Esther replied.

Veronica said: 'We would like you to think Olympics.'

'Ah,' Esther said.

'As a prospect,' Maldwyn said. 'A prospect to be secured against the mighty efforts of other bidders.'

'2012,' Veronica said.

'Distant, yet not so distant, believe me,' Maldwyn said, 'not when the many potential exigencies are taken into account.'

'Maldwyn, it's a fact, exigencies can be a living sod,' Esther said.

'But they can also be dealt with, triumphed over,' Maldwyn said. 'What would be our *raison d'être* otherwise?'

'I see that,' Esther said.

Veronica said: 'The Government and the Mayor's office are minded to put London forward as possible hosts for the Olympics of 2012. As I've mentioned, the matter is only at "concept-for-development" status at this point. You may, in your necessarily down-to-earth fashion,

Esther, ask what that bit of back-room gibberish means! Let me make it more or less intelligible, will you? A project idea starts as a general proposal, and proceeds – if it *does* proceed – to one, presentation of salient factors; then to two, concept; followed by three, concept for development state and finally, development. For the Olympics invitation to be at three indicates what is categorized as "substantial intent". In other words, something with a high possibility of fruition. I believe the concept a good one, and its development into more than a concept possible and, indeed, probable. I think London is formidably qualified to succeed with its bid, and so does Maldwyn.'

'Absolutely,' he murmured. 'What Veronica meant about "in the widest sense", you see. The Olympics. Could things actually *be* wider in the sporting world? Parameters – extensive.'

'All right, that's fourteen years ahead, you'll argue, Esther – nearly a decade and a half. Yes, it is,' Veronica said. 'But the decision will be made in 2005 at the latest. Applications must go in a long while before. And the preparations for the application must begin an even longer while before. We have to start worrying about London's "image" pretty soon in fact. At this stage general, basic, background aspects of the capital are what's on our minds, Maldwyn's and mine.'

'London must be established from the outset in international eyes as an impeccable, capable, wholesome venue, its assets unquestionable, inveterate,' Maldwyn said.

'I think you see which way our thoughts are moving, Esther.'

'We do not to any degree imply a reflection upon your work,' Maldwyn said. 'That would be quite outside our remit.'

'Quite outside, quite outside,' Veronica replied. 'Certainly, certainly.' Veronica now brought a real businesslike crackle into her voice. 'Esther, we speak law and order, of course. I know you'll agree these are priorities.'

'Well, they are ideals to which you have devoted your working life, so, obviously, you prize them,' Maldwyn said. 'A demonstrable track record.'

'Certainly, certainly,' Veronica replied. 'And, Esther, you will realize it is crucial that from the earliest possible date – such as, yes, now! – London's reputation for peace on the streets is at least preserved and, if possible, enhanced.'

'A challenge,' Maldwyn said, 'but what are the Games about but challenge? In our small, admin-centred way we are mimicking the spirit of those Games – the Olympic spirit – in our efforts to secure the Games and that Olympic spirit for our capital city in 2012.'

'You will wish me to come to the particular, Esther,' Veronica said. 'London is blessedly free from terrorist acts: a considerable plus. Other grounds for anxiety exist, though.'

'Any modern capital city is likely to have social problem areas,' Esther said.

'Certainly, certainly, Esther,' Veronica said.

'It would be naive to gainsay this,' Maldwyn said.

'And we would not attempt to,' Veronica said. 'But we have to recognize such difficulties and attempt to counter them. For instance, there are two large estates hereabouts, very near the centre of the city, where criminality may appear embedded, intractable – may, to be precise, have gained at least an element of dominance.'

'Or that is the perception,' Maldwyn said. 'And perceptions are, of course, so vital. It is perceptions that will decide whether London is a suitable venue.'

'If the situation at Whitsun and Temperate is not remedied it will clearly harm London's campaign,' Veronica said.

'Or the perception of that situation,' Maldwyn said.

'The murdered journalist, Gervaise Manciple Tasker, appears to have had some sort of interest in both estates, and his death can be seen as – is bound to be seen as – part of the prevailing tensions,' Veronica said. 'Does it not, we have to ask, incorporate these tensions in a single, terrifying symbol?'

Fuck! Fuck off, both of you! But Esther actually said: 'We are determined to resolve the Tasker case. The inquiry progresses.'

'This is not inner city trouble,' Maldwyn said, 'rather what the sociologists, pinching from Frederic Thrasher, of course, call "interstitial" – meaning it affects areas occupying the interstices, that is, the districts between inner city and outlying suburbs.'

Esther wondered which of them, if either, had any real power. Obviously, someone behind them did – someone in the Mayor's office and/or the Home Office: the people who'd sent them. To get access to Chawse, even for a token few minutes, would require clout, their own or their bosses', most likely the second.

Veronica said: 'We hear that Paris might well be a contender for 2012. A formidable rival, Esther. New York City could be another tough opponent. Manchester failed to secure a Games lately, so there's obviously no sentimental preference for the UK among Olympic decision-makers. If London is to get them, they will have to be won. It follows – I think you'll accept, Esther – it follows that we can do without the sort of negative qualities so troublesome at the moment in the Temperate Park and Whitsun Festival estates, and which have led to what must be seen as a depressingly typical killing.'

'Or the perception of this negativeness,' Maldwyn said.

Esther didn't care much about whether the Olympics came to London or didn't, but she could see that some would. And she saw, too, that Whitsun, Temperate and Tasker might shake London's chances. These two, Veronica and Maldwyn, could have no notion what it was like dealing with Whitsun, Temperate and the Tasker case. But it wasn't their job to deal with Whitsun, Temperate and the Tasker case. Their mission was to get London looking nice and spruce for the committee who'd pick the short list of contenders for 2012, and then choose the winner. As part of their mission this pair had come to let Esther know that although there might seem to be plenty of time, there wasn't.

'I want to assure you, Esther, that all concerned believe you, with your experience and skills, remain unquestionably the officer who can, as it were, turn this adverse set of circumstances around,' Veronica said. 'Commander Chawse of course agrees. Any replacement coming in might, it's true, bring fresh vision and dynamism, but could not conceivably have your "on the ground" knowledge. Such a replacement would be starting with a very considerable handicap and, even if his or her talents were exceptional, might be unable to rectify these very unpromising conditions. Or not swiftly enough.'

Esther could read their thinking. It assumed that solution of the murder and winning back the estates would be related. The killer, killers, of Tasker most likely came from one of the firms and a credible, processable arrest would show that the law did still operate on Whit and Temperate. This would be the start of general cleansing. There might be something in this idea, but not much.

'Someone got shot,' Esther said. 'That's the long and short of it.'

'It might be the short of it,' Veronica said, with a sweet, injurious lilt. 'Certainly a man was shot. But the long? The long must entail, surely, the significance of this death in the larger scene. The, yes, alarmingly symbolic elements here.'

'Larger scene . . . ?' Esther said.

'Than the mere death,' she said.

'Veronica doesn't mean "mere" in the belittling sense of that word, naturally,' Maldwyn said at once. 'Plainly, no death can be mere.' He magicked up sadness to his face. 'But she is using "mere" as equivalent to, say, "isolated". The death is part of a wider scene.'

'A touchstone,' Veronica said.

Maldwyn said: 'Please don't imagine for a moment we are here to tell the police their job.' He chuckled more than briefly, to show how preposterous that aim would have been had it been their aim.

And Esther did not imagine it was, but knew it was. Therefore, wished to bellow 'Fuck off, both of you!'

'We do feel it is especially worrying that the man Gervaise Manciple Tasker, murdered because of some kind of link to the estates, should have been a journalist,' Maldwyn said. He reran sadness. 'Obviously it would be bad whatever Tasker's occupation. Someone is dead and a family grieves. We all recognize this and sympathize. But the fact that he was a reporter is bound to produce extra quantities of damaging media attention. Editors are liable to highlight the dangers of estates like Whitsun and Temperate and ask – pointedly and repeatedly ask – why these dangers are allowed to persist, why nobody has been brought to book for the slaughter of Gervaise Manciple Tasker.'

Veronica got activated again. 'A novelist called Abel Vagrain – quite well known – *The Insignia of Postponement* and so on – is interested in the situation on Whitsun and Temperate, especially the murder of Tasker. He has been in touch with both press offices – the Mayor's and ours at the Home Office – looking for what he calls, I gather, "context briefings" about the estates. Maldwyn will confirm what I've been told by one of our spokespeople at the HO, that Vagrain seemed to have more knowledge of matters on Whitsun and Temperate than could have been gained only from media reports. And he knew of Thrasher and interstitial.'

'Our officer felt the same about his seriousness,' Maldwyn said.

'The implication must be that Vagrain is already far into his researches and hopes to use the Whitsun/Temperate enmities as setting for a new work,' Veronica said. 'You might think a writer would be deterred by Tasker's fate from attempting similar inquiries. The child playground display obviously aimed to scare others off. The fact is, though, that this killing becomes not a no-no but a sort of bonus for Vagrain – another dramatic, exploitable element in his fiction. As he'd see it, death livens up a chapter or two. This is how novelists are. Their only focus is on what they can use in a tale.' She would be about thirty-three or thirty-four, slim, dark, eye-bright, square-faced beyond what would have been an adequate squareness of face.

'A television arts show gave a mighty boost to Vagrain's *The Insignia of Postponement*, as you probably know,' Maldwyn said. 'What we don't want is a repeat of such a publicity fuss several years from now, when Vagrain will have finished and then published the story. It could be a critical moment in the Games strategy. We would have to combat *réclame* for a novel by Vagrain saying – and saying at bookish length and with literary weight – saying, that parts of London are wild, lawless, murderous. He has the kind of status that would ensure best-seller ranking abroad as well as here.'

'And abroad is somewhere we have to impress, and defeat,' Veronica said.

There was nothing mean or obviously snide and vindictive in Veronica's face. You could see faces like hers looking out from bus windows or searching for bargains at the local car-boot sale. Her cheeks had small, shallow hollows near her mouth, which would fascinate some, Esther thought. A man might want to take her for a hefty feed somewhere to see if they plumped out. When Maldwyn or Esther was speaking, Veronica would slump forward and rest her head on the table as if she'd swallowed poison. Esther spotted no grey at her roots.

Veronica had on a high-necked, four-button black jacket of cotton, or a mixture, with four buttoned-down pockets, the top two on her chest slightly askew. Esther thought these a clever idea because they modified the otherwise general severity of the style. The many buttons could suggest miserliness or control-freakdom. Her skirt was a coordinate, black-navy, to just above the knee. She wore a thick gold necklace.

'I think you understand the urgency of our message, Esther,' she said.

'Definitely,' Esther said. Yes, they wanted her to go up to Whitsun and Temperate and look out Pellotte and Amesbury and say genially and woman-to-men, 'Come on now, lads, cough who beat up and killed Gervaise Manciple Tasker for me, please, otherwise, you see, it might disastrously queer London's prospects for the 2012 Olympic Games? The Government and the Mayor's office are *so* anxious. You probably haven't thought of it in that light till now, Adrian, Harold, or one of you would obviously have come forward before and given us a name, names, plus very best wishes to all those helping build London's case for the Games. They might not have been the correct name, names, just those of a person, people, you wanted to get rid of, but you would have longed to make some sort of imitation civic gesture, in keeping with your respective high positions.'

'Incidentally, Maldwyn is very much a grapevining person,' Veronica said.

'It can be a plus,' Esther said.

'This telly programme we've been talking about, *A Week in Review*,' Veronica said. 'Maldwyn has discovered that . . . but I should let him tell it for himself.'

'Media people – I bump into quite a few,' Maldwyn said. 'It's the normal course of things. *A Week in Review*, I gather, has invited your husband to become a panellist. More importantly, he's accepted.'

'Frankly, we wonder about the wisdom of this,' Veronica said.

'Absolutely no reflection on Gerald Davidson's abilities,' Maldwyn said. 'Does anyone do Hindemith better? Gerald, Hindemith and the bassoon seem made for one another.' Maldwyn rarely looked at either of them when he spoke. In fact, he closed his eyes for much of it, like some university don needing to concentrate on simplifying a big, complex thought for the stupid undergraduate he tutored. His voice could assume almost any intonation, but never even approached rage or contempt during the meeting. Esther would put him at, say, twenty-six, although his hair had begun to back away from his brow. He was middle height, burly running towards fat, thick-fingered, bull-necked, his skin paler than pale, almost into pallor. He wore a zip-up, navy woollen jacket trimmed at the zip and pockets with strips of khaki, dark moleskin trousers, inexpensive blue and white training shoes. He had magnificent teeth but didn't make a thing of showing them off, as if afraid he'd be confined in people's impressions of him as the lad with the teeth.

'We're bound to be unhappy about any Pellotte connection via *A Week in Review*. As Maldwyn hears it, the programme's regular chairman is seeing Pellotte's daughter, Dione – a meaningful relationship. Or Pellotte intends it to be a meaningful relationship. There are obvious concerns on his side, and probably Dione's, about Bale's apparent flagrant compatibility with Priscilla Sandine, on that *Insignia of Postponement* show.'

'Plus Bale lives on Temperate,' Maldwyn said.

'This is potentially a mix of dangerous elements,' Veronica said.

Maldwyn said: 'On the other hand, as you'll probably know, Esther, the producer of the programme has a place on Whitsun, and was observed in long, seemingly amicable discussion with Pellotte and his bagman, Dean Feston, on Gideon Road. Also they called at his home, 19a Bell Close. They used a taxi. Did they want to disguise the visit? Pellotte's BMW might be regarded as too well known. No taxi driver would dare to speak about the trip if instructed not to by Feston.'

'You'll understand our anxieties when we find that the husband of the officer nominally in charge of policing those two problematical estates intends to become a part of these very dubious circumstances,' Veronica said.

What the hell did she mean by 'nominally'? Did it signal Veronica thought Esther had only a frail hold on things at present and might not be around here much longer?

When Esther went home in the evening she helped Gerald choose his best profile by holding a mirror at various angles around his head. 'The left, I think,' he said.

'Unquestionably.'

'Not that the right is totally unacceptable.' He grabbed her wrist in one of his martial arts grips to turn the mirror so it did his right again.

'Not unacceptable at all,' Esther said.

'But the left marginally better.'

'I'd say so.'

'I want to let the director and producer at *A Week in Review* know which side of the camera I should prefer when I speak.'

'Whichever, you'll come over brilliantly, Ger.'

'I hate it when you suck up to me. It sounds so phoney.'

'Some people don't want you to appear on the show at all,' Esther replied. 'I'm not going to be pushed about by them. So, I speak encouragement. "Let us now praise famous profiles." But I'll work on the sincerity aspect if you're going to be picky.'

'Which people don't want me to go on?'

'People around.'

'It's fucking envy, is it?' Gerald said.

'Other considerations.'

'Which?'

'Almost everyone has one profile markedly more attractive than the other,' Esther replied. 'You can see it in police dossier photographs.'

'I don't say "markedly".'

'You're lucky in that respect.'

'I hate it when you suck up to me. It's phoney.'

'Honestly, it's not meant to be, Gerald, dear, but you'll understand the difficulties, I know.'

Twelve

It really grieved Adrian Pellotte when someone in the firm tried skimming off the top, and cornering money that rightly should have come to the treasury of Happy Gardening Solutions. They were on their way to see someone in that dismal category now. Pellotte found disloyalty almost impossible to understand. If you belonged to a company, drew your income through a company, you surely owed it your full, honest allegiance.

Of course, Pellotte knew that many would say the amount of money involved here with Gordon Basil Hodge – less than £21K – they'd say this bagatelle probably did not justify an a.m. door knock by him, Adrian Pellotte : that is, Adrian Pellotte *personally*. It meant risk and it was footling. But Pellotte believed he should let it be known once in a while around Whitsun that he – yes, he personally, Adrian Pellotte himself – he, Adrian Pellotte, still checked the accounts for fiddling, and could become so hurt by these attempts at deception that he felt it correct to show his, yes, again, his *personal* pain and disappointment on the spot, such as Hodgy's nest in Larch Street. Pellotte's pain and disappointment might be acute, but they did not disable him.

People needed to be reminded that Adrian Pellotte was more than a mystical, pervasive presence on Whitsun, occasionally glimpsed being chauffeured across the estate to collect from and supply sales executives. When it suited, Adrian Pellotte could and did take a down-to-earth part in things. Even someone as minor as Hodge might have to be made an example of *pour encourager les autres*, as the phrase went. The BMW outside his front door would inform neighbours that a procedure, reproachful and serious, driven by dis-appointment as much as anger, was probably under way at Gordon Basil Hodge's. They'd listen out. They'd absorb the lesson. They'd pass on that lesson to others on Whitsun. What they would *not* do is pass on anything to the police, suppose the emergency services became involved at the address later as a result of the visit by Pellotte and Dean. Pellotte regarded his actual participation as to some degree a public relations matter, but also a chance to reacquaint himself with basic fieldwork skills not often called into play these days.

Dean Feston drove the BMW over towards Larch. Dean had obviously been doing some thinking, and had a fair whack on general topics to speak about now. Dean wouldn't degrade himself by discussing Hodge and how to deal with him today. A skimmer could never deserve that kind of attention. Nor would Dean refer to his arrest, with Gabrielle Barter Cornish, on suspicion of involvement in the death of that grossly, persistently, invasive journalist. Dean would regard such behaviour by the police as an automatic, blind, impulsive, not worth a word. Dean liked discussions to be on larger issues. Pellotte could put up with it. Sometimes what Dean said did matter. 'Very regrettably, some fail to realize the hold a child – son or daughter – has over the feelings of a father, Adrian,' he stated now.

'In which respect, Dean?'

'We've traced those four relationships of the TV producer, Larry Edgehill. All hetero, but, crucially, he's got no kids to our knowledge. People like that, they can't properly understand the bond, the sense of parental obligation. Despite those two meetings with Edgehill, I wonder if he'll appreciate how vital, supremely vital, it is for him and his continued well-being in a quite physical sense to make sure of Dione's safety and general contentment. I mean, really exert himself on this, not just something token. In his own interests, Adrian. OK, he's someone at present fit and strong and able to maintain a long conversation while stooped that day in Gideon. This despite a pretty sedentary existence. So, I don't deny he's entitled to feel comfortable with his selfhood, however fragile. But I'd hate to believe he takes your goodwill on this kind of topic for granted, Aid.'

'We'll return to Edgehill again if necessary and be much more pointed about what I expect from him as a duty – reasonably expect from him as a duty. Much more. I believe he'll try on our behalf, Dione's and mine. I feel he saw the urgency. A call at his own property – he's bound to appreciate the significance of that.'

'You're always inclined to think generously of people.'

'How else can one live satisfactorily, responsibly, Dean? How? How? Despair otherwise. Positivism – the search for it must be unceasing.' To quite an extent, Pellotte believed this, and, so, he decided he'd give those opening chats with Edgehill a little while yet to take effect. Occasionally, Pellotte thought well of patience. And for now, in any case, the firm's routine business and related matters had to be carried on. The session with Hodge would be a sorting-out encounter. Dean had spoken of this kind of measure when explaining to Edgehill why, originally, they hadn't doorstepped him. Such a visit, with Pellotte's car, could produce unfavourable repercussions and gossip throughout the estate. Although Pellotte hoped the present call would be fairly untroublesome and quick, he realized there might be snags, complications, even foolish time-wasting.

This morning, Pellotte felt exceptionally eager to avoid these because he and Dean would go on to a meeting later at handsome and fascinating Faunt Castle in the country. The Anthony Powell Society was holding its biennial conference there. Dean and Pellotte both belonged. They loved the novels of Powell, the twentieth-century English writer who wrote about the upper classes. Faunt Castle was thought to be the model for Stourwater, one of the great houses, important in Powell's books. Pellotte and Dean needed to look bandbox smooth when they arrived there, not bloodstained or limping or anything uncomely like that, particularly Dean who had agreed to give a keynote talk. Dean knew Powell's work well. He'd needed something substantial to read in jail and a twelve-volume novel like Powell's *A Dance to the Music of Time* really suited. Dean considered the first book in the series best, *A Question of Upbringing*, because some of it was set in Eton. Although Dean had not been at Eton, or anywhere much at all, he enjoyed reading about school-boys cooking sausages in their rooms, and their pranks outwitting the masters.

But Dean also had a considerable non-literary side. Now and then he could spot the hidden essentials of a problem. Pellotte listened to Dean's thoughts about the TV producer, and saw some sense in them. Those conversations with Edgehill – on Gideon, and then at his place, 19a Bell Close – certainly did not satisfy Pellotte entirely. Dean might be only an aide, a chauffeur, a sidekick, but now and then he could judge a situation. Why else would Pellotte employ him?

'Adrian,' Dean said, as they neared Hodge's place in north Whitsun, the glib, duplicitous, pulverizable sod, 'I've been able to do a detailed language analysis of some statements made by Edgehill in that second interview, the domicile session, rather than the Gideon interview.'

'Well, I expect so.'

'I felt it would be unfair to set too much store by what he said in Gideon, because he could not be relaxed and properly thoughtful when crouched.'

'Agreed, Dean.'

'But in his drawing room, with tea, a more conducive situation.'

'Why we went there.'

'His words on that occasion may, I think, be reasonably subjected to scrutiny. Such as his remark about potential unrest, even violence, among mavericks in the firm – *your* firm, Adrian – over Dione and Bale. Presuming to pronounce on *your* firm, in that regard.'

'Oh? Something dodgy there?' Pellotte said.

'His words: "You can take care of all that, I imagine. Par for the course." What do we *make* of such a statement, Adrian?'

'He wanted to reassure. That's how *I* took it.'

'"I imagine".' Dean replied.

'What? You imagine what?'

'No, I mean the way he said it. "I imagine".'

'Oh? How *did* he say it?'

'It's sort of cool, offhand, superior Mr TV Executive speaking. Now hear this! As though he doesn't give a fuck *what* we do – can't be bothered at his altitude with definitions – but he fucking *imagines* we'll manage it somehow or another because we are we.'

'I don't notice that kind of thing, Dean. It's subtle.'

'What I mean about you, Adrian – generous to people. Almost to a fault, I have to say. 'Or take "par for the course".'

'"Par for the course"? He's suggesting we've usually got matters under control, Dean. It's a golfing term, meaning a normal perform- ance given the nature of the ground. Yes, he wanted to reassure.'

'This was tacked on.'

'Which?'

'"Par for the course." I noticed the way his voice went down but immediately picked up again. "You can take care of all this, I imagine." Then a pause. And, as if he decided he hadn't been chilly and dismis- sive enough, he extends the insult, makes it more general. "Par for the course".'

'Insult? Surely, he's saying we don't have to worry because we know how to deal with such matters. Likewise, we'll handle it if there's any further bother over the playground journalist, Tasker.'

'Oh, that. But what's Mr Edgehill telling us, Aid?' Dean said.

'Well—'

'He's telling us he's got us summed up and classified in his TV executive mind and that he considers you and me a couple of very capable career thug-hoods, accustomed to wiping out opposition on more or less a fucking day-to-day basis.'

'Possibly he has a—'

'He comments, we can "take care of all that". What does "all that" refer to? He speaks like it's a bucketful of things, not worth the bother of listing. But, in reality, "all that" concerns guarding your position at the head of this firm and, crucially, it ultimately concerns your dear daughter, Dione. But to Edgehill these are trivial problems which can be "taken care of" in a standard, bloodletting style. "Take care of" – just a soft-talk way of describing utter brutality – a disgusting slight on you, and those who do your bidding. Possibly a hidden reference also to Tasker – who was "taken care of".'

'Yes, Tasker. Occasionally people do have to be "taken care of" in our scene,' Pellotte said, 'Not as we might "take care of" an elderly relative or stray cat, but "taken care of" in our own manner such as, for instance, this trip to Gordon Basil Hodge. I'm afraid Gordon might have to be "taken care of".'

'*You* know about these possibilities, Adrian, and *I* know about them, but is this something an outsider should speak of to us so frankly, so matter-of-factly in his own extremely average property? And then, when we're discussing possible uprisings among the staff, what does he say? "But these are only your tribesmen. They're not going to disrespect you, Adrian, surely." A delightful term – "tribesmen"? What does it make our people sound like? What does it make *you* sound like? I hope I would never slip into racism, but isn't he talking to us as if we're some primitive, spear and loincloth lot in Africa or South America, you as face-painted jungle headman? "They're not going to disrespect you, Adrian, surely." He's picked up that word, "disrespect", because he thinks this is how villain roughs talk here. It's condescending, offensive. If anyone's showing disrespect, it's Larry Edgehill.'

'Well, I—'

'What does all this suggest, Adrian?'

'Well, I—'

'It suggests that, although he's having what seems to be a nice, serene, tea-based conversation with two Whitsun neighbours, he's thinking the whole time, I've let a couple of lout gangsters into my home and must get them out fucking fast. All right, in some ways he is *not* an outsider. He lives on Whitsun. But he goes off to work in television every day, and a top job in television, not shifting scenery. Untypical for Whitsun, I think you'll concede that. He is hardly a true part of the community as you and I are, Aid, and proud to be. I think it's possible he would like to find a place right *off*

Whitsun, if he could afford it. Well, just as Rupert Bale wants an exit from Temperate . . .'

'Edgehill is—'

'Take this: I mentioned to him – knowing it would be your wish – I mentioned that you could arrange for his car to be fully honoured and swathed in security on the estate if he bought one. He gives the big ignoral. Why? There could be two reasons, neither very comradely. First, he doesn't intend staying here. Second, he does not wish to seem indebted, beholden to Adrian Pellotte. "Thanks so much for the offer, Dean, but stick it up your arse. *I'm* not one of his fucking tribesmen. I wear a shirt, changed every day."'

They reached Larch Street and did a couple of slow circuits of the block, to check for police vehicles about on inquiries or patrolling. If officers saw Pellotte's car parked at Hodge's house they might make guesses and decide to try a bit of nosing. 'We're only doing our job, Adrian.' So, what's their job? To nose. This would possibly turn out awkward later in any court case about what happened to Hodge in this possibly boisterous scenario. Although civvy witnesses on Whitsun could be easily discouraged and/or bought, this didn't apply to some police, and finding out which it *did* apply to often took a while, with the danger of errors.

Pellotte saw nothing to trouble them on the first reconnoitre, but he told Dean to repeat it, taking in a couple of extra streets this time. 'Maybe you give too much attention to Edgehill's phrasing, Dean,' he said.

'And then his remark, "A new friendship based on shared musical tastes sounds good for both of them, Dione and Bale,"' Dean replied. He put on a clipped, teacherly voice for that. 'Those two, Dione and Rupert Bale have both just emerged from emotional crises, yet Edgehill thinks – or *pretends* he thinks – that if they hear a bit of Haydn and Mozart they'll immediately feel OK again, and a healing romance will kick in. "Get someone to play a few bars of *The Magic* fucking *Flute* and she'll be fine." Flippant? Deeply heartless?'

They stopped outside Hodge's place and sat for a moment watching it. The second round-the-houses tour had been OK, too: nothing on the lurk.

'Certainly, we can return to Edgehill if necessary and become more pointed,' Pellotte said. Dean often needed to be quietened down. He'd let anxiety run him, anxiety drifting towards rage sometimes if he thought Pellotte or the firm endangered. On the up side, this kept Dean alert. But occasionally he frothed about trivialities.

He seemed to think only he saw the seriousness of certain problems. He'd go at them super-hard. He regarded Pellotte as too laid
back and kindly.

Although such underling qualities remained pathetically strong in
Dean, Pellotte realized he might want to bring him towards heir-
ship in due course. Someone must take over Whitsun and Happy
Gardening Solutions when Pellotte felt he'd had enough and wanted
to withdraw. No job for a daughter, nor for a son-in-law. Not one
like Rupert Bale, anyway. One of the most crucial obligations of
leadership was to ensure a suitable succession. Think of the Queen,
worried about Prince Charles and his speeches and farming notions.

'You've always been good at the step-by-step approach, Adrian.'

'What other approach is there? Which other approach is rational?'
Pellotte said, pulling on gloves. Dean lacked subtlety and the larger
vision. Could they be taught, or was the defect in his DNA? 'If
Hodge has the cash handy and will cough in full at once we take
it and forget about anything fully punitive for now, Dean. He'll
probably call it "an administrative slip-up".'

'Oh, he's got the words, all right. Sometimes I wonder if you're
too tender and forgiving,' Dean said.

'Perhaps just a temporary spell of . . . well, moderation. At this
juncture.' Pellotte thought that the sight of him, Adrian Pellotte
himself, personally, rather than staff, in Larch on the doorstep might
swiftly free up any loot squirrelled by Gordon around the house,
the congenital thieving bastard. Adrian did not want those 'repercussions', especially today. Dean's paper on 'Lady Widmerpool's
Schoolboy Chum' in the Powell tale, *Books Do Furnish a Room,* was
scheduled for quite early, and it could be a drawback if he'd failed
to recover his settled pulse properly because Hodge turned foolishly
obstructive, as people sometimes could when in a money dispute.

According to the dossier, Hodge had an old style .45 Sokolovsky
automatic, a model described a few decades ago as the most expensive pistol in the world, and probably still capable. It was like that
posturing twerp, Hodge, to go for something glamorized by history.
Pellotte and Dean carried nine mm Brownings, thirteen rounds
apiece. But Pellotte hoped none of these weapons would be used
today. He didn't want to go into the Powell conference smelling of
cordite. Dean had a drily witty way of delivering literary talks, and
breathlessness after possible excitement at Hodge's house might mess
up his timing and ability with consonants.

Even if there were only non-firearms violence, Pellotte would hate to see torn, bloody knuckles taking hold of a lectern in such a setting. Faunt Castle had become an arts and culture centre with hireable rooms at low cost, and Pellotte didn't want its reputation shaken by crude signs of violence. Dean had introduced him way back to Powell's work, and Pellotte felt real gratitude. Dean had read the twelve books many times over, of course, while serially jugged. Dean said he'd thought now and then that the overall title should be changed to *A Dance to the Music of* Doing *Time*. Dean's astonishing memory and the many lock-up re-readings meant he could repeat pages in their entirety from several of the *Dance* volumes.

Pellotte did not mind too much having to listen over-and-over to these very unnecessary fucking performances. After all, as Pellotte saw it, the main point about Dean was the certainty that if a blitz squad came over from Temperate one afternoon meaning to disfigure, maim or kill him – him, Adrian Pellotte – Dean would try very nearly everything to prevent it. Yes, very nearly everything.

Naturally, they had packed the BMW boot with complete changes of clothes and shoes as well as moist face flannels and towels, first-aid gear, blood transfusion equipment and an oxygen cylinder with mask, for their personal use. Pellotte recognized that the visit might turn out complicated, with possible rips and/or staining and contusions. But he hoped all this gear would prove unnecessary. Between them he and Dean should be able to see off Hodge if things went that way, but Pellotte would try to avoid any type of rough-house *pro tem*.

Hodge and his family had an interesting property. When Pellotte and Dean knocked, he came swiftly to the door, wearing a blue roll-topped sweater and navy jogging trousers. Pellotte felt at once that these clothes did not look at all the kind of outfits convicts on their way to execution wore in, say, Texas, but at a push they'd do. Pellotte considered the clobber and Hodge's bubbling attitude made him seem extremely relaxed – the two-timing, embezzling rat. Of course, he might have spotted the BMW doing its preparatory circling just now and readied his larcenous, filthy self. One of the special strengths of doorstepping was shock, and this might have been lost.

Hodge cried: 'Adrian, Dean! Here's a happy surprise. I understood you were away today, out of town at a conference on Anthony Powell. He said it "Pole" though, didn't he, so as to knock the Welshness out of it? But, obviously, I've been expecting a visit.'

'Yes?' Pellotte replied. 'You saw the car?'

'Saw the car? No,' Hodge said, 'but I meant on account of this exceptionally tricky Dione situation. You're bound to seek support. And I . . . I am equally bound to provide it. Am proud and delighted to provide it. Not to mention the shit flying your way because of the journalist who met his deadline, as it were.' Hodge stood back in the doorway. He made a real sympathy thing of this, like an Eskimo welcoming travellers out of the blizzard and into his igloo.

The exterior of the house was unattractive, the same as all the others round about, but Hodge and his partner had done the inside minimalist, probably under top-notch professional advice not necessarily gay, and to Pellotte it looked wonderfully spacious and light, the walls pastel shaded and with, here and there, a good, framed surrealist print, but nothing crudely bright and unnerving. The dots, broccoli heads, JCBs, biplanes, panthers, trombones and halberds in these pictures seemed to fit in with one another very well.

Letitia, Hodge's partner, must be out. The firm's personnel records showed Hodge had two daughters – Delphine and Maisy – both away at boarding school in Cheltenham, now near the end of term. One girl was by Hodge, one previous. Pellotte thought such first names fair enough for this kind of family. They had a total difference in sound, and if Hodge shouted for one of them during a vacation because he urgently needed somebody to get help, it would be obvious which he meant, not as if he had a Jane and a Joan, or a Celia and a Delia.

Hodge took Dean and Adrian to the lounge, and they sat in excellent blue leather chairs, the arms and legs shiny tubular steel of what seemed prime quality, and possibly fashionable among some. Little other furniture. Hodge didn't drink or, apparently, keep alcohol in his house and brought from the kitchen three glasses of barley water on a tray decorated with what looked to Pellotte like Old Masters illustrations, including one by Bronzino. Even on barley water, this lad, Hodge, could really smile. The smile had a kind of true authenticity to it, a false kind. The smile helped make him a fine street salesman. Pellotte recently watched a TV rerun of the Oliver Stone film, *Nixon*, which began with a sales director instructing a subordinate on the value of a smile, and showing him one. But this looked a foully unbelievable, trickster's smile, and referred, of course, to President Nixon's. But Hodge's smile had terrific depth and, if you did not know him, you could easily believe it meant unrestrained friendship. Punters – including punters new to Gordon – *all* punters felt confident as to quality of the stuff he offered, and reasonableness of price, from Ecstasy and resin through skunk to H.

Suppose things could not be resolved, Hodge would be an undoubted loss to the trade, but Pellotte had to think about the ethics of the situation, and if Hodge did represent unfortunate finagling within the firm he could not be excused. It would get to be a contagion otherwise.

'No, Gordon,' Dean said, 'not to do with Dione or the journalist, God rest his soul, but—'

'I knew you'd be getting around everybody, lobbying to see who are your allies in the Dione matter, Adrian,' Hodge said.

Dean said: 'No, that's not it, Gordon. We—'

'Well, I want to say straight out that I'm with you all the way on this one, Adrian,' Hodge said. 'I expect you heard the buzz and decided in your kindly fashion that you must drop in and show your gratitude. But no need, I assure you, Adrian.'

'Which buzz, Gordon?' Pellotte asked.

'That I've been talking your case to people in the firm – people potentially extreme. I mean extreme in a negative sense. I've argued for Dione's absolute right to a love life – if I may so call it – no matter where the man comes from. This is surely fundamental for a democratic state. Good Lord, we're almost into the new millennium! Don't tell me we're reverting to "arranged" courtships, as prevail in some countries. I've demanded restraint of colleagues. Really, demanded it. Plus, I've attempted to choke off unpleasant rumour about the death and so on of Gervaise Manciple Tasker, Dean. I do believe I can impose some influence. There are people on Whitsun – our people – who would use their own methods to end that relationship between Dione and Rupert Bale, as you know, Aid. They claim to feel stained by it. So far, I've been able to hold them in check. Difficult work, but entirely worthwhile. And you've had a whisper about my efforts, have you, Aid, on both the Dione and Tasker front? The Dione situation being hugely more important, naturally. I'm thrilled you can regard me as so much an ally that you make this personal call, despite your commitment to the cultural occasion at Faunt Castle today and tomorrow, I gather.'

'You're twenty-one thousand pounds fucking short for October, give or take a twenty,' Dean said.

'We can't overlook that, Gordon.'

'Certainly not,' Hodge said. Pellotte thought Hodge's very amused but still entirely convincing smile said it would be crazy for anyone, including him, Hodge, to think they *might* overlook it. 'Or, actually nearer twenty-three, by my reckoning.'

Hodge: spare, mid-height and long faced – the sort of face that might look sulky and hostile, but ready nearly always to turn to smiles, though, obviously, not if he was getting beaten shitless, for openers. His eyes managed integrity and friendship at consummate speed from a neutral start. He wore a couple of rings on his right hand, both triple amethysts, as far as Pellotte could make out, and one of those bulky watches on his left wrist, just below the edge of the sweater arm, with several dials, for different time zones, or blood pressure readings, or barometric forecasts, or luminous compass bearings to guide underwater diving explorers in a black lake.

The firm ran a £10,000 prize competition for 'Trader of the Year'. Hodgy had scooped it three times, though, admittedly, he'd been second on the last occasion, but moved up to first when the original winner, Gladstone Milo Naunton, got shot dead in a territory spat by something of very small calibre, but effective. This occurred only twenty-four hours before formal announcement of the award.

In a way, Pellotte admired those who used small calibre guns because they indicated precision and the coolness to achieve it. Almost anyone could blast a target's head or chest away with a .45, but a .22 had to be pinpoint. He wondered where Hodge kept the .45 Sokolovsky. He didn't have it on him. A harness under the sweater would cause an obvious bulge, and so would a pistol in his jeans. The Sokolovsky was a big gun, as pistols went. Pellotte and Dean kept the Brownings in the side pockets of their jackets. Probably, Hodge would spot the outlines, and he should know, anyway, that these were their usual weapons. But that might be for the good – deterrence.

Gladstone Milo Naunton's removal during that turf trouble could have caused chaos. However, Pellotte had ordered at once that Hodge must go to top place following the death: a kind of walkover, a walkover over a corpse. Some colleagues and associates of Gladstone had wanted him to be named as 'honorary' or 'posthumous' winner in tribute to his work in the period, but Pellotte pointed out as tactfully as he could that the contest was not to find 'Deceased Trader of the Year'. He insisted the competition must look forward as well as to the period just past, and this required someone living to collect the distinction. Tasker, the journalist, had been quizzing people on Whitsun about this difficult management episode, and Pellotte thought his curiosity very unnecessary. Financially, he certainly helped Gladstone's live-in and probably principal boyfriend, Bert (Albert) Jutland Marsh, for the present. That was only basic humanity.

Dean said: 'I've gone over the figures taking into account all due variables, and, in fact, allowing a one point five per cent shortfall factor in your favour for poor street weather from the eleventh to the thirteenth, and for that special police clampdown on discos and raves in the third week. We still come to a twenty-one thousand pounds plus gap. Adrian likes to run a tidy operation. It's . . . well, it's of his essence, a passed-down attitude of his family, like politics with the Kennedys, or the Redgraves and theatre.'

'Famed for it. Extensively and justly praised for it,' Hodge said with full enthusiasm in his tone. 'Mention Adrian's name far, far afield and people will immediately refer to the notable abstention from hand jewellery and then very soon afterwards to the tidiness of his operation.' He glanced down at the amethysts, his horse-collar face shifty for a moment in possible shame at his own skittish trinkets. 'Ringlessness, tidiness, these are synonymous with Adrian. This is what I tell people agitating now about Dione and Bale. I ask them how . . . *how* they can turn against a chief of Adrian's solid, earned reputation merely because his daughter chooses to step out of line.' Quickly, he softened this: 'That is, again, in *their* embittered, palsied view, to step out of line. It's not a view I or several others in the firm can share. I say to the anti-Dione lobby, "Please judge Adrian Pellotte as Adrian Pellotte, not just as the father of a supposedly headstrong, heart-strong woman. Consider his enormous mercantile achievements over almost a decade, his status on Whitsun and afield. Would you *dare* act against him in person? Yet, by acting against Dione, or even against Rupert Bale, you would, in fact, be acting against Adrian." In their rabid state they don't seem to have realized that.'

'So where's the fucking absent takings, Gord?' Dean replied.

'Of course, I realize this is also a concern for you, Adrian,' Hodge said. 'Comparatively very minor as against worries over Dione and the dead journalist – a lucre matter only – but still indubitably a concern.'

'No question you owe it,' Dean said.

'Undoubtedly,' Hodge said.

'So, where?' Dean grew edgy, impatient. 'Listen, Gordon,' he said, 'not to press unduly, but I'm billed to give a lecture on a book topic. It's in the printed programme. This is a quite educated gathering – people from northern universities and so on, and Boston USA.'

'I'd heard about that,' Hodge said. 'Admirable. I think it's grand to have interests outside the work environment.'

'I can't be late,' Dean said. 'It's disrespectful to the author concerned and to other members of the Society.'

'Certainly,' Hodge said. 'I'll admit that this, what you might call "missionary work" on behalf of Adrian and Dione among the disaffected in our organization, has preoccupied me, rather. And the Tasker whispers. Hence, my self-accounting sessions fell behind a little – the major payment handed in, of course, but then these little catch up sums sidelined momentarily.'

'Understandable,' Pellotte said. 'Thank you for your intervention, Gordon. I speak for myself and Dione.'

'Where is it, for fuck's sake?' Dean Feston said.

'The money?' Hodge replied.

'The money,' Dean said.

'Naturally, I have it ready,' Hodge said. 'But, yes, nearer twenty-three than twenty-one. That might be a result of your kindly pro-Gordon October weighting, Dean! Sorry for the delay. Of course, I had a feeling you would call some time before Christmas re the Dione tensions and Tasker, and decided we could settle up then – though, as I say, I didn't think you'd come on such a notable day as the opening of the Powell conference. The money's in two packets.' His right hand held the glass of barley water, and with the left he struck the leather-covered metal arm of his chair quite a blow, most probably suggesting exuberance and/or amusement. 'I love the idea of very ordinary supermarket carrier bags carrying more than ten grand each in tens, twenties and fifties, don't you – all fifties naturally double-checked as kosher?'

'So where is it?' Dean said.

'Extremely ready,' Hodge said.

'Fucking get it then. Or do you want me to?' Dean said.

'But you're going into the country and will have to park the car in an unfamiliar setting for the day during Society proceedings,' Hodge said. 'Secure? It won't be like Whitsun Festival estate there – people familiar with your vehicle, Aid, and therefore giving it full, proper homage, plus everything aboard. Crime always up pre-Christmas even out in the sticks, as people think of present-buying and booze and cashew nut and crackers stocks. Shall I hold on to the money for a more convenient time? No trouble. I don't mind the risk of having it on the premises.'

'We noticed,' Dean said.

'Obviously, you can't bank that much cash in a lump,' Hodge said. 'The laundering alarm bells would sound off.'

'Our worry, not yours,' Dean said.

'Gordon, who particularly of our people was thinking of reprisals against Dione and Bale?' Pellotte said.

'I don't want you to fret about that, Adrian,' Hodge said. 'They'll listen to me. *Have* listened to me, so far.'

'Who?' Pellotte said.

'Because basically they know I'm right,' Hodge replied. 'Beneath all the rage, they suspect their position on Dione-Bale is bigoted, harsh and obsolete. Farcically obsolete and bigoted. Or, at least, they know I won't shift from my stance, and that they'll have me as an enemy if they continue with plans of that negative, vicious sort against Dione or you, Adrian, or you, Dean, or Bale. That threat, implied threat, is enough in many cases.'

'We'll take the money,' Dean said, finishing his barley water without a tremor. 'It will be fine in the boot.'

'If you think so,' Hodge said, and looked at Pellotte.

'Yes,' Pellotte said.

Hodge left them. At once, Dean went to the opposite side of the room from Pellotte, so that if Hodge came back blazing he'd have to deal with counter-fire from two very separate directions. Dean had his hand in his jacket pocket. Pellotte thought this looked a bit low-level Hollywood and kept both hands in his lap. Hodge soon returned with two bulging Asda carrier bags. Dean moved forward and took them at once. Of course, Pellotte wondered whether, if they hadn't called today, Hodge would have ferried that loot down to Cheltenham with him when he drove his daughters, Maisy and Delphine, to school for the new term after Christmas, and used it as part of due fees. Probably the bursar would be used to payments in cash because so many parents who could afford boarding for the kids had incomes from dodgy sources. Logo of the bursar guild: 'Don't tell me where it came from.' Deprived of those funds, would Hodge have to withdraw the girls and put them into state education? This thought gave Pellotte true distress. Sympathy, gripping him tight, caused him momentarily to hyperventilate.

And things might be even worse than this for the Hodges. Handing over that Asda-bag money to Pellotte and Dean was only a short-term solution. What if, on reflection, Pellotte, advised by Dean, decided Hodge could not after all be forgiven for trying to pull such a scam and had to be properly dealt with, mainly as a warning to others? Pellotte feared that perhaps he would feel compelled, duty-bound, to take an all-out reprisal against Hodgy. How would those girls get on if they had no father, or only a father too badly knocked about to work and earn for at least ten years? Hodge's career depended very much on his smile, yet a time might arrive when smiling became permanently difficult, even impossible. Although Pellotte subsidized Gladstone Naunton's relict, Bert Jutland Marsh, this seemed a different kind of situation from possible poverty in the Hodge household. Hodge had wilfully cheated, calculatedly risked discovery and retaliation. Some might argue he had it coming. And what did the sod mean by continually mentioning the murder of Tasker and its aftermath? But Pellotte decided to remember Maisy and Delphine in a positive, financial sense should Hodge suddenly become a non-breadwinner.

'You'll keep me in the picture, Gordon?' Pellotte said.

'About any potential insurgency over the Dione/Bale question? Oh, yes. It's a privilege, Adrian.'

Dean said he wanted to use the lavatory before they left, customary with him, even when he had not been drinking barley water. Pellotte knew what Dean intended. If there was nobody about, he'd take his shoes off for silence and do a rapid tour of the house, while supposedly behind the locked loo door. Then he'd return to the lavatory, re-shoe and get the flush going, so it would seem as if he'd been inside there non-stop. He'd assess from items in other rooms whether Hodge had been spending big, possibly cornering from takings much more than the twenty-one, or supposed twenty-three, that caused this visit. People could be stupid with money – showy and careless. Dean loved collecting insights and expanding his dossiers. This was the sort of skill that Pellotte found remarkable and praiseworthy in Dean, for someone whose father, so he said, had played a pub piano and done nothing much besides. Dean would have an eye open for the Sokolovsky, too, though that did not seem a danger now.

Obviously, the way Hodge had graciously upped the figure to twenty-three was one of the most ancient tricks in the game: you hung on to filched money for at least weeks hoping nobody would notice, but, if they did, you added a bit, to show how stupendously deep-down honest you were, despite the apparent silly, pardonable reckoning glitch. And the carrier bags, all prepared: a lovely, homey, workaday touch. Hodgy almost deserved to get away with it, the pilfering sod, especially if he'd really been doing something among the crew to ease the Dione-Rupe situation, and quell that Tasker slaughter gossip. Dean could check fairly soon on this, but to Pellotte it sounded like make-believe, of course.

He recognized that Hodge was probably right about the danger to the money if left all day in the parked BMW boot, and was *definitely* right about the lunacy of banking such a flagrant heap in the bank's deposit wall safe. Pellotte thought Dean would spot these difficulties, too. When they left Hodge, Dean did, though, put the carrier bags into the boot, alongside their emergency kit, in the event blessedly unused. Pellotte couldn't tell whether Hodge saw these extras and deduced what they meant, might have meant, might yet mean. He shook hands intensely with the two, wished them an enjoyable conference, showing another excellent replica of total genuineness. He stood at the door until the car moved off. Then he smiled that smile and waved.

Pellotte knew Dean must regard his rooms survey as rushed, skimped, hardly professional, yet Dean seemed to feel he'd got an adequate picture. 'Nothing outlandish in the rest of the place, Adrian,' he said. 'Some jewellery boxed on a dressing table, all run-of-the-mill or crap standard. The rings and watch he's wearing are worth a bit, but less than a grand all together.' Normally, Dean would have wanted to count the bank notes at once. He believed in counting and exactitudes. He lived by confirmed data. He always behaved as if Adrian could be a little slack over detail and needed Dean's thorough, meticulous input. Today, though, because of his scheduled talk on Powell's book at Faunt Castle, Dean clearly did not want any more delays. Or no more *avoidable* delays.

Dean drove around the corner into Pine Street and, in fact, stopped briefly. They brought both carrier bags from the boot and quickly began to load their pockets, including trousers, with as much of the cash as would not grotesquely distort their clothes, concentrating on the biggest denominations, fifties and twenties. During his many years as a trader, Pellotte had grown very familiar with old notes in bulk. They were the essentials of his career, as was, say, a scalpel for a surgeon or a cow for a vet. Normally, he and Dean would have a briefcase for money they collected, but he knew the science of pocket utilization, also, from his earliest days dealing. The amounts collected then would not really have justified a bag of any kind, although reasonably substantial. He recalled that, for optimum storage, currency notes should be placed horizontally in jacket side-pockets but vertically in trousers. Although the inner breast pocket of the jacket could also take some notes vertically, the quantity had to be limited or a crude bump in the tailoring showed.

They made the transfers quickly now. Although people in Pine might observe through their windows Dean and Pellotte working with the money, Pellotte guessed it would not strike them as unusual. They'd know the car, and also know it did a lot of collecting around Whitsun, a lot of in-cash collecting. And nobody would ring the police. People on Whitsun did ring the police about *some* troubles and nuisances, but not about Adrian Pellotte garnering money. For them, that's who Adrian Pellotte *was*, most probably – someone who garnered.

Dean had brought rubber bands for the funds. Neatness he always aimed for. The rubber bands helped. But their pockets could only take about half. Some of the notes they decided to replace in the boot with their Brownings, under some old newspapers in a green plastic crate. They had to accept that degree of risk, or make their garments farcically untrim, like Marlborough Man.

As a keynote speaker at Faunt Castle, Dean, in particular, knew he should maintain high suavity. There'd be some very distinguished tailoring at the conference and it would be sad if he appeared unkempt through gross boodle wads distorting his couture. On account of the setting and expected upper-crust flavour of the conference, he had only two of his shirt buttons open today, rather than the usual three. Dean estimated this would be just right: a bohemian element tinged parts of Powell's work, and Dean could be seen as matching that, but in a muted, very unmedallioned way. Adrian wanted to accommodate some notes in the top pocket of his jacket, although they had decided at first not to use this one in either of their suits because, unless folded into a real, pronounced, tit-like wodge, cash would protrude a little above the upper edge and look brash and vulgar, as if deliberately to proclaim they had plenty. Dean thought that might be suitable for a gathering of bookies or soccer agents but off-key for an Anthony Powell gathering. Dean recognized this as the kind of casualness Adrian could fall into, and saw he must apply a gentle corrective. He convinced Pellotte it would be better from the point of view of image to leave all the surplus in the boot under the papers with the guns.

In fact, Adrian Pellotte thought Dean looked pretty nearly all right when he gave his lecture. Of course, Pellotte knew about the money ballasted aboard and could see that Dean's jacket had become slightly misshapen and too tight, despite their care. But others would probably not notice and, in any case, might assume he always fell short of total smartness, and forgive him, regarding scruffiness as natural to some scholars, self-taught or otherwise. Tomorrow, though, when Pellotte and Dean returned to the two-day conference, the money would have been left in the firm's safe and some delegates might spot how Dean's turnout had improved and his weight apparently gone down. That wouldn't matter. They'd think he had on a better cut suit. And similarly for Pellotte, except that he wouldn't be doing anything as noticeable as Dean at the lectern today, and so his tailoring shouldn't get focused on.

Faunt Castle was still impressive, although turned over these days to community projects. Pellotte loved ramparts and towers, that kind of thing. Of course, he could have bought Faunt Castle if tempted and restored it to a home, while keeping all ancient features. But that would be a stupidly flashy use of wealth. He would stay on Whit. For these two days, however, he'd enjoy Faunt and its genuine stone and beams. He considered Dean's talk this morning in a long mahogany-panelled room went damn well. He had done quite a bit of research – to be expected of someone so systematic when he approached a challenge, whether literary or commercial. He focused on the Lady Widmerpool character mentioned in the title of his paper, a beautiful, destructive, evil-tempered, *grande horizontale*, in and out of innumerable beds and several *Dance* volumes. At the end of one volume she is almost certainly fucking a current Eton pupil called Calthorpe on school premises at tea time, having during her life tried – not very satisfactorily – fucking at least two *Old* Etonians, including, of course, as Dean suggested, her husband, Lord Widmerpool. He waited miserably outside in the street for her to finish with the boy, who was related to two previous Calthorpes, actually school contemporaries of Lord Widmerpool, but then only Kenneth Widmerpool. Dean's talk was about the splendidly circular shape of *Dance*, here exemplified in educationally networked upper-crust shags across the years.

When making one of his most brilliant points during the talk, Dean leaned forward excitedly. He must have forgotten how swollen he was by the Hodge money and bumped hard into the lectern with the stuffed inside pocket of his navy double-breasted suit. This clearly brought him a rough shock through the chest for a moment and made him falter, as if he had taken a thumping body blow. His eyes met Pellotte's in the audience. They seemed like a clobbered, dazed boxer's halfway through a disastrous round, imploring, from his corner guidance, or prayer, or the surrender towel. Pellotte gave a brief, silent handclap, to show Dean he was winning – and would always win.

Dean felt grateful. Adrian's signal made him struggle harder and with more conviction to get his breath back to normal and frame his words more or less coherently. Slowly, he recovered and managed a small smile to Pellotte. It thrilled Dean that they always helped each other in their different styles. He reached a neat conclusion and received good applause, including 'bravo' shouts from two or three delegates.

After the talk and a question session that followed, there was a fifteen-minute break and he and Pellotte went over to the gallery wing of the building. On loan from the Wallace Collection in London, the original Poussin work that gave Powell his impulse for the novel hung there, the painting itself called *A Dance to the Music of Time*. Dean considered Poussin came quite close to making the grade, and he knew Adrian agreed more or less fully with this.

A woman behind them spoke, or rather, called out. Of course, Dean instantly recognized the voice. It started all kinds of memories, and thoughts about now and the future, too. 'Dean – your talk – *so* fascinating, so understanding of womanhood – but wouldn't one expect that?' she said.

'Karen!' Dean said. He and Pellotte had both turned.

Karen Tyne stood there smiling at them, in that way of hers.

'You'd put real thought into it,' she said. 'And *such* humanity! Do you know, for at least a couple of minutes I think I ran a temperature, it excited me so!'

'You belong to the Society?' Dean said.

'Joined this year,' Karen said. 'I'm really into novels these days.'

'They're worth the effort,' Dean said.

'Well, what a treat!' Pellotte said. And he meant it. Karen – one of Dione's most long-term friends, perhaps from as far back as prep school. He liked her. During the run-up to Dean's divorce a few years ago, Pellotte thought there might have been something fervid between Karen and him, though Dean had never spoken of it, nor Karen, nor Dione. Dean could be very tactful/secretive. So could the women, probably. Pellotte considered they all had a right to silence, if that's what they wanted.

'Things all OK?' Karen said.

'Which?' Pellotte said.

'Dione-Bale,' she said. 'I hear bits, not all.'

'Adrian, a father, so some anxiety. That's a big relationship, parent-daughter. Don't I know from my own family?' Dean said.

'I think she has some guilt,' Karen said.

'In which respect?' Dean said.

'Oh, obviously, the estates – Temperate, Whitsun. The hates. She knows she's defying all that, and putting her father at risk,' Karen said. 'Putting herself and Rupe at risk, too.'

'No, no, I won't have that,' Pellotte said with anguish, 'not Dione herself.'

'She underplays that side of it, as you'd expect of Dione,' Karen replied. 'It's all a bit tense. As a matter of fact I ran across someone lately who might be researching the estates, and the conflicts, for a novel.'

'Who's that, then?' Dean said.

'Well, of course, of course, you might know of him!' Karen said. 'His latest book was on the Rupert Bale TV programme.'

'Vagrain?' Dean said.

'A brilliant item,' Karen said.

'Researching?' Dean said. 'I'm not sure we'll want some stranger poking about in the cause of literature or anything else.'

'There was that journalist, wasn't there – the terrible death?' Karen said. 'I told Abel Vagrain, but it didn't seem to dissuade him.'

'We like our privacy on Whitsun, don't we, Aid?' Dean said. 'And we feel we're entitled to it.'

'That woman was on there with Bale discussing the novel, wasn't she?' Pellotte said.

'Priscilla Sandine?' Karen said.

'We're assured it's very much a business arrangement,' Dean said. '*Only* a business arrangement.'

'I don't say impossible,' Karen replied.

'I want Dione to be OK,' Pellotte said.

'As do we all, I'm sure,' Karen said.

'I worry a bit,' Pellotte said.

'Often these kinds of things sort themselves out,' Karen said.

'Which kind?' Pellotte said.

'Uncertainties,' she said.

'Next time you see them together, Karen, I'd like to hear what you think,' Pellotte said. 'How they're getting on. I'm too involved. You'd be more clear and detached.'

'This is not a request to snoop, not at all,' Dean said. 'But there are unsettling aspects. That's what I meant, referring to fatherhood and its cares – noble cares, but cares. Just give it some very friendly, well-intentioned observation, Karen, and if the fucking Sandine woman seems to be hovering, a note of that, please. These would be acts by you of normal . . . normal comradeship.'

Karen said: 'There are many wholly innocent pairings in television of man and woman, the only link being the programme, with
absolutely nothing further to—'

'When you say you ran across Vagrain, how would that be –
running across him?' Dean asked. 'In what circumstances?'

'An uneven novel, *The Insignia of Postponement,*' Karen replied.

'There's not an Abel Vagrain Society, is there? You don't belong
to that as well as the Powell outfit, do you?' Dean said.

'The symbolism in *Insignia,*' Karen said. 'That old-style diving suit.
And the boots. Crude. Laughable. Leaden – like the boots! But some
other sections very OK.'

'Tell us about Vagrain,' Dean said.

'What put me on to him . . . or, that's to say, what caused me to
run across him . . . I watch that programme because of a hate figure
of mine who appears occasionally. I try to will him to touch a live
cable and get shrivelled in front of the cameras, or at least have a
haemorrhaging fit. I do a sort of voodoo. Actually, he wasn't on the
show that night.'

'Ince,' Dean said.

'Right,' Karen said. 'From Cambridge.'

'I remember you told me. And he *is* hatable,' Dean said. 'We
wonder about him now and then.'

'Following this, I managed to get to one of Vagrain's book-store
signings,' Karen said.

'Plus conversation?' Dean said.

'One can see another side of the author,' she said.

'Not just words on the page,' Pellotte said.

'Right,' she said, 'though these, of course, remain paramount. One
gives the words, as it were, a living context.'

'There's a very worthwhile flesh and bone aspect from actual
contact at a signing and so on, I expect,' Pellotte said.

'The theme of your paper, Dean – so perceptive and humane on
. . . what did you call it? – yes, "the unhidden, unbidden, flagrant
compulsions of promiscuity",' she said. 'Pamela Widmerpool's I mean.'

'Thanks,' Dean said.

'Flagrant because . . . well, because it *is* compulsive,' Karen said.
'In her.'

'That's the gist,' Dean said.

'It's been a while, hasn't it, Dean?' she replied. Karen touched his
arm for a second. 'And how *are* you? Generally, that is. You're looking
so damn well. Have you been in the gym bodybuilding? I think

you've put on some pounds. It suits you. Greatly. Oh, yes, greatly. You look so upper body solid. Formidable.'

'Sterling,' Pellotte said. 'We should move.' People were beginning to return to the auditorium. She turned and went ahead.

Dean said to Pellotte: 'Adrian, I might not come back to Whitsun with you tonight, other things being equal.'

'No, I don't suppose you will. Which other things?'

'You'd better have these.' He passed Pellotte the car keys. 'See you here tomorrow. Make sure you put the Hodge boodle safe.'

'Will you be all right when you take your jacket off and lose nearly all your upper-body physique?' Pellotte replied. 'I suppose she must have a car here. There should be a nice country hotel not far off.'

Dean went swiftly after Karen, put a hand on her shoulder and spoke into one ear. She nodded. Dean rejoined Pellotte and they resumed their seats in the auditorium.

'I'm really looking forward to it,' Dean said.

'What?' Pellotte said.

Thirteen

'He says he knows you, ma'am.'

'Yes,' Esther replied.

'He says he wants to talk to you on a "one-to-one basis". His words. Only to you. We're not getting very far with him.'

'Right.'

'He says he's got something significant. That's another of his words, "significant". To do with Gervaise Manciple Tasker. He uses all the names. Like official? And about Pellotte and Dean Feston. He could be just mouthing.'

'I'd better come.' She replaced the internal phone and went down to custody. Detective Sergeant Sutton took her to Interview Room Four. 'Hello, Ivor,' she said.

'Mrs Davidson. Good. Thanks.'

'What's been happening?' she said. 'I've heard an outline. But—'

'Alleged.'

'Yes, alleged. Passing forged notes. Attempting to.'

'There's more to it,' he said. 'Much.'

'I guessed that.'

'Something significant.'

'Fifties and twenties, yes?' Esther replied.

'I'd like to talk to you alone,' he said. 'On a one-to-one basis.'

'Fine,' she said.

'The recorder off,' he said.

'Fine,' she said. The other people left. Esther sat opposite him.

He gave a big, loud, comradely sigh. 'This is quite a bit different from usual, isn't it?'

'Well, yes.'

'Which is why I thought it best to ask for you.'

'Right.'

'I mean, we have . . . we have an arrangement. You'd agree?'

'Absolutely.'

'I help you good sometimes. You'd agree?'

'Absolutely.'

'I give you whispers.'

'You're a registered informant, Ivor.'

'That's what I was getting at when I said "different from usual".'

'The setting?'

He waved his hand at the bare, small room – a few straight chairs, the table, all of them anchored, the recording apparatus. 'Not our normal sort of meeting spot. Supermarket car parks. Railway platforms. Malls.'

'We switched them about. Best like that. Safer like that. Elementary precautions.'

'But now in here,' he said. He gave another contemptuous, forlorn wave.

'Where did the forged notes come from?'

'Alleged.'

'Where did the alleged forged notes come from?'

'That's the point, isn't it?'

'Are there more?' she asked.

'It's a situation, isn't it?'

'What kind?'

'I don't know. I can't see the edges of it – how far it goes,' he said.

'We might be able to work that out together.'

'How am I supposed to know if they're forged? Do I hold every note up to the light?'

'You've got a lot, have you?'

'If there's cash in my pocket, I like to spend it, not put it under the microscope. My nature.'

She saw he wanted to sound unmiserly, loveably open-handed. Many informants realized they were regarded as sneaky and furtive. They *were* sneaky and furtive, had to be. So, when they saw a chance to act grand they grabbed it – to compensate. 'It can be difficult with bogus notes,' she said. 'Some places won't take fifties at all. They put up notices.'

'Disgusting, really, isn't it?'

'What?'

'Abusing the nation's currency.'

'Disgusting. Did a shop refuse the notes and call us?'

'Presents – with Christmas coming up.'

'How much involved?'

'Two hundred and some.'

'All forged? Alleged forged.'

'Might only be one or some. I don't know. They didn't tell me.'

'From one source?'

'You'll remember where I live,' he replied.

'Pine Street, on Whitsun. Is that important?'

'My address – it's in your safe, with my code name, yes? Luke Totnes.' He smiled, as though comforted to know he had an approved, established place in the organization – the police organization – although, for now, he'd finished up in this room. That was also part of the organization – the police organization – but not a favourable part for him. He'd chosen the alias name himself. Totnes, in Devon, had some magic for him – a girl, perhaps, or childhood holiday. And he said he liked the flavour of 'Luke' – maybe the mildness of the vowel sound. You kept a nark's name hidden, even from other police. Information could leak in more directions than one.

Of course, it would be wrong to call him Luke now. He had been pulled in under his proper name. Luke Totnes equalled Ivor Frank Caple, a capable, low category thief who did some confidential talking to Esther when it suited him. Now? She felt this shouldn't be held against Ivor Frank Caple/Luke Totnes: most informants only informed when it suited them, either as an earnings boost, or to get softer treatment in a prosecution. Esther was unusually high rank to run a registered, official, informant, but he'd talk to nobody else.

Caple: burly, large-faced, open-faced, strong-faced, grey-moustached, firm-jawed, fiftyish, cheery-looking even now, though with brief scowls at the room and what it meant for him. Some might be prepared to trust Caple on his appearance alone, and Esther would admit he probably brought her truth more often than make-believe. This would put him in the top seven per cent of informants. The moustache showed genius. It had bulk, density, packing the under-nose region and pushing out on to his cheeks but not farcically reaching the ears: these whiskers recalled earlier good eras – Victorian enterprise and sense, Edwardian solidity.

'Your other self is secure,' Esther said.

'Let's imagine a scene,' he replied.

'Let's.'

'For instance, I might be at the window of my place in Pine Street, though not necessarily observed.'

'Well, yes, I expect you might be at times. Neighbourhood watch.'

'Tell me this, then, Mrs Davidson, whose car's out there? Whose car out there on this a.m. occasion?'

'In our scene?'

'In our scene.'

'This is not an easy one to answer.'

'A well-known car.'

'Give me a clue.'

'Like new. Not a scratch anywhere. Original wing mirrors, most probably.'

'Pellotte's?'

'You'd already had a clue from the sergeant, yes? He mentioned names – Pellotte, Dean Feston?'

'Doing what in Pine Street?'

'Stopped.'

'A call on someone. A dealer? Who's in Pine Street? They're coming to your place?'

'Not a call. They're on the pavement, stuffing themselves with cash. Working fast.'

'Stuffing themselves?'

'Their pockets. The boot's open.'

'They're taking money from the boot?'

'The boot's like an operating theatre.'

'Meaning?'

'Equipment.'

'Which?'

'An oxygen cylinder. Blood transfusion gear. Big green first-aid box.'

'Many cars carry those.'

'And spare suits, shirts.'

'Cash from where?' Esther asked.

'Asda bags. Two. Full.'

'Yes, but from where?'

'You ask the key questions. Why you're in that job.'

'But would you know from where?'

'If I say Larch Street? Most probably.'

'Around the corner.'

'Who's in Larch Street?' Caple said.

'Gordon Basil Hodge?'

'Brilliant recall, Mrs Davidson! But to be expected. A brain like yours! You've got him dossiered, haven't you?'

'Collection by Pellotte and Dean from Hodge?'

'That sort of thing.'

'Routine.'

'Think so? What was the word around about Hodgy?'

'He's won best trader awards, hasn't he?'

'So the dossier says, I expect. That's old info, though. What did the voices tell us now, up-to-date?'

'Which voices?'

'Voices generally.'

'Gossip voices?' Esther asked.

'Gossip, but spot-on gossip. That's obvious, isn't it?'

'Is it?'

'*Now* it's obvious. Because of the BMW stopped in Pine Street.'

'Which spot-on gossip are we talking about?' Esther said.

'Ask yourself, why two bags of boodle?'

'Takings.'

Caple laughed. 'Well, yes, you could call them that. Hodgy taking from the firm. Trying to.'

'Skimming?'

'Pellotte himself, in person, present.'

'Pellotte collects regularly. Everyone sees the BMW harvesting.'

'This is a morning, doorstepping call, I'd say, plus paramedic backup kit and the emergency wardrobe. Not routine. The opposite.'

'Oh. Is Hodge all right then?'

'OK so far, I think. But short of two Asda bags.'

'The emergency clothing in the car boot?'

'Unused.'

'How do you know? Perhaps they'd changed into the suits they were wearing when you saw them. The garments in the boot might have been the stained ones. Are you sure Hodge is all right?'

'The clothes were clean.'

'The spot-on gossip you mentioned said Hodge was diverting Happy Gardening Solutions loot, did it?'

'Clever voices, weren't they?' he said.

So, how did all this bring revelations about Gervaise Manciple Tasker? Esther wondered, but didn't ask. Number Three guiding rule with informants: let them tell it their way. Don't badger. Don't push. Number One was: they know where they're safest so let them pick the meeting spot. Two: assume what they tell you is three-quarters wrong. 'All the Asda-bag money into their pockets?'

'Not all. It's too much. Their tailoring would look ridiculous.'

'Why not just take it to the office safe – Happy Gardening Solutions? That's usual. We think it's laundered through company books.'

'They're making for somewhere else,' he said, 'and are timetabled. Where? There's been some more gossip around. It says they'll be away at a castle. A conference, to do with books they both like, especially Dean, relating to some author. Famous. Some in hardback. Not porn. Faunt Castle. No secret they're going. Everybody knows and has a chuckle. Those two, in love with books! How nice! They're proud of it, I bet. For something like that they'd want to look all right, not fat with cash. They pocket as much as they can in case the car's raided or pinched. They're going to be off Whit. Takers at the Faunt car park won't know they shouldn't touch the holy BMW. To them it would be just a BMW – luxury model, good for a glean or a drive away.'

Esther could see how the tale might develop. 'They put some of the money back in the boot, did they?'

'Alongside the oxygen, in a blue plastic crate, to help keep things tidy. They shoved the extra money under newspapers. And their pistols. Brownings. They're famed for Brownings. From their jacket pockets.'

'They flourished guns?'

'Not flourished. Just didn't bother hiding. This is Pine Street. This is Whit. This is Adrian Pellotte and Dean.'

'We're working on it.'

'They wouldn't want to go to a literature conference in a castle with automatics aboard, would they? Off colour. And they had to make pocket room.'

'How much do you reckon?'

'In the Asda bags originally, I'd say at least twenty K, and maybe up towards twenty-five.'

'How much goes back into the boot, under the papers? You'll know that exactly now, won't you?'

'Ah . . .' he said.

'What?'

'You're on to it.'

'On to what?'

'How things will turn out,' he said.

'They drive off towards this castle, Faunt Castle?'

'There's eleven thousand four hundred in the boot.'

'And you could guess at something like that, from watching them.'

'I knew it was pretty good. Used notes, no numbered list anywhere.'

'But some forged and antiqued. At least some. Obviously, you couldn't tell that then. Did you tail them?'

'Tail them?'

'To the castle.'

'Tail Pellotte and Dean Feston! Not fucking likely. Sorry! Not at all likely, Mrs Davidson. Couldn't be done – not secretly. They're too fly, too alert, know the game too well. We're talking about the chief of Happy Gardening Solutions and his heavy.'

'Right. But, of course, you didn't need to tail them. You knew where they were going. Faunt Castle will be on the map.'

'I keep my car in a friend's multi-lockable warehouse yard. It's on Whit, but I have to pushbike there. It takes a while. So I couldn't have tailed them, even if I'd been stupid enough to want to.'

'It gave you a break-in idea, did it?'

'What?'

'Them loading their pockets. They're obviously scared someone might force the boot while they're into lit at Faunt. So, get as much of it about their person as they can manage. But more or less half is still there. "Very promising," you say to yourself. "And I know where the car will be for most of the day, unattended."'

'Many would surely think like this, Mrs Davidson, if they'd seen the money moving.'

'As you had.'

'This is why observing from a window can be useful. It's dirty money, anyway. Crooked money. Drugs money. They can't have a proper right to it. Courts confiscate that sort of money.'

'You, too. A true hijack. You were doing society a service,' Esther said. 'Did you know how to get a BMW boot open? I don't suppose it would be alarmed. Pellotte doesn't want the police called to his car.'

'Now, listen: I'm not under caution.'

'No.'

'None of this can be used.'

'None of it.'

'And no recording.'

'No recording.'

'I thought, "They're going to be off Whit. All that pious, timid respect for Pellotte's car won't apply." It has always niggled me, you know.'

'What?'

'The BMW. Its shine and size. The untroubled life it gets.' His cheery features went twisted and sour for a few moments. 'The rest of us drive something small and old and bottom of the range even when it was new, so if it does get done or taken the loss is nothing much.'

'Envy's a deadly sin, Ivor.'

'So damn smug the two of them look, cruising Whit. Yes, I know BMW boots. Not impossible.'

'Evidently.'

His face became upbeat again. 'Faunt, the castle, ever seen it, Mrs Davidson?'

'I don't think so.'

'Beautiful. Not huge, but lovely. Middle ages, though mucked about with since obviously. Grey walls and towers backgrounded by the greenery of old trees. A centre for social and cultural stuff now, but you can imagine it as someone's home, although with towers. And a moat. Swans. There's a place like it in the books, I think. Why Faunt was picked for the conference. That's the talk. Several pricey vehicles in the car park. Four-by-fours. A Bentley. Three BMWs. Couple of Lexuses. Perhaps he's that kind of writer. Classy.'

'You do the boot, lift the carrier bags, get back to your car and scarper?' Esther said. 'I don't suppose you'd take the Brownings.'

'What would I do with Brownings?'

'Defend yourself, when Pellotte and Dean come looking for their deficit eventually?'

'Guns are not me, Mrs Davidson.'

'Good.'

'But it's tricky in that car park. Plenty of people about. Some conference folk, most likely, and others, too. It's a community centre, you know. All sorts going on there as well as the literature. People coming to learn Italian and ballet steps. I have to look as if the BMW is *my* BMW. Like casual? And there might be CCTV, though I couldn't see it. The money's still in the bags, both about half full. They're bulgy. I've brought a black leather, very executive, valise with me in case I'm lucky.'

'You pushbiked over to your car from Pine Street carrying a valise?'

'Don't report me to traffic for one-handed cycling, will you?'

'Bit obvious?'

'Necessary.'

'Dean's news gathering service will probably hear about it.'

'I'm entitled to own a valise.'

'And a bike. But he'll wonder if you were after treasure. Theirs. A chunk will have gone missing, won't it? Most probably, he's got your address in his data cupboard. He might suspect some window gazing.'

'All right, perhaps I could have done things a different way. I didn't. I was rushed. So, at Faunt I take the money out of the bags in the boot and make four, neat flat piles. Then I wrap these with the newspaper and put them into the valise. This left the Brownings very obvious, but did I worry? I pull the boot lid down. Although it won't shut properly because of a bust lock it stays down. Most likely it will swing up when they're driving home, especially if they don't notice it's been done. Some rage then, I should think. Oh, dear, dear!' He half giggled, half smirked. 'I'm still acting matter-of-fact – like I'm here for the conference or another activity and have papers and so on in the valise to do with my visit. There's a reception desk in the castle visible from the car park, which means, also, the car park is visible from the desk. I can see a woman staring out towards me and the BMW. I don't like it. What's she going to think if I walk to my old Peugeot from the BMW carrying a plump case and drive away, not even having gone into Faunt? Who's she going to tell? Will I see a blue light behind me after a couple of miles?

'So, I walk urgently up towards reception, as though ashamed of being very late, yet pleased to be here at last. I say to her: "The conference, please?" "Pole?" she replies.

'I couldn't make out what she meant. Did she think I was Polish? Did it matter if I was? Or was the author Polish? Maybe some other meeting on, to do with exploring to the North or South Pole. I said: "Right." You see, Mrs D., it didn't really matter where I ended up in the castle as long as she believed I belonged *somewhere*. She pointed to double doors on the other side of the reception foyer and I crossed to them and went inside. Quite a big room, fairly crowded, but with a few empty places at the back. This would be part of the original castle, the ceiling high, the walls bare stone. Might have been the Great Hall once, for feasts and merrymaking. Terrific. I love authentic old buildings. History I'm in favour of, times when Whit and Temperate didn't exist even. I took a seat, placing my valise under it.' He bent and re-enacted this with the custody chair, but no valise.

He straightened. 'Now, a surprise,' he said. 'Who do you think was lecturing? Dean! He sounded pretty good, as though he'd really done some reading. He spoke about all sorts of characters in the books like they were actual people he knew very well, but quite different from the people he knew on Whit. Maybe when he was banged up alone they became like friends – company in his cell. The money gave him quite a lot of extra chest and most probably around the hips, also, but I couldn't see that because he spoke from behind a lectern.

'Once, he seemed to forget he'd bulked himself out and bumped against this lectern and obviously knocked the wind out of himself. It made him lose the line of his chat for a while. I thought he wouldn't recover. But Dean's a fighter and managed to get back to the topic all right. This was about some woman in the tales called Pamela who sounded a real goer – sorry to be so frank, Mrs Davidson – but it *is* literature. Finally, although married to a Lord, she's still at it all over the place. But only a Life Peer. Dean said this proved life moved in circles, with this toff slapper in the middle pulling all sorts into her bed and linking them up. And I thought, yes, maybe life *was* a kind of circle. Consider it, Mrs Davidson, I'd managed to glimpse Dean and Adrian Pellotte in the street splitting the funds. Then I came to Faunt and lifted the money they hadn't already lifted for themselves. Following this, I pop into the conference with these happy gains in my valise. And by a sort of fluke I listen to Dean give a talk which, because they obviously had to get there in time to do it, made them divide the money like that, meaning I could come to hear his performance, with about half of it nabbed, in my bag and right in front of him, and he with a quarter of it around his body right in front of *me*.'

'Yes, a kind of neatness to it,' Esther said.

'He got some good applause at the end. I felt glad. He deserved that. I didn't stay for any more of the conference, though. It seemed wisest. They might go to check the car. The chairman announced that in one of the galleries there was a painting about a dance which people might want to look at, but I went to the Peugeot and drove back to Pine Street.'

'We haven't had any report from Pellotte that his car was broken into and cash taken.'

'No, maybe not. What's he going to say – "£11,400 of Happy Gardening Solutions' crack, charlie, H and skunk money has been outrageously lifted, officer?"'

'Perhaps it wasn't a sound idea to start using it so soon,' Esther said. '*Trying* to use it. They'll be listening out for tales of big spending. And Pellotte is going to be deeply cross about fractures to his myth.'

'Which myth?'

'The perfect BMW. A buckled boot. He'll be like anyone else on Whit or Temperate.'

'Ducky idea, isn't it?'

'He won't want to show signs of frailty at present. A ruptured car is frailty. He's trying to handle a crisis.'

'That TV stuff, and his daughter?'

'Some people in the firm watch him for weaknesses. They'd like to push him out and take over. You might have started a—'

'The papers,' Caple replied.

'Which?'

'The ones from the boot to wrap the money.'

'Newspapers?'

'Old newspapers. When I get home after Faunt I drop off the take in Pine Street, then go over to park my car in the warehouse yard and cycle back – valiseless now. First thing, obviously, I must count the earnings. Suddenly, though, I see his face. It stops me. For a couple of minutes it stops me, Mrs Davidson. All that money, waiting to be totted up, but I pause. Yes, I pause.'

Drama. 'Whose face?'

'Gervaise Manciple Tasker's.'

'How? Where?'

'When I'm unwrapping. In one of the papers.'

'He was a journalist.'

'There's an article he'd published and a photo of him as the writer, the way they do, and under it "Gervaise Tasker". No "Manciple".'

'That would be his working name. What kind of article?'

'Oh, about some topic.'

'Well, yes, it would be.'

'What they call investigative. To do with an MP. Backhanders etcetera.'

'Which?'

'It's not important.'

'It might be.'

'No, it isn't. What's important is that I'd picked up four newspaper pages as wrapping when I took the money. So, I see his face on one and I wonder about the rest.'

'They're *pages* from newspapers, are they, not complete issues?'

'Pages. I'd thought they were whole newspapers in the crate, but no. Pages. From different newspapers, different dates, different kinds of articles. But they've all got a picture of Gervaise Tasker. I've kept these at Pine Street, if you want to look. I had them spread out on the table – the money in stacks at one end where I'd been counting, and now the newspaper pages at the other. This was a kind of – well, a kind of revelation.'

'In which way?'

'They're interested in him.'

'You mean interested in the kind of reporting he does?'

'Yes, maybe his kind of reporting, in case he did it one day about Whit and Happy Gardening Solutions. And Temperate and Abracadabra Leisure. But also they've got identification pictures of him, haven't they? Different pictures. Various angles. All round. Suppose they wanted to send someone or more than one for him. This could help make sure they got the right man.'

'How do you mean "send someone, or more than one, for him"?'

'Yes, send someone, or more than one, for him.'

And Esther decided then that Pellotte and Dean, and Happy Gardening Solutions could not be implicated in Tasker's death. If they were, Dean would never allow potentially awkward evidence like that to pile up in the car, and stay there after Tasker's death. Adrian Pellotte might act lordly and careless, not Dean. They could have been *interested* in Tasker and his objectives on Whit and Temperate. Dean did like to gather information, build his facts store, register incursers. That was different from killing Tasker, or having him killed, though – and different from sending 'someone, or more than one, for him'.

Detective Sergeant Abner Cule had had doubts about Pellotte's and Feston's involvement from the start, because, for one thing, the forensic people said the bullets that killed Tasker were not from a Browning nine mm, the usual weapon of both. But, of course, they might have sent 'someone or more than one' to do the job, and such a hit man, or hit men, would use their own preferred gun. Or Pellotte and Dean could have used a different pistol, knowing the Browning was a giveaway. And Esther had also wondered whether Cule's reaction came because he hadn't cracked Dean in the interview. Cule, proud of his abilities, possibly thought this failure wasn't a failure at all but meant Dean couldn't *be* cracked because he was innocent.

Now, though, after Caple's description of the newspapers, Esther's thoughts did turn away from Pellotte and Dean and went elsewhere. She recalled that Temperate church sidesman in Tasker's notes and his words of blessing: 'Mene. Mene. Tekel. Upharsin. Ufucker.' And she recalled Belinda's hint that Esther's guesses at Camby or Laidlaw for the Tribe meeting might be wrong. Belinda had clammed then, wouldn't say more. But there'd been a strange moment: at one point, hadn't she referred to Temperate people at the club as 'personnel?'

Unusual word. A slip? A pointer? Who was Personnel in the Temperate firm's hierarchy: Joel Jeremy North, according to Tasker's notes. The sidesman? The Tribe figure? Perhaps if Amesbury's leadership had become fragile, others beside the two deputies might want to show they were in the running as successor, and would prove it by the decisive disposal of Tasker, considered a danger to the company. Esther focused on North.

'This is a discovery for you, isn't it, Mrs Davidson?' Caple said. 'I look after you, as ever.' She heard the winged chariot of *quid pro quoism* hurrying near. 'I know you're stuck – the Tasker investigation going nowhere. And the buzz says bullies from the Home Office and the Mayor's office grow stroppy. But now – now you have these papers. They're waiting for you in Pine Street. What could be referred to as a breakthrough.'

'Thanks, Ivor.'

Big matey sigh again. 'And then this carry-on about the dud notes and the shop. You might be able to do the same.'

'Same as what?'

'*You* look after *me*.'

'As ever.'

'Now you know the full tale you can see I'm spotless, a victim, that's all. Someone passes me phoney bills, but I don't recognize them. Who would, except an expert?'

'Or a shop,' Esther said.

'I say "passes me phoney bills" but you'll query this. All right, it's not quite true, I know. Nobody passed them, in the usual meaning of passed.'

'No, not the usual meaning.'

'But I thought you'd be able to explain the special details to your people, without saying too much, of course.'

'Of course.'

Esther went with Gerald to N.D.L.tv's studios to meet some of the people concerned with *A Week in Review.* Gerald would not take part in the actual broadcast this evening but could familiarize himself with the place, and the procedures. There'd be a drinks reception first. Then, as she understood it from Gerald, they could watch the show from the hospitality suite and, afterwards, re-meet the panellists and programme staff as they relaxed. The invitation to Gerald had specifically mentioned Esther. She thought she'd enjoy things, as long as Gerald stayed reasonably civil and controlled. He'd been fairly unfebrile lately. Perhaps N.D.L.tv had been warned that Esther should be present to manage him. She knew Gerald was referred to here and there as 'the loon with the bassoon'.

The producer introduced himself, said how pleased he was they'd come, and that a busy and distinguished musician like Gerald had agreed to take part in a future show.

Esther glanced around the room: 'I don't see the Sandine dynamo,' she said.

'Not tonight. Panellists vary. But Sacheverell Biggs, our drinks man, is blessedly always here!' He approached with his tray. Esther took white wine, Gerald, Glenlivet.

'Will you miss her?' Esther asked.

'Who?' Edgehill replied.

'Sandine,' Esther said.

'In what sense?'

'She lit things up lately, didn't she?' Esther replied.

'You could cut the sex with a cheese wire,' Gerald said.

'We have some lively people and topics tonight,' Edgehill said.

'And Bale chairing?' Gerald said. 'He's great. Or great when Priscilla Sandine is there to do some igniting.'

'Great, regardless,' Edgehill said.

'I see him by the door with the Pellotte woman,' Gerald said. 'Has she come along to show who owns him? She gave us a blast about Sandine.'

'No need for such enmity,' Edgehill said.

A middle-aged woman holding a glass joined them: possibly gin-and-bitters. Esther felt she should recognize her. 'Ah, here's Nellie,' Edgehill said. 'Head of News and Current Affairs. She often invades for a free drink.'

Yes, Esther had seen her at police news conferences occasionally. Nellie Poignard? Big, hearty-looking, vigorous.

'This is grand,' she said.

'What?' Esther said.

'To catch you on the premises, Chief Superintendent,' Poignard said. 'I'm constantly trying to get Larry to give me useful insights. He's hopeless. Or secretive. You might be better.'

'Insights?' Esther said.

'The estates. He lives on Whitsun. I tell him something mighty is brewing up there – and on Temperate. We have two leaderships with problems, Amesbury in Temperate, Pellotte in Whitsun, both desperate to hang on to their thrones. They'll do anything to secure themselves, including all-out warfare. I ask Larry for privileged glimpses. He acts blank, blank, blank. No barometer at all.'

'All's set fair, as far as I can see,' Edgehill said.

'Oh, stop! The pointers to imminent trouble pile up,' Nellie said. 'Above all, of course, that killing. The journalist. And the foul display.'

'An ongoing inquiry,' Esther said.

'Progress?' Nellie said.

'Ongoing,' Esther said.

'We've found he went out to Happy Gardening Solutions and to St John's Church on Temperate,' Nellie said. 'Reconnaissance?'

'I thought we were here for a sodding arts programme,' Gerald replied. He would grow dizzy and eye-popping if Esther became central to the chit-chat, not him, when the only reason they were here was him and his fame.

'And now a different car outside Pellotte's house,' Nellie Poignard stated.

'Oh? That's meaningful?' Esther said.

'I get up to Whit and Temperate occasionally, just driving around for the . . . well, for the flavour. More than ever recently. I smell crisis. It's a BMW, but not ADP 12. If he's bought a new car he'd have transferred the cherished number plate. So, has ADP 12 been vandalized, broken into, needs garage treatment? My God, what would this say about his position on Whit and in the firm? People don't fear, idolize him any more? Insurrection? What's next? Yes, what's next?'

'Who gives a twopenny toss?' Gerald said. 'These damn degenerates.'

'Cars go in for servicing,' Esther said.

'Missing for days. I've done several trips.'

'Obsessional, Nellie,' Edgehill said.

'Even BMWs need repairs now and then,' Esther said.

'That's what I mean,' Nellie Poignard exclaimed. 'Why? ADP 12 has been savaged?'

'Wear and tear?' Esther suggested.

'ADP 12 is this year's model,' Nellie said.

'Or damaged elsewhere,' Esther said. 'Perhaps he's been lent a courtesy car.'

'Ask sweet Dione,' Gerald said. 'She certainly knows how to open her gob. We ran into her and Bale at a concert.'

'But what kind of answer would we get there?' Nellie said.

'Tell us about tonight's items, would you, please, Larry?' Gerald snarled. 'I know that ultimately this evening I'm going to have my mind engaged with something worthwhile. Ulti-fucking-mately.'

And ultimately Esther, Gerald, Dione Pellotte and Sacheverell Biggs watched the programme together in Hospitality.

'Hell, it's true,' Dione said, 'Rupe's a dud without that shag-me-do, juicy bird Sandine.'

Biggs said: 'He won't drink before a show. Mistake. They have to talk so much shit that only a few good toddies can get them through.'

'I expect you watch every week, do you, Sacheverell?' Esther said.

'I'm usually here alone.'

'Ah,' Esther said.

'What happened to your father's car, Dione?' Gerald said.

'Car? Did anything happen?' Dione said.

Fourteen

'I told him blunt, no messing, Mr Edgehill, you wouldn't want to get pulled into something like that,' Udolpho Wentloog-Jones said. 'These are unsafe times, what with the journo and other matters.'

'You echo one of my colleagues at work.'

'Oh?'

'"Unsafe." She thinks there's going to be big, tumultuous bother.'

'Bright. But, of course, he *would* say there's no intention to pull you into anything like that, not in a major fashion. He says he only wants to ask for your help on the very outside edge of the situation – hardly into it at all, really, according to him – and definitely only a one-off. "Intercession." That's the term he used. A lot. He says he needs somebody to provide intercession on that one-off basis, only that – the one-off basis.'

Edgehill had called in as usual for his morning papers. He said: 'What makes him think that I—?'

'So, Hodgy asks, would I just speak a word to you, nothing beyond that, and only this once? Naturally, he's heard you had a big chinwag with Pellotte and Dean in Gideon the other day. Everybody's heard that, haven't they? A major buzz item on Whit. And, he says, a *friendly* big talk by the look of it, nothing to do with putting the frighteners on, or with reproaches leading later to a swat, as might be the usual cause of a conversation with those two. Well, you told me that talk was mainly to do with the arts – a really civilized discussion, although roadside. He thinks this shows you must be on decent, comfortable terms with them.'

'It was a conversation. That's all. Unexpected. No special meaning.'

'The BMW becomes part of the setting for this happy conversation, and they'd never use it to run you down, in the present state of things between you and them. As a matter of fact, I've seen them around in a different car lately.'

'I heard about that.'

'Servicing, most likely.'

'Or repairs,' Edgehill said.

'His car doesn't get vandalized. Who'd risk it?'

'No, I meant adjustments to the engine, the exhaust – that sort of thing.'

'Anyway, what he's getting at, when he says about intercession, is you've obviously got good access to Adrian Pellotte and Dean and you'd be able to offer it – intercession. They called on him – at his place, Larch Street. That can be an unhelpful sign. But this time they were in a hurry – on their way to something special. He's afraid they'll come back to attend to things, though.'

'Which things?'

'Sort of "on hold" while they were elsewhere.'

'And what's his name again?' Edgehill replied.

'Hodge. Gordon Basil Hodge. GBH, as he's known sometimes, meaning grievous bodily harm on a charge sheet. But he's not really like that. He wins awards for pushing. Remember that sad situation with Gladstone Milo Naunton, God rest his soul? But Hodge is all right. I come across him often – in the way of business. More or less a mate. Yes, Larch Street.'

'The newspaper business?'

'The business.'

'The business in the sense of—?'

'The business.'

'He wants me to intercede on what account?'

'Yes, intercede. Or to put it simpler, speak a word.'

'To Pellotte and Dean?'

'He knows you look in here most mornings for your *Sun* and *Guardian*, getting a good range,' Wentloog-Jones replied. 'That's why he thought I'd be able to pass a request. On his behalf. Like interceding about interceding.'

'He's got problems with Adrian Pellotte and Dean?'

'This can happen.'

'What kind of problems?'

'Any problems with them are going to be serious. They don't go in for small problems. They had a collection of particular stuff in the boot of the BMW,' Udolpho replied.

'What particular stuff?'

'When they called on him,' Wentloog-Jones said. 'He saw it for himself.'

'What kind of stuff?'

'This BMW, ADP 12, will obviously be just a car most of the time, like anyone's vehicle. And useful for when they want to chew the fat with you on Gideon in an amiable and artistic fashion.

But if it pulls up outside your front door with particular stuff in the boot, that's a different aspect.'

'What particular stuff?'

'I didn't want GBH hanging about here to meet you, like by accident. Pellotte doesn't believe in accidents, except the ones he causes. I can do without that kind of trouble. I've got a business to look after.'

'A newspaper business?'

'Of course, what else?'

'*You* don't want to get pulled in.'

Udolpho served some other customers. After they'd left, he said: 'Like you, Larry, I am not indifferent. In a way he's a chum, a business chum, and he has needs.'

'Is he in the newspaper business?'

'A business chum.'

'The other business?' Edgehill said.

'The word would get around if the meet-up happened here. There's what's known as a centrality about this newspaper stall. It's a hub for many. They talk. And Gordon won't call at your place in Bell. Same reason – the word might get around. Pellotte could work out what was going on – Hodgy trying to find allies. Allies against *him* – Adrian Pellotte. I said, phone you, but Gordon doesn't like phones – scared of intercepts, and in any case he wants . . . he says he needs the face-to-face, so he's not just a cold-call voice out of nowhere pleading for favours. He'd like it on a more friendly, equal-to-equal foundation.'

To Edgehill he'd be a voice out of nowhere pleading for favours wherever and however they spoke. 'I've got to get my train, Udo. If he's in touch again say I don't think I can help. I'm sorry, but he's misread things. Badly misread things. I'm not on matey terms with those two. They wouldn't listen to anything I said about Hodge, even if I'd met him. I've no idea what's in the BMW boot when they visit.'

'I think he might do the same.'

'Same as what?'

'Wait in the station and get the train with you, the same train like bump into you. One of those accidents which aren't.'

'The Tube? Why do you say that?'

'I think he will.'

'A rush-hour train for heavy conversation? Some chance!'

'Travel along, then talk to you where you get off – Chancery

Lane? He seemed to have heard it's Chancery Lane. The studios are up that way? He's done research. In the streets there it will be all right to get a chat going. You won't be recognized in a different district, either of you.'

'He told you this?'

'Told me some. I worked out the rest.'

'Stalking?'

'It's necessary. Well, as he sees it, it's necessary. Things are poor for him. As he sees it. Shall I tell you what to look out for? About five foot ten, thirty-one to -four, dark hair – a lot of it, wedge-piled at the front – most likely a jogging suit, navy or black. Or maybe a denim jacket on jeans. Long face. Inclined to smiling. It doesn't mean much – not the way he feels now – but he makes the effort. Scared. There are two children.'

So, Edgehill glanced about for someone matching this at the entrance to Whitsun Festival Station. If Udolpho was right, it must be where the first contact would be made – before Edgehill became hard to spot in the commuter crowd on the platform. *If Udolpho was right.* Surely, he *couldn't* be right. Why the fuck would Hodge believe Edgehill had enough influence with Pellotte to persuade him to call off . . . ? Call off what? A hunt? A vengeance sortie? A punishment operation? A postponed execution?

He saw nobody loitering near the turnstiles who came anywhere close to Udolpho's description, whether round- or long-faced, jogging suit or denim. He saw nobody smiling and loitering near the turnstiles. He saw nobody loitering near the turnstiles at all. People at this time in the morning did not smile or loiter. If Edgehill located a feasible Hodge, he had at least three choices. He could make as though to get on the next train, but, once the supposed Hodge followed him aboard, leave it swiftly. Or he could unexpectedly, swiftly disembark at Holborn, the station before Chancery Lane, just as the doors started to reclose, keeping Hodge stuck. Film and TV drama constantly used these kinds of last-minute train-hopping ploys in chase stories. He knew the techniques. Or, of course, Edgehill could do everything normally and let Hodge make contact when they both alighted at Chancery Lane. That wouldn't commit Edgehill, but it would be a human and humane, large-minded, uncowardly way to deal with these apparent troubles. And Edgehill felt some curiosity.

Actually, after a while, he began to turn the situation upside down. He'd started by scheming to avoid Hodge. Now, because he'd failed to locate him, he felt defeated, incomplete – he *wanted* to locate him, *needed* to locate him. He didn't. He boarded a train and failed to hop off at Holborn. Nobody accosted him in Chancery Lane on his walk to the studios. He slowed from his normal pace. God, might it be too late to intercede, supposing, that is, Edgehill ever *could* have interceded? Where the fuck *was* this thirty-one to -four year old long-faced, smiling figure in a jogging suit, or denim and jeans, five foot ten inches of him under a frontal ton of wedge-forming black hair and father of two? Wouldn't it have been wrong, knowing of Hodge's distress, to pass by on the other side – pass by on the other side of Chancery Lane station: i.e., the Holborn stop?

At noon there was a routine meeting of programme makers – Drama, News/Current Affairs, Sport, Arts, with Flo Tait in the chair. She said: 'I get good, though very unofficial, intimations about *A Week in Review*'s chance of a Best Programme Award at the upcoming Media and Press Presentations, Tuesday week. It's unofficial because they don't do a long list, but I gather we're longlisted!'

'Great,' Edgehill said.

'However, what's the future?' Flo asked.

Nellie Poignard, burly and untentative, said, as if tentatively: 'Very, very preliminary idea, Flo, which I've spoken of to Larry, to Larry as Whitsun resident, not Larry as producer of *A Week in Review*. An idea not in any sense formulated at present, but we're wondering about an in-depth survey of the estates, Whitsun and Temperate, with filming – the objective being to chart the endemic tensions and their apparent sudden increase. Our indications are that something fairly cataclysmic is building there. When I say "there" I appreciate this is vague, given that we're talking about two estates. But probably in the frontier territory, the continually disputed frontier territory of the substances business. We think we see a . . . well . . . we see a root and branch situation that would give a programme countrywide, network, interest, not just the London end. Even *inter*national.

'This is social housing, still fulfilling in many ways its original tremendously worthwhile purpose, yet somehow that purpose has been compromised, shaken, and the estates turned into battle grounds where ignorant, but well-heeled, armies clash by night, and day. Surely we have a duty to show this and to look for the reasons.' Nellie paused, held up two hands, as if in surrender on a battle ground. 'I'm aware, of course, that I speak as an outsider to at least one here who is very much an *in*sider – yes, I refer again to Larry.'

'The estate is certainly characterful,' Edgehill said.

'The Tasker killing remains unaccounted for. And then, not so long ago, we had the turf battle death of that Whitsun pusher,' Nellie said, 'Gladstone Milo Naunton, who would have won Trader of the Year except he got shot. We covered both slaughters in the news at the time, as one-off crimes, obviously, but we're seeking now the wider viewpoint, the context, so the programme will have a universal touch. It will say something about civic decline and criminality everywhere. Why I talk of "root and branch". The barons, parading in their limos, feared, revered by some, full of money and power.

'We've done serious research. Two villains on Whitsun, I gather, are arts fans, would you believe, and actually Anthony Powell fans – the upper-crust novelist. I'm told one of them gave a paper at a Powell conference. This is quirky. Fascinating programme material. Additionally, Gladstone Milo Naunton's ex-lover, Bert Marsh, still lives on Whitsun, apparently pensioned by the super-baron, Adrian Pellotte. A sort of family, in the Mafia sense. Wonderful deep, complexity to the scene. What we need. Plus, talking of books, I get whispers about Vagrain. Abel Vagrain? Was featured on Larry's show a while back. Now, the word's around he's planning some sort of book on Whitsun and Temperate – maybe fiction, or documentary, or faction. Whichever, it shows there's major interest. He's a consider-able figure, crap writer or not.'

'Oh, that's harsh,' Edgehill said.

'Or *because* he's a crap writer and reaches all those readers who want crap and wouldn't be able to tell it from caviar,' Nellie replied. 'He's not put off by Tasker's death, apparently, nor the wars. In fact, of course, the violence is what attracts him, might be the makings of his book. Anyway, we feel we must be in on this topic, too. We shouldn't let ourselves get scooped, by him or, say, the BBC or ITV1.'

Flo switched herself on full. 'No, indeed,' she said. 'No, no, no.'

'And isn't there an angle special to us – admittedly a trifle deli-cate, but intriguing?' Nellie asked. 'I hear that the topmost – the only? – Whitsun baron has a daughter who's making it with Larry's frequent presenter, Rupert Bale – a Temperate resident. More tension? That's what I'd expect. It's all pretty ripe. This guy – the girl's father – Pellotte, Adrian Pellotte– the tale is that if he parks his BMW outside a house, the lad or lass inside has very severe trouble, some-times terminal. Generally, a skimming matter to be righted. Is there someone called Hodge in dodgy circs at present? Larch Street? That's the gossip. And Pellotte and Dean Feston, his baggage man, splitting

big funds between them in Pine, up near Hodge's house. Hodge
and Naunton were Pellotte's best operators it's said. So, all told,
various bad knocks for the Whitsun firm. Explosion or implosion
certain? We ought to be getting background filmed in good time,
Flo, stored for the eventual moment.'

'Perhaps, perhaps. But, yes, parts of it *are* delicate. That shouldn't
stop us, though. Let me have something on paper, would you?' Flo
said.

Sport and Drama took the rest of the hour. In the afternoon
Edgehill and Tom Marland lined up a couple of items for the next
A Week in Review, then at just after six p.m. Edgehill left for home.
As he neared Chancery Lane Station he became conscious of someone
about five foot ten inches with a hair wedge up front walking along-
side him, and staying alongside him.

'Gordon Basil Hodge of Larch Street, Whit?' Edgehill said.

'Best done like this,' Hodge said. He gave a hugely accomplished
smile, glittering in the street lights, probably the kind of thing
Udolpho had mentioned: definitely a plus in this long, donkey-chops
face, but lacking any basis, any cause. Still, a lot of smiles were like
that, and not all of them in mental hospitals. 'Too flagrant if I'd
joined up with you this morning,' he said.

'Udolpho thought you'd do it like that.'

'What I mean,' Hodge said. 'I edit what I tell Udolpho.'

'He's a friend of yours, isn't he? You don't trust him?'

'Udolpho hears a lot, blabs a lot. Pellotte and Dean call in there
for papers and scuttlebutt, you know. It's wisest you're not seen with
me – not someone in your role.'

'Which role?'

'Potentially, you're in a sensitive spot. I can appreciate it.'

'Sensitive? How?' Edgehill asked.

'We must apply discretion and more discretion. Things can get
difficult. You've heard of the journalist, Tasker, I expect.'

The pubs were full and noisy with office staff on their way home,
or not. They went into the Nonesuch and stood in a corner. Edgehill
bought beers.

'You and I, we're connected, in a way,' Hodge said. 'Which is why
I – why I feel you wouldn't mind being asked to help me.'

'Connected how?'

'Dione. Pellotte's Dione. I'd say we're both concerned there. When
I ask myself why you and they should hold that long Gideon road
conference, and thereafter, I can only come up with one answer,'

Hodge said. 'Dione. Some people read the BMW meeting all wrong, in my view.'

'Which people?'

'On Whitsun. They imagine it's to do with the trade. I'd say not a bit.'

'How could it be?'

'No. It's Dione. Adrian Pellotte would think you're able to help with the Dione-Rupert Bale romance, because you regularly employ Bale. Have I got it right? This is why they wanted to talk? Udolpho says you told him it was all about the arts! We had a giggle over that. Sorry, I don't buy it. Pellotte's got problems on Whitsun with some of his outfit – the nuttier, more poisonous, more violent ones – because Bale's Temperate, of course. I've gone about – I swear this is right – I've gone about trying to smooth them down for him. Why I said we have similarities. *I* try, unprompted, to help, and he comes to you seeking *your* help. And that obviously gives you a true, robust status with him and Dean. It's important, brings you power.'

'Haven't noticed,' Edgehill said.

'By the way, don't underrate Dean Feston. He can do damage as much as Adrian. They're making a fuss about some pretty piffling amount. Not much over twenty thousand. Did they mention it to you, as mates to a mate? This little sum could easily get overlooked by me during all the work pressures. You'd agree on that, I'm sure, especially when, as an extra task, I'm busy flitting around to people and trying to put them right about Dione. But, consider: *I* can't go to Adrian or Feston and tell them they're being unreasonable, hasty and footling. I'm not in that kind of position. They value me as a salesman, but that's it. Plenty of us around. Naunton was almost as good. But you, Mr Edgehill – Larry – you're different. There's a special familiarity you and they enjoy, and they obviously have a special regard. You could suggest in a very gentle, tactful but effective way, that taking the overall picture, a minor lapse by one of their most established, loyal and successful people is not to be made overmuch of. It would be an acquaintance of their own calibre putting a fair point to them, and I feel they'd accept the sense of it, even some vicious lout like Dean.'

'I'm not in a—'

'Obviously in my kind of trade I meet all sorts, form good connections with all sorts. Taxi firms. Well, as you'd expect. Punters strange to the area jump into a cab and want to get taken to a B and B, or a girl or a dealer offering something to snort or swallow or veinline.

I talk quite a lot to taxi people and vice versa. And so I understand Adrian and Dean were at your place without the BMW. That would be a very secret, respectful, significant call. It shows they have exceptional esteem for you. It's massively enviable. I shouldn't be mentioning the taxi driver to you. He could have bother if they knew he spoke to me. You're the kind who would not disclose such material, I'm sure. Of course, I didn't talk to Udolpho about this second meeting between you and them.'

'He says they called on you, but *with* the BMW and some things in the boot. What things?'

'Yes, in my view most Whitsun people have the wrong notion about that Gideon road session, Udolpho, included,' Hodge replied. 'Of course, none of them knows of the call by taxi – by taxi, for God's sake! – at your own property, which gives a highly serious aspect to it all, much more so than the Gideon encounter. Maybe the Dione topic was only hinted at in Gideon, but at the taxi call they could go into it properly. Udolpho – he doesn't swallow the arts explanation, naturally. He thinks it concerned Dione, as he'd tell you, but also he believes Adrian wants to expand the business, diversify, and that's another reason he's interested in a confab with you. Udolpho reckons the whole trade game is changing. He and others believe Adrian's probably tired of all the wasteful, bloody battling on the estates and hopes someone like you can take their business into a quite new realm – the uptown broadcasting and media community. There's undoubtedly a fine, safer, steadier market there, and Adrian and Dean might feel they're missing out on it by being stuck on Whitsun. Which, as Udolpho sees it, is where you come in, although he wouldn't talk of it to you.

'In your kind of influential job, you could make routes into this sector for them to offer their wares. That's Udolpho's theory. And, as I say, the theory of others. Coke, the comfort of the middle classes, more or less regardless of price. You, a possible conduit – hence the Gideon negotiations. As they interpret them. Udolpho says, look at the way the death of Gladstone Milo Naunton has been left unpunished – just some monthly, token handout to his sweetheart, Bert Marsh. What does this indicate? Udolpho says, and others say, Adrian and Dean are losing interest in the estates and its awkward troubles. They want to get among bigger, more select pickings, and they've come to see the routines of vengeance as stupid, not worth their attention. Udolpho considers they're looking elsewhere, with your help.'

'It's idiotic.'

'Certainly. Me, I don't go with it, Larry. All right, the seeming indifference on Gladstone Milo Naunton is strong, but I still think they approached you for something more precious to Adrian even than the business – his daughter. That's why I feel you have big influence with them. That's why I ask you to use a fraction of it for me, Larry. Make them see their reaction is extreme.'

Edgehill fought off that stupid impulse to offer aid whenever he was asked for it, regardless of whom it came from. 'No, I won't have another, thanks,' he said, 'I must get along.'

Fifteen

Esther went out to a Sunday morning service at St John's on Temperate. She wanted to talk to the sidesman mentioned in Gervaise Manciple Tasker's notes, and perhaps to the female vicar. Esther looked at dossier pictures of people in the Temperate Acres firm and thought she'd matched one with the laptopped description by Tasker. The sidesman might be – ought to be, on her reckoning – yes, ought to be, Joel Jeremy North, personnel director of Abracadabra Leisure, and therefore of Harold Perth Amesbury's Temperate operation. She hoped for a chance to buttonhole him. She couldn't expect anything better. She had nothing to justify an arrest. Profanities in church wouldn't do, and, in any case, she had only a third party account of the profanities in church, and the third party wasn't available to confirm.

This week's sermon dealt with the destruction of the walls of Jericho, and Esther enjoyed it. The vicar had a real, spittle-laced enthusiasm for the shouting and trumpet blasts that knocked those walls flat. So, walls might not stand for ever. Esther liked the idea. She wanted to think this included walls of silence. These were unintelligible to people from the Home Office and the Mayor's office.

Esther had been right to identify Joel Jeremy North. He was acting as a sidesman again and took Esther to her pew. 'Is it Detective Chief Superintendent Davidson?' he'd said quietly. 'Perhaps glimpsed occasionally on TV News following a crime? St John's indeed welcomes you. To do with?'

'You. What else?'

'Many possibilities.'

'Perhaps we could talk afterwards.'

'Certainly. I'm here to facilitate your visit, in the hope that it might lead to regular attendance.'

At the end of the service, the vicar stood at the door again, as described in Tasker's notes, and shook hands with people leaving. 'Where would we be without the Old Testament?' Esther said.

'You'd lack a first name.' So the vicar recognized her, too. 'You've come about the dead newspaper man?'

'Do you hear anything?'

'In which regard?'

'The death and pre-death slapping regard.'

'He did turn up here. I expect he made notes, and you've seen them. They don't like people of that sort coming to St John's and pretending to be pious.'

'Which sort?'

'Poking about.'

'*I'm* here to poke about.'

'They won't like it. I hope this doesn't hurt your feelings.'

'How about you? Do *you* like it?'

'The church is open to anyone. We're not behind a wall. Our theme today.'

North was with his wife and two young children. They ran off to play with friends in the churchyard. 'You're police,' Mrs North stated. 'Jeremy says you're police. Whoever heard of police going to church on Temperate? What's the underlying purpose? Well, I know what the underlying purpose is. You want to talk to Jeremy. He told me you want to talk to him. But then I ask, what's the underlying purpose in wanting to talk to him?'

'That's logical,' Esther replied.

Mrs North was short, small featured, unrobust, except for her voice. She wore a simple, stylishly cut blue trouser suit, with a silver kerchief formed into a large, round knot under her chin. Usually, that knot would have given her a jaunty, even jokey, appearance. Not now. Although at a distance her face would appear only neat, attractive and cheerful, from where Esther stood she could see a fair whack of hate. Policing could often bring you some of that. This woman regarded invasion of the church as . . . as invasion, and to be confronted, resisted, ferociously discouraged. The vicar seemed to share this feeling. As a requirement of the job, she must have got herself so attune to Temperate and its ways that she would suspect any intruder. Esther? Gervaise Manciple Tasker? Temperate Acres would have its community cop, and the locals had probably come to accept that. Esther in St John's was extra: dangerously, offensively, intolerably extra. And Gervaise Manciple Tasker?

'Jeremy says you're high up,' Mrs North said. 'A Chief Super. My, my. That means you deal only with big items. Not lost dogs.'

'Have you lost a dog?'

'I ask, what big item says you have to go to St John's, Temperate?'

'Oh, a death. When you get high up you deal a lot in deaths.'

'Which?'

'A journalist,' Esther said.

'I've read about this in the press, Liz,' North said. 'And it was on television. A murder, wasn't it, the body in a children's amusement park, shot but with signs of a beating earlier?' He made his tone aghast and glanced protectively towards his own two daughters, playing a game of chase.

'Yes, regrettable,' Liz North said, 'but what's all that got to do with St John's?'

'I'd like to find out,' Esther said.

'He came here?' Liz North asked.

'I gather,' Esther said.

'What's that mean, "you gather"?' Liz North said.

'There's information,' Esther said.

'What information?' Liz North said.

'The vicar remembers him. You, as a sidesman, Jeremy, I wonder if you do, too.'

'Why do you wonder that?' Liz North asked.

'Someone strange to the church might need a sidesman,' Esther said.

'So you decide it must be Jeremy. My God, that's why you're here, is it? You've got your dirty, suspicious, big-rank eyes on Jeremy.'

'I show a lot of people to places in the church,' he said.

'A man of twenty-eight, on his own, would that be usual?' Esther said.

'Why not?' Liz North said. 'It's a church. There's no age bar. No gender bar. You don't have to have a family.'

'The press and TV showed pictures of him taken a few years ago,' Esther said. 'You didn't recognize him then, Jeremy?'

'Well, the thing is, I wouldn't be expecting to recognize him, would I?' he said. 'St John's has never been involved in this kind of thing before.'

'No, I don't suppose so,' Esther said.

'What does that mean?' Liz North said.

'What?' Esther said.

'"No, I don't suppose so",' Liz North said.

'No, I don't suppose so,' Esther replied.

'It's sarcasm,' Liz North said. 'Like saying "No, I don't suppose many churches do get involved in murders". As if that's too obvious to need saying. There's a . . . there's an underlying purpose to your words.'

'As far as you know, you've never met Tasker?' Esther asked North.

'Possibly not in the church. It could be a business matter.'

'To do with Abracadabra Leisure?' he asked.

'Sort of,' Esther said.

'What does that mean?' Liz North said.

'Sort of,' Esther replied.

'I don't think I ever did,' North said.

'You come here and corner us with our children in a church ambience,' Liz North said, 'because you think we'll be a soft touch, no lawyers present, obviously. It's sneaky. It's like police, especially top police.'

'You know a lot of top police?' Esther said.

'And then I hear from Jeremy that your husband goes to one of the Temperate pubs with his gang and shouts all sorts of poison. He knows he's safe, because of you, the big officer.'

'I hope he's safe,' Esther said.

'Of course he is,' North said. The children returned. North clasped them both affectionately to him, the affection very, very equal. Esther had a sense of real power in his arms, though he wasn't using all of it now, naturally. He might have been strong enough on his own to get Tasker's body from a car and on to the children's slide.

Sixteen

Bert Jutland Marsh lived on Whit supported by a very tidy spouse-pension from Adrian Pellotte. This followed the death of Gladstone Milo Naunton, Bert's former lover, in a two-hour territory battle around William Walton Avenue, that famed frontier area. At home in Moorhen Street, Bert heard the communication box on his front door crackle, indicating someone had pressed the button and was about to speak. He listened but didn't recognize the voice or the name when it came. 'Mr Marsh, I wonder if we could talk briefly. It's Abel Vagrain.'

'Don't know you,' Marsh said. 'You selling? Bettaware?'

'Personal.'

'How did you know I was Mr Marsh?'

'Good to see old-style and historical first names coming back – Albert, Jutland.'

'I don't go in for personal things these days. They're best left to others.'

'About your ex-partner, Gladstone Milo Naunton.'

'You police?'

'No. What makes you think so?'

'Giving all his names. Police do that, and courts. Makes people think no chance of dodging out. Nailed in triplicate.'

'It's how I noted it down.'

'Noted it down from where?' Marsh said.

'References.'

Marsh said: 'You found references to Gladstone somewhere?'

'Tragically dead.'

'Yes, tragically. And nothing done about it.'

'By the police?'

'By anybody,' Marsh snarled. 'Did you know Gladstone? Is that it? Is that why you're here?' More anger swirled in Marsh. 'Listen, I was the only one he truly cared about. It's a fact. If you've come here to say you knew him – really knew him in a fucking *fond* or fond *fucking* way – you can piss off, because I was the one he treasured, despite his damn waywardness from time to time, and only from time to time. Always he returned to me and in a totally committed fashion nearly.'

'Regrettably, I never met Gladstone.'

'All sorts say now they knew him – knew him close, I mean. Easy for them to say it. He can't show it's not true, can he? Your name – not one I've come across on Whitsun, although a lot of strange ones here now.'

'I'm from outside.'

'Outside where?'

'Not from either estate.'

'You expect me to open up to someone who just turns up in the dark from what you call outside saying it's to do with Gladstone?'

Marsh had every security fitting, including the voice box, cost no concern. Gladstone saw to that far back. Everyone who could afford it saw to that on Whitsun, but especially someone in Gladstone's type of active career, and, naturally, he could afford it: front door solid wood – not your two slices of mahogany veneer stuffed with porridge – chains, two bolts, three locks, two of them mortises, and a fire extinguisher right alongside the letter box, to douse flaming arson rags, plus tongs and a shovel for shit packets. The letter box had a wire cage around it in case of posted rats, which could be shot or knifed in there, meaning blood and mess around the hallway, but better than having them run about the property and undoubtedly breeding in the eager fashion of rats. It grieved Bert Marsh that Gladstone had organized home precautions yet couldn't keep clear of the bullets in the boundary struggle with Temperate for William Walton Avenue. Always William Walton.

Marsh hated the names of some of these streets. Another avenue was called Gustav Holst, also famed for music. The council wanted to make the streets, avenues, roads, sound distinguished, like taking people who lived here up a level. This made the names ridiculous and full of dud hope. William Walton? Everyone knew he was quite a composer, but you did not get much harmony in the avenue – nothing but fucking warfare and casualties, because it was a frontier between Whit and Temp.

The front door had a spyhole. Marsh did not recognize this visitor, standing bent over a bit for the voice box. He looked thin, almost tall, in a dark overcoat, white scarf with six tassels each end, no hat, very flat dark hair – what Marsh thought of as 'Hitler hair'. However, moustacheless. About forty.

'Forgive me for just turning up like this, Mr Marsh.'

'Got anti-theft nuts on your wheels?'

'I come to you because I'm interested in Gladstone as typifying a certain kind of present-day life.'

'I store many memories of Gladstone, yes. This could get up some noses and result in peril for me. You've heard about that reporter, I suppose?'

'My purpose is serious, and might, in fact, help preserve those memories. I'm a writer. If I could come in and talk of these matters it would—'

'You more press?' Another fucking reporter. One dead, then the next one turns up. Always trying to get through the front door. The white scarf most probably true silk. Journalists did nicely on their exes. And they'd think a white scarf with plenty of tassels at each end helped make them dashing.

'No, not press, a writer.'

'Reporters write. Notebooks. Shorthand. I saw a lot of reporters not long ago. That's plenty, thanks.'

'When Gladstone Milo Naunton was killed? This is how I found your name and so on. I've been researching old newspapers on the Net. The newspapers didn't give the number, just "Moorhen Street". I knocked some doors, asking if people knew Albert – or possibly Bert – Marsh, and what number.'

Marsh felt a sudden fiery pain in his chest. Shock would work on him like that sometimes. Now and then he thought, heart attack. 'You knocked doors on fucking Whitsun? Any old door?'

'Just in this street. No real trouble.'

'And someone told you?' Marsh said. 'That's well out of order.'

'I'm interested in the setting,' Vagrain said. 'The two estates – Whitsun, Temperate. Tensions. What you hinted at just now.'

'It's getting worse. Everyone says so. They think carnage any day. I mean massive.'

'Yes?'

'You sound damn eager. You sure you're not press? Carnage they live by, don't they?'

'This will be a story, a made-up story. A novel. Different from the press. But not unrelated to the actual. Based on the real, but the real given shape. Different names for places and people, naturally.'

'I'd get into this book, with a different name?' Marsh half fancied the idea. Such chances didn't happen very often to Whitsun people who'd lost their partner in a turf fight. 'Gladstone Naunton, as well?' He kept up his staunch loyalty to Gladstone and felt pretty sure he might always. If he didn't, those years together would have no meaning. They *must* have meaning, even though Gladstone didn't stay too absolutely faithful, the busy, gaudy slut, bringing possible disease home regardless. Gladstone had a flair for handguns, but so did some folk on Temperate. It wouldn't look too good on his grave-stone – 'He had a flair for handguns'.

'Yes, Gladstone's central,' Vagrain said. 'His death—'

'Not just the death. Gladstone would have won a prize,' Marsh said. 'An estate prize, hardly known about off Whitsun. Not like the FA Cup. What's referred to as "in house". Hodgy got it, although he definitely came well behind on the year's sales charts. A shame. Well, the word is Hodgy's got enmity from Adrian and Dean now. Skimming? That's ingratitude. Gladstone was shot when into true duty at William Walton, which is real Whitsun ground, whatever those Temperate slobs think. A soldier can have what's referred to as a posthumous Victoria Cross, meaning he did something brave that killed him, but Adrian Pellotte stopped anything like that for Gladstone. Oh, I admit they look after me since Gladstone died, and me only, definitely not those others he went with, the non-stop tart, but it still doesn't seem OK to say Gladstone couldn't have the award. This is to do with morale. Important. The firm paid for the funeral, a first-class box, and the drink-up after, yes, with vintages, but he deserved proper recognition.'

'Proper?'

'Why haven't we killed the killer or killers? Wouldn't that have made his death seem more worthwhile, and help us forget he lost the prize? You're right when you say "typical". In a way, Gladstone was what would be known as a "typical" of Whitsun. They owed him better treatment. This should have been a full and instant vengeance job.'

'Can I come in briefly?'

'Got a card? The press always have a card. I'd like to see a card that says you're *not* press.'

'Yes, a card. Also . . . also it could seem a bit much, just descending on you like this, so I brought a dust jacket from a work of mine, *The Insignia of Postponement*, for more identification. My name's on the front, of course, and a picture on the rear fold-over.'

Bert opened the door on the top, middle and bottom chains. The caller handed in a visiting card and the glossy paper cover between the top and middle. 'Oh, this is how you spell Vagrain,' Marsh said.

'French far back. We came over with the Huguenots.'

'I heard that was some trip.'

'Centuries ago.'

'You're well settled now, though, not like some of these illegals. A stack on Whitsun. Adrian doesn't like it. They make running Whit more difficult for him. These newsters don't know Whit traditions. How could they? Different cultures. Some come from really rotten places over there. They've known people definitely worse than Adrian, blood on their teeth, and so they're not properly frightened of him and respectful. This could damage what's known as "social cohesion", which Adrian so greatly values sometimes.'

Marsh unfastened the door and Vagrain came in. Marsh refitted the chains at once. If you went around saying those who did Gladstone ought to be done you had to be non-stop careful those who did Gladstone didn't turn up and do *you*. There was Gladstone dead and Tasker, the reporter, dead. Marsh felt warned. Stupid not to be.

He tried to guess how Vagrain would regard this room and the furniture and pictures, seeing them for the first time. Gladstone put iron bars over all the downstairs windows, it being Whitsun, but they had curves and swirls so they could be decorative, and were not just straight bars like a jail or dispensary. Marsh thought Vagrain would most probably be impressed by this room as one part of the setting he was after. Gladstone himself chose most of the furniture and the blue carpet. He bought many of the pieces totally above board in proper antique shops. Hardly anything in this house came off the back of a lorry, and definitely nothing that would fetch above £750, say, at auction. Beautiful but stolen stuff offered by mates of his, Gladstone would generally not even look at, no matter how much of a bargain. He did not want any pricey-looking items, with a strong, evil, crooked tale to them, in property he owned. *Joint*-owned, of course.

They sat in Edwardian bucket-style armchairs that had been re-covered not long ago with red leather. Pellotte would look in occasionally and decide this or that needed smartening. Marsh never saw the bills. He poured rums. 'What made you curious about this estate?' he asked.

'A girl at a publicity-do for my book, *Insignia*, in a Hampstead shop put me on to it.'

'The girl was from Hampstead but knew about Whitsun Festival?' Marsh said.

'It's amazing what you can pick up simply from a casual meeting like that.'

'Well, *especially* from a casual meeting like that. It's what I meant about Gladstone. But I hope you wore a—'

'In the way of ideas.'

'Oh, those.'

Vagrain said: 'I don't think Pellotte got mentioned in any of the newspapers reporting the Walton tragedy.'

'He'd avoid that. Publicity is not Adrian's thing. He's like me – longs for privacy, guards it. That's why it was so damn dodgy to go knocking on doors in the street.'

Vagrain had been lifting his glass to his lips but stopped now. He seemed very puzzled, sort of paralysed, the glass nearly touching his mouth, yet he cut the movement. He said: 'Dodgy – merely to ask people your address, Bert? Why?'

Vagrain did not get it at all, did he, the fucking thicko? You'd think a writer would be able to feel a situation much quicker than this.

'Neighbours know someone in a white silk scarf with tassels worn loose called on me,' Marsh said.

'That matters?'

Marsh wanted to say in a still-friendly, quiet, unpanicky way: *of course it fucking matters, you turd brained twat, because some people will think I might be blowing secrets. Whitsun runs on secrets.* No. Crude.

'Word will get around,' he replied. 'On Whitsun word does get around if you don't take care to stop it getting around, which most people do.'

'But so what?'

'People will hear you're going to put this situation into a book.'

'Is that bad?'

'It might be.' Marsh made a decision then. It would be wisest to take Vagrain to see Adrian Pellotte right away at his place on Whitsun. Marsh wanted this visit to Moorhen Street by Vagrain to be known about and open. It would be known about, anyway, because Vagrain did his bloody stupid, careless door knocking in the street like a Jehovah's Witness, but not enough like a Jehovah's Witness. And people passing must have noticed him and that clever mouth and fucking white scarf crouched over the voice box for so long with his bleat. Better Adrian heard about it all direct and honest by Bert, not from possible gossip.

Perhaps Adrian wouldn't mind seeing Vagrain. Adrian was into books and authors. And most likely by being helpful to Vagrain, Adrian would want to show he didn't get people such as the journalist removed because they came doing probes and then writing stuff. That is, he would want to show he didn't get people such as the jour-

nalist removed if he didn't get him removed. Or if he did. Especially
if he did. Bert had to keep in mind how good, regular cash came
by messenger every week from the firm just for having been with
Gladstone on a decent domestic basis at the time of his slaughter.
This money could stop absolutely, just as Gladstone's trading prize
got stopped absolutely by Pellotte. And worse than that could happen
if Pellotte ever thought Marsh had fed confidential tips on the quiet
to Vagrain about Whitsun. It might be regarded as unforgivable.
Adrian liked books, but there were books, and books.

Vagrain had been examining a picture-print of the Pope's Swiss
Guard at the Vatican. Now he broke from the art. 'What I'd like,
Bert, is simply to watch the street for a while through your upstairs
front window.'

'Watch? Who you looking for?' *God, a hunt, after all? Was he really
a writer?*

'No, not looking for anybody specific. It's only to get the *sense*
of the street, the pageant of day-to-day activity, the pageant of, as
it were, normality. Invaluable to a novelist.'

Whitsun didn't have any normality. What one lot considered
normal, others regarded as sick or crazy or disgusting or foreign.

'Not on, old son,' Marsh said. 'People would think it's undercover
surveillance. I'd get *all* the windows smashed – as starters.'

'Surveillance? *Surveillance.*' Vagrain sort of held this word up to
examine it all round, like sexing a kitten. 'Well, yes, in a sense I
suppose it would be. I need to *survey* the patterns, the routines, of
their days. "Surveillance" is only a heavy word for totally harmless
observation.'

'Surveillance up here means police, and so would observation,
not an author on the look out for normalness,' Bert said. 'Perhaps
this will surprise you, Abel, but hardly any authors come to Moorhen
Street and stare out through windows. That author Adrian and Dean
are fans of, Anthony Powell, but not said like that – Pow-well – but
Pole – he never comes up here to Whitsun or Temperate and stares
out of windows collecting atmos. It will be bad for me if people
think I let police use my place for snooping. They'd decide I must
have an arrangement with that dame detective, Esther Davidson.'

'I'd be discreet, keep behind the curtains.'

'They'd expect you to be discreet, wouldn't they? Officers on
surveillance don't stand in the middle of the glass flashing their
fucking buttons and night sticks. People here are *used* to curtains.
They know about discreet.'

Vagrain gave a small smile and nodded. 'The fact that I mustn't do it – that you warn me off so vigorously from doing it – that, in itself, is a unique glimpse.'

'Not having a glimpse from the window is a glimpse?'

'It's a glimpse at the prevailing conditions here, isn't it? On Whitsun, someone innocently standing at a window, even if concealed by curtains, would be regarded as a menace.'

'*Especially* if concealed by curtains. Neighbours would ask, "Who's that trying to conceal himself behind the fucking curtains, and why? And what's Bert Marsh letting him do it for on his property?" Nobody's going to answer, "Oh, of course, of course – silly old me! – it must be an author taking a fruitful gaze at normalness.'

'I need to get the feel of specific pavements under my shoes,' Vagrain said. 'It's how I work. I must have contact.'

'These pavements are like other pavements, but probably more dog shit than Mayfair way. People up there scoop and bag it, considering the environment. Whitsun might do less of that. They think a bit more dog shit in Whitsun won't be crucial one way or the other as far as reputation and aroma goes.'

'Some novelists can concoct a place without ever having been there. For myself, though it—'

'I could probably get you in to see Adrian Pellotte,' Marsh replied. 'If you're looking for the flavour of Whitsun, Adrian's pretty essential. Unique. He *creates* the flavour. No, he *is* it.'

'You've got access?'

'He pays me a consultant fee. What's referred to as "a retainer".'

'Consultant on what?'

'They'll probably be at home now. Dean lives near Adrian. You might be able to meet both, pile up the glimpses.'

'Great!'

'But let *him*, or possibly Dean, start the topics. Don't do any interrogation. They'll tell you what they want to tell you.'

'Understood.'

Marsh went to the telephone in the kitchen, shut the door and rang Pellotte. 'Someone here wanting to see you, Adrian. He called hoping I could direct him to your place. Well, I replied, "Possibly," not knowing your view.'

'Has he got some insights?'

'What kind, Aid?'

'We've had an attack on the car lately – fixed now, but a nuisance. I had to use a replacement to get to the second day of a conference.'

'Unbelievable. *Your* personal BMW?'

'And problems arising from that. Materials taken from the boot.'

'Well, no, I don't think this caller knows about your car and so on.'

'What then?'

'He's interested in the estate. For a tale.'

'I think I might have heard of him.' Pellotte went silent for a few moments. Then he said: 'We're watching a television awards programme. It's live. A special friend of my daughter, Dione, is part of the team that might win. In fact, I'm sure they'll win.'

'Exciting,' Marsh said.

'Yes, I have a real premonition they will.'

'You've made contact with some of the judges, Adrian? Or Dean has?'

'But I expect it will be over by the time you get here,' Pellotte said. 'All right. I'll see him.'

'Thanks, Adrian.'

'How did this visitor locate *you*, Bert?'

'He's done some research. Newspapers – about Gladstone.'

'Gladstone in William Walton?' For a moment, Pellotte sounded uncomfortable. So the princely sod should.

'I was mentioned there,' Bert said. 'Oh, Adrian, look, I said a consultancy – not just the pay-off pension re Gladstone. A retainer. It sounded better.'

'Right. What kind?'

'Like Public Relations? Quite a lot of that about these days. Devoted to tending your image, Adrian. Ensuring respect and affection.'

'Right. I'll ring off now, Bert. The telly programme's getting to the bit I'm interested in.'

'Fingers crossed,' Marsh said. He returned to the lounge. 'We'll go, then, shall we, Abel? Best take *your* car. It's probably still OK. You haven't been here long. Stupid to leave it, though.'

As they drew away from Marsh's house, he saw a Fiat coming slowly towards them down the street with Hodgy driving. Marsh lowered his head, to stay unrecognized. He guessed Hodge must be on his way to visit him. It would figure. The word was around: Hodge had bad trouble and a bad outlook now with Adrian, despite the in-house prize. Gordon Basil Hodge must be touting for people who might take pity and say something nice about him to Pellotte. Nice and possibly life saving. Not the kind of request to do by phone. Most likely, Hodge had tried elsewhere first. Many knew Bert Marsh kept a fine, friendly link with Adrian following Gladstone's death. But Bert wanted that link to stay friendly, even though Pellotte had failed to get any tit-for-tat scheme against Temperate going yet. For ever? Bert thought Hodgy would have to sort things out with Adrian and Dean for himself, poor bastard. All right, Hodgy needed extra funds because of those kids away at school etcetera. Fine. He should have considered, though, what the result might be if he tried to get the extra how he did. Marsh stayed crouched and face down in the passenger seat.

But, he and Vagrain had been at Adrian Pellotte's place for only a quarter of an hour when GB Hodge himself arrived, excited, glowing. 'All at once the idea hit me, Adrian, really hit me,' Hodge said. 'I realized something. I realized I had been dealing with things all wrong. Suddenly, I knew I should be more direct. That's why I'm here, in your home, Adrian. Face to face. Too devious – that's what I was till now. You'll reply, "Devious how?" In this way: I've tried to persuade people who might be able to say a word in my favour to approach you, instead of coming straight to you myself. Larry Edgehill, for instance, from TV. I feel almost ashamed of it now – seeking his . . . well, his sympathy, really. So weak. Pathetic.'

'Edgehill?' Dean said. 'Why him?'

'The connection to Adrian – and you,' Hodge said.

'What connection?' Dean said.

'That Gideon conversation. Much noted. Perhaps about your lovely daughter, Adrian, and her relationship with a regular on one of Larry Edgehill's programmes. Considerable talk concerning this around Whitsun. I felt it would be an honour to have my problem linked with hers, as it were.'

'Conversation? Gideon? Oh, just re the arts,' Dean said. 'Adrian admires his programme. As a matter of fact, it won a big award tonight. We watched the judging on BBC1.'

'And then, half an hour ago, I'm on my way to try for Bert's support, also, knowing of his excellent relationship with Adrian, dating back to Gladstone. But as I arrive at Bert's home, I see him driving away – or, actually, being driven away from his house. He's sitting low in the passenger seat, so comfortable looking, so content. A new partner for Bert? I asked myself. That would be brilliant. Bert has grieved, has sincerely grieved, but perhaps the time for grieving is gone and life begins to lighten. William Walton will still darken part of his soul – a very tender and valid part of his soul, yes, but not his total soul from now on. I turn and follow, curious as to their destination. Perhaps a celebratory supper at some quality restaurant. Maybe I can get a word with him there. But, no. They wished to make a happy announcement where that announcement is most due, and most appropriate. To Adrian. To Adrian, with his earned role as chieftain in our community, guardian of our community. And – great good luck! – I'm behind them, tailing! Which brings me here, at last. A move I should have made at the start of all this.'

Dean did introductions: 'Mr Abel Vagrain's a writer. And Gordon is a much esteemed commercial associate, Mr Vagrain. We don't especially mind you coming here, Gordon – entirely without a fucking appointment, as far as I can recall.'

'Certainly,' Pellotte said, 'although we have guests.'

'A writer?' Hodge said. 'I thought I knew that name. And how did you and Bert meet?'

Vagrain felt half drowned by the Niagara of Hodge smarm, and the Hodge haywire interpretation of things. He said: 'Gordon, as to Bert and myself – it isn't exactly how you describe. I—'

Dean said: 'Those items we recovered from the Larch Street property with your very kind and ready assistance not long ago, Gordon, gave us some problems.'

'Oh?' Hodge replied.

'Some disappeared,' Dean said. 'And then we get a rumour that a lad from Pine is taken in for trying to pass what might have been some of these as genuine. Didn't you tell us they were all kosher?'

'Which kind of items?' Vagrain said.

'These will be items of a certain sort, I should think,' Marsh said.

Pellotte served claret all round. He said heartily: 'Dean is unhappy about these developments.'

'Anything wrong, it will be totally inadvertent, let me assure you, Dean, Adrian,' Hodge said. 'Look, I would hate to overstay. But, can I speak openly?'

'Adrian favours total openness in many circumstances if not most,' Dean replied.

Hodge said: 'I ask myself: How can I best wipe away all memory of that foolish minor though embarrassing recent tardiness error, especially if some items were false? And, in answer, my thoughts take me naturally, inevitably, starkly, to the matter of Gladstone.'

'We have Gladstone's street murder very much in mind,' Dean said.

'But at present unresolved,' Hodge said.

'No, not unresolved. Adrian would very much resent that word,' Dean said. 'It suggests slackness. We'd prefer "pending".'

'Under consideration,' Pellotte said.

'Of course. Of course,' Hodge said. 'But how would it be, then, if I, Gordon Basil Hodge, promised to take on as my own individual duty that matter still outstanding, still pending, still under consideration? There are people over on Temperate chortling about what happened to Gladstone. Chortling. Hugging themselves, the bland fuckers. They regard the death as a triumph. These people have to be traced and dealt with. Properly dealt with. What's more, they've managed, as I hear, to direct the blame for that reporter's death on to us. Do I gather that you, Dean, and Gabrielle Barter Cornish, were questioned?'

'A rubbish move,' Dean said. 'Davidson panicking under pressures from the politicos. She's bound to be nervy, living with that fucking daft bassoonist.'

'Whitsun pride requires forcible action,' Hodge said. 'Absolutely no reflection on you Adrian, or you, Dean, but postponement of a hit-back for the Gladstone matter has puzzled some folk on the estate.'

Marsh said: 'Mr Vagrain has a book about the insignia of postponement. I've seen the jacket. I don't know if that's about the delay re Gladstone.'

'Delay in which regard?' Vagrain said.

'Well, I, too, have an announcement to make, here, tonight,' Hodge said, 'perhaps not as significant as Bert's and his new partner's, but substantial, nonetheless.'

Vagrain watched him, and picked phrases that he might one day use to describe in a novel Hodge's behaviour now and his state of mind: boldness sparked by despair, cockiness stoked by terror, an agonizing mix.

Hodge said: 'In the presence of Bert himself and his new, very special, friend, I now gladly take on that mission.'

Although Hodge had misread the link between Vagrain and Bert Marsh, of course, Vagrain loved his style – the solemnity, the grandeur, the sitting-room resonance.

Hodge said: 'I dedicate myself to the task, a Whitsun answer in similar kind to the brutal termination of one of its own. I will find those responsible and show them they have been judged, condemned and must, in their turn, die. I shall be acting not simply as Gordon

Basil Hodge, but proudly, *so* proudly, on behalf of you, Adrian, you, Dean, you, Bert and all the Whitsun community. I ask, can there be any better way of proving my entire and absolute loyalty to you, Adrian, and the firm?'

Marsh said: 'Thanks, Gordon.'

'And now, I will leave,' Hodge said, 'so that you may enjoy one another's company, without an intruder.'

When he'd gone, Vagrain thought: my God, he's talking about killing someone. Or more than one. He's the self-designated avenger. It came wrapped up and oracular, but that's what it meant. He didn't much care that I was here, listening, because he thinks I'm tied lovingly, gayly, to Bert Marsh – thinks I've lately become part of the staunch, inviolate Whitsun team through espousal.

Dean stood suddenly from the armchair where he'd been sitting. Vagrain heard what seemed to be a man's voice just outside the front door. Dean put his right hand under his jacket up towards the left shoulder and went quickly into the hall. Pellotte stood, too, but his hands remained down at his side. Radiant coolness would be one of his things. He stared towards the door leading to the hall.

In a moment Dean cried out with loud pleasure, 'Ah, Dione!'

A woman said: 'Did you see the show?'

'But of course,' Dean said. 'A brilliant and due victory. Congratulations.'

'I've brought Rupert,' the woman said. 'All right, I know this is off Temperate, off his normal territory. But such a terrific occasion! Top award for *A Week in Review* – almost always chaired by Rupe. We wanted to surprise you, but someone was leaving as we arrived and said, "Hello." He seemed to think he knew us.'

'Gordon Basil Hodge,' Dean said. 'He'd guess – daughter visiting Dad. And I expect he sees TV.' The three of them – Dione, Bale and Feston – came back into the room. At once, Vagrain recognized Bale from the television.

'We felt we should come out at once and share the splendid news,' she said.

'Splendid, indeed,' Pellotte said, 'but as Dean remarks only what has been well earned. A very predictable victory. Great.'

'Yes, so deserved,' Dean said.

'But we didn't realize we'd be stepping into a party, Dad,' Dione said.

'Party?' Pellotte chuckled and glanced around the big room. 'Well, not quite.' He made introductions. 'Bert and Mr Vagrain called in looking for some background on Whitsun Festival. Mr Vagrain's an author. But you know that.'

'Well, of course. We did one of his books,' Bale said. 'Grand. *The Insignia of Postponement.*'

Marsh said: 'Is it to do with—?'

'Excuse me, Mr Vagrain,' Dione said, 'but I get damned annoyed when people mention the TV discussion of your book. It's supposed to have been brilliant because Rupert and some woman splurged sex. That cheapens the novel. Makes it seem secondary to the way they presented it. The damn bassoonist husband of that woman pig, Davidson, was on about the impact of Rupert and the telly slut the other night at a concert. So infantile.'

'Now, Mr Vagrain's planning a tale set between Whitsun and Temperate,' Pellotte said. 'I'm not sure how I feel on that . . . But, anyway, this is why he's here with Bert. A long-time colleague, Gordon Hodge, arrived soon after Bert and Abel Vagrain with a business proposition. You bumped into him in the front garden. He spoke a greeting and spoiled the surprise, did he? And as for Dean – he turned up earlier than any of them. He's been busy lately on pressing business near Faunt Castle, after the Anthony Powell conference. Returned by public transport.'

'Do I know her?' Dione said.

'Her?' Vagrain said.

'Karen Tyne, a good friend from kiddiedom, told me she was going to the Anthony Powell,' Dione said. 'Did you run into her there, Dean? You remember Karen?'

'Tyne?' Vagrain said. 'Karen Tyne?'

'Definitely a considerable reader,' she said.

'Dean was always an admirer, weren't you, Dean?' Dione said.

'Karen Tyne? Lives in Hampstead?' Vagrain said.

'You've met her? She's exceptionally literary,' Dione said. 'But not exclusively bookish. She gets about. You *did* come across her there, did you, Dean? Well, like old times!'

Pellotte served Bale and Dione claret from a magnum. To Rupert Bale, the atmosphere seemed all right so far. It was his first visit to the Pellotte house. He expected some tensions. And there might be discoveries: Gordon Basil Hodge – hadn't that name come up in dinner table talk before the awards announcement tonight at the Savoy?

Pellotte handed out fine china side plates and then went to the kitchen and brought a Stilton cheese on a wooden tray. He passed around a barrel of cream crackers and spooned a portion of the Stilton for everyone. 'My wife's in Barbados with some lady friends. She'll be sorry to have missed you all,' he said. 'They go for a month most years. Husbands extremely uninvited!' The long wide room contained four big, loose-covered settees and half a dozen easy chairs, plus a mahogany bookcase, possibly converted skilfully from an old display stand in a chemist's shop. There were side tables and a huge Chinese carpet on dark-varnished hardwood boards. Bale guessed Pellotte must have bought two council houses alongside each other and had them turned into one property. Although he could have afforded a Mayfair mansion, he probably wouldn't feel happy or secure living away from the estate. He had a kind of sacred, devilish bond with the punters. A spiritual matter.

'We thought it only right that we should come out at once, Mr Pellotte,' Bale said 'More personal than the phone.'

'Call me Adrian, please,' Pellotte said. 'Tonight I'm mightily privileged – all these visitors, some unscheduled. And now you and Mr Bale, Dione! Grand!'

'He's Rupert, Dad,' she said.

'Yes, Rupert, please, Mr Pellotte,' Bale said.

'Rupert,' Pellotte said.

'Adrian, then,' Bale said. He felt this to be nuts. There could be no proper closeness with Adrian Pellotte. Bale didn't have any notion of what Adrian Pellotte was. Well, yes, Bale *did* have a notion of what he was. Everyone who lived on Temperate or Whitsun had. That offered Bale no comfort: he didn't have any notion who Pellotte was beyond the drug running, attendant necessary thuggery and regard for Anthony Powell.

'Yes, a wonderful triumph, that recognition of the programme,' Pellotte said.

Bale tried to work out from Pellotte's face and words whether he had landed the victory for *A Week in Review*, by money dabs to the judges and/or threats to the judges, and/or the promise of several years' discounted top-bracket coke to the judges. But Pellotte didn't have the kind of face that told much. In Rupe's opinion, this did not mean it was a jail face, accustomed to offering long haul blankness to the screws. No, it was a stay-*out*-of-jail face, accustomed to offering generally a show of refinement, sweet humour and calm to those he considered more or less undangerous. And his words now seemed wonderfully benign and chummy. Some things said about him at the Savoy pre-awards meal earlier tonight had startled Bale though.

He had been sitting between Hector Pye-Oram, *A Week in Review*'s usual studio manager, and Selina Mysan, often a panellist on the programme, and editor of the bookish magazine, *Page Upon Page*. Selina went in for big, irrational laughs that would sometimes bring relief if discussion on *A.W.I.R.* became stifling: laughs sort of 'in their own right', unrelated to anything that had been recently said or done or ever would be. Selina must be pushing seventy now, excellent on London literary and similar gossip after years with the magazine, contemptuous of tact.

And she had boomed: 'Well, aren't you the lucky one, Rupe?'

'To be alongside you in the plushness of the Savoy? Absolutely.'

She went into an expansive, multi-furl laugh: 'Gallant! But I meant you and Dione Pellotte, of course. Some family to bring on to your side via romance!'

'Lucky but maybe also a teeny bit brave?' Pye-Oram asked. 'Her father, formidable.'

'Don't see that,' Bale said. Of course, Bale *did* see it, did see risk. And he knew people had begun to talk about him and Dione. In his office the other day, Larry Edgehill told Rupe he had been more or less ambushed on Whitsun by Dione's father and baggage-man, and quizzed over Bale's future. 'When I say quizzed, I don't really mean quizzed, of course, Rupert,' Larry had said. 'I was being *instructed* to look after your career because you have to buy somewhere off Temperate Acres and take proper care of Dione. Don't talk about this, Rupe. You might get a new programme, anyway. We don't want it to look as if Pellotte fixed that.'

'As it happens, I saw Dione's daddy-o himself at an Anthony Powell conference,' Selina had said.

'Powell's one of his interests. Dione told me,' Bale said.

'Yes, *one* of his interests,' Selina said. 'Loot's another. And he knows how to wield it. Perhaps we should be grateful.'

'In what sense?' Pye-Oram said.

'In an awards sense,' she said.

'What's that mean?' Pye-Oram said.

'His pal actually gave a keynote talk,' Selina replied. 'He stood at the lectern and, do you know . . . he stood there looking . . . yes, looking full of money. Remember that phrase from, I think, *The Great Gatsby* – somebody in the tale seems "full of money"?'

'Daisy Buchanan. Gatsby says her *voice* is full of money,' Bale replied.

'This was his suit,' Selina said.

'In what respect?' Pye-Oram asked.

'In a fucking money respect,' Selina answered, and another thorough laugh crackled. 'The best sort! His suit a-bulge with currency. And Pellotte's, too. I loved it. But *loved* it. So *raw*. So *blatant*. So absolutely *street*. I mean, the conference, hyper-literary and well behaved, and these two flaunting profits. That's the kind they are.'

'Which?' Bale said.

'They'd been garnering dues, hadn't they? Trade barons and also lit fans. Delicious!' Selina said. 'People sell for them and are entitled to commission – *only* commission. If they try to cream off more, they catch severe trouble. Maybe they've got some two-timer or slow payer in their network– so they pop in and sort him out. Those pockets are undisguised, elemental, living power. You're mightily fortunate to have that sort of influence working for you, now you're cuddling up to Dione, Rupe. Result? We get shortlisted like this, and maybe even win – the rumours say so. Win! *You're* lucky, and *we're* lucky because we appear with you. We get drawn along in your sparkling wake. Yes, Hector's right, too: Pellotte's formidable.'

Bale said: 'But what's he to do with the awards, with the short-listing?'

'Oh, quite.' Selina belly-laughed. 'He's probably a very loving, very proud, father, you know,' she said. 'Concerned for his daughter. And, by extension, concerned for those she takes up with, such as you, chairman Rupe.'

'His money reaches the judges – is that what you mean?' Bale asked.

'He *is* money. And the judges are known.'

'That's preposterous,' Bale said. But Selina heard plenty, some rumour, some truth.

Momentarily, she paused again from knife-and-forking. She spoke quietly now, to take in only Bale and Pye-Oram: 'Rupe, rest assured that, when people ask whether you and Sandine only got that rare magic going over *Insignia* because you were shagging the arse off her on an established basis, I refute this. Obviously, I don't know whether you *were* shagging the arse off her, but a denial seems wisest. It would be bad for gossip like that to get about.'

'This is what I meant by bravery,' Pye-Oram said. 'You with Dione Pellotte while the Sandine thing is still very in the minds of everyone.'

'And then I hear of a long chat on the main Whit Festival road between Pellotte and his aide and someone who might be our dear producer, Larry Edgehill. I ought to ask him, but it's occasionally better to know something without its being known, you know.'

Yes, and Rupert kept quiet about what Larry had told him. In any case, Larry had asked for secrecy.

Pye-Oram said: 'Pellotte, a bit of a mystery. When I was still into a habit myself I bought from a lad on Whitsun called Hodge, Gordon Hodge, Hodgy. Gordon Basil Hodge – part of Pellotte's outfit. The sort who'd produce those "dues" you mentioned, Selina. He said Pellotte could be an absolute gem, charming, sort of father of his people, if you played along. Meaning, of course, if you paid up in full. Not otherwise. His manners then are tearing off heads.'

'*Did* Hodge play along?' Selina said.

'He had grand notions. Image. Kids in private school. I moved from him. He seemed dangerous, not helpful to know and deal with. Then I got myself clean, anyway. Perhaps Hodgy's still around. I doubt it, but he might be.'

And, yes, he *was* still around. At Pellotte's house after the Savoy, Bale realized he'd just crossed with 'Hodgy' in the front garden.

'I imagine she was at the award do tonight,' Pellotte said.

'Who?' Bale said.

'Sandine,' Pellotte said.

'The panellist?' Vagrain asked.

'Yes, Priscilla Sandine,' Dean said. 'Late twenties. Whiz-kidette. Columnist and would-be film maker. A flat in Ealing. Lives solo. Two accesses to the flat. Via the front door, naturally, but also a fire escape. A Bertram Caliph Sommerdale alarm system. There appears to be no regular timetable to her movements, except a walk for the news-papers just after ten o'clock on Sundays, using a pedestrian crossing near the post office both going and coming. Say twelve minutes in all. This is rain or shine, always alone and never bothering with an umbrella. Am I right, you saw *On the Frontier* at the theatre with her? The Auden-Isherwood bilge. You two sitting together.'

'That's the usual sort of thing,' Bale said. 'Panellists often go to the theatre or cinema or concert hall together.'

'Slightly apart from the others?' Dean said.

'I always think of William Walton as being like that,' Bert Marsh said. 'This is the fucking trouble with it.'

'Like what?' Dean said.

'On the frontier,' Bert said.

'I think the other one *does* live in Hampstead now,' Dean said.

'Karen?' Dione said. 'Yes, Hampstead. She came into some money. And she's partner in a couriering firm. Have you been there?'

'Been there?' Vagrain replied.

'I believe you met her at a signing, Mr Vagrain?' Dean said. 'In the Voluminous shop.'

'Of course, *you* live on Temperate Acres, don't you, Mr Bale – Rupert?' Vagrain said. 'This is luck! Distinguished representatives from each, Whitsun *and* Temperate present together. That must be rare. Useful in my research. Balance.'

'Rare enough,' Pellotte said. 'I'll concede that. I believe, though, that Rupert and I can get on. All the same, I was saying, before you arrived, Dione, Rupert, that I'm not convinced about the wisdom of a book based on Whitsun and Temperate.'

'I'd put the idea on ice for a few years, Abel,' Dean said.

'Daddy can be like this sometimes, Mr Vagrain. Known as "a domain matter". Spoken in a big, weighty voice.' She said the words in a big, weighty voice. '"Domain matters" get exceptional treatment. Whitsun and Temperate would be a "domain matter".'

Bale also considered now, and considered again, Pye-Oram's tale about the pusher called Hodge and his fear of Pellotte, if he turned against you. It gave Rupe a mild shiver, but intrigued him, too. In Rupe's thinking, it made Pellotte's actual support of him – Rupert Bale – even more valuable by contrast. 'Someone mentioned Hodge at the Savoy,' Bale said. 'Just an aside, really.'

'Who?' Pellotte said.

'Daddy doesn't like people nosing into the business,' Dione said.

'Is Hodge of some significance, then?' Vagrain asked. 'Oh, great! These insights could be of enormous help with the book. I'll talk to him.'

'They were discussing me at the awards dinner, were they?' Pellotte said, 'then got on to Hodge?'

'Is Hodge in some way dubious?' Vagrain asked.

'Was a connection implied between Adrian and Hodgy?' Dean asked.

'There's talk, and there's *loose* talk,' Pellotte said. 'People like Hodge might mention all sorts if asked for information by an outsider – by you as a distinguished writer, Abel. Hodge would want to impress, regardless of veracity. We certainly could not recommend him as a source for your work, Abel, I'm afraid.'

'Sad, really about GBH,' Dean said.

Seventeen

Esther found she awoke some mornings with the words 'To hell with the Olympics' either in her slowly surfacing head or actually on her lips and spoken, though she couldn't be sure at what volume. Usually, Gerald would be already up, working out piteously on the rowing machine downstairs, so the curse remained unheard, except by her guardian spirit, if she had actually uttered it, and if she had one.

Anyway, to hell with the Olympics. They were more than a decade off, suppose they ever came to London at all, but causing her big, present-day trouble and angst just the same. People – powerful, focused people – wanted a spruced and serene Whitsun and Temperate soon – or sooner – and she had two unsolved killings around her neck: a commonplace, territorial William Walton killing; a keep-your-nose-out-scoop-merchant killing.

And now talk of a potential third. That's what it undoubtedly was.

She'd got pretty well nowhere with the original two: Dean Feston and Gabrielle Barter Cornish brought in for chats, and released after chats; other chats at St John's with the vicaress and Joel Jeremy North, plus Mrs North – very plus Mrs North – equally un-progressive.

Number Three? Possible number three? At present she had Larry Edgehill, television producer, seated in front of her desk at Central. He seemed knocked about by guilt and possibly fear. 'Normally, I don't know that I'd mention this kind of thing,' he said. 'It's a sort of grassing, I suppose. And that means very dangerous. I'm scared. But . . . well, I know you to at least some extent, and, of course, your husband, via the programme and so on, and it . . . well, it becomes easier, perhaps even necessary. Yes, perhaps even necessary.'

'I know Gerald is pleased to be coming on *A Week in Review.*'

'He'll be fine, I'm sure.' Edgehill stayed silent and blank faced for a moment. Then he said: 'That's not really what I want to talk about. It's to do with the Whitsun situation, and perhaps beyond Whitsun.'

'Yes? Nothing sensitive you say now will involve you in trouble. I'll see to that.' *Talk to me, talk to me, if you've got something real stored there, 'real' meaning fit to base a charge/charges on right away, and able to stand up in court. I begin to unravel. I've heard you live on Whit, haven't I, so you get insights, intimations, murmurings?* Edgehill had telephoned and then arrived half an hour later. She'd guessed it would be to do with more than the programme.

'I'm concerned about someone called Hodge,' Edgehill said.

'Yes?'

'I feel a responsibility for him. It's stupid, I suppose, but I do.'

'He's unsafe?'

'He asked for help and . . . well, I ignored it.'

'What kind of help?'

'Have you heard of him? Gordon Basil Hodge, Larch Street, Whitsun.'

'Were you in a position to help?' Esther replied.

'Perhaps.'

'How did you know each other? Is he a neighbour?'

'Not a near neighbour. He'd picked up some gossip about me. It made Hodge imagine I could get him out of a mess. He arranged a meeting – in the street. He thought I had some influence.'

'Influence via the programme? Via TV?'

'In a way, yes.'

'Which way?'

'As a go-between.'

'Between?'

'Between him and some business heavies he'd upset.'

Editing at work here. But she knew the names would come eventually. When people were uncertain whether they should spill, they spilled in droplets only at first. Eked. It meant they could change their minds, back out. But, in any case, Esther thought she could supply much of the detail already. Hadn't there been the custody conversation with Ivor Frank Caple, code cover Luke Totnes, hauled in for passing dud notes? Esther could learn from that. Caple had been ready to guess for Esther where the counterfeits had most recently come from – Gordon Basil Hodge of Larch Street, Whitsun. Perhaps Caple guessed right. After all, past form showed he got fifty per cent of his information OK. Gordon Basil Hodge might have been skimming, and seriously enraging his master, Adrian Pellotte, and Pellotte's chaperone, Dean Feston: 'some heavies he'd *upset*' as Edgehill mildly phrased it. Caple: could she do anything for him? He was still inside. Tricky. But she'd try.

'I might have driven Hodge into stupid risk-taking,' Edgehill said.

'Because you failed him – that is, of course, in *his* view you failed him?'

'Maybe my view, too. I feel irresponsible – cowardly. So, here I am, taking a risk, trying to compensate – trying to get brave.'

'You're worried that he'll look for some other method of getting these heavies off his back? A more dangerous method? You have evidence?'

Edgehill thought, she knows some of this already, the secretive bitch. But how? Does she talk to Udolpho? Or, to put it the more likely way, does Udolpho talk to her, on the quiet, just as he talked to Edgehill on the quiet? What was it he'd called his newspaper shack – a thing of 'centrality', a hub? This morning, when Edgehill looked in for the papers, Udolpho had said in a real comfort-ye voice: 'He doesn't want you to fret about it, Larry, not suffer guilt. He understands. I think he knows now it was wrong to approach you that way. Like presumptuous? If you ask me, he's come to see that someone in your media executive position would have to be so careful about what you might get pulled into.'

'That wasn't why I—'

'The real point being, Larry – he's all right now. He's got the future beautifully organized. Morale up.'

'Well, I'm glad,' Edgehill had said.

'Like from a sudden vision. It's shown him the way.'

'Grand.'

'He's that sort.'

'Which?'

'He'll always come back from what looks like the dumps. He's not one to fold – no collapse. You two had your chat up Chancery Lane and it didn't turn out right. At first – disappointment. Even some rattiness, I wouldn't be surprised. One drink only with him, then vamoose, as I understand it. You know the way the mind can go topsy-turvy for a little while in someone pressured like Hodgy. But then a reappraisal. Return to coolness and a switch to Plan B. This is what I mean about coming back. Gordon Hodge is the sort who'll make sure he has a Plan B. Defeat? He's got no time for it. There are two daughters away at a terrific school paid for with much gold. That's his sort. And great taste, I understand, as to the inside of his property.'

'It wasn't that I *refused* to help him, Udolpho. I *couldn't* help him. I don't have the kind of influence he imagined – not with the people he feared might become . . . well, troublesome.' And this was certainly on the way to being true.

'Troublesome would have been on the cards, yes,' Udolpho said. A couple of commuters had showed for papers and cigarettes. Udolpho served them. When he and Edgehill were alone again, he said, 'Perhaps a lot of Whitsun folk got the wrong ideas from that conversation on Gideon Road.'

'Yes.'

'My impression is, Gordon Hodge recognizes this now.'

'I hope so.'

'More direct,' Udolpho said.

'What is?'

'These are words he used re his forthcoming schemes, which are in hand. When I say "in hand" I'm referring to beyond just thoughts and ideas. "More direct." The kind of words I'd expect from Gordon.'

'What does it mean, "more direct"?' Edgehill said.

'Oh, yes, much more direct. That's my impression.'

'How, exactly?'

'He's not one to spell everything out.'

'No.'

'Sort of oblique? Many people who get things under way are like that. They talk oblique, but when they act, they go straight at it. This is a kind of superstition. They don't want to say too much in case it all just stays at saying it.'

'Right.'

'Also, the walls of this place, if you can call them walls. Not exactly sound proof. When Gordon talks, there's often a – there's often a security side to things. Keep it vague? But some of us can interpret.'

'I understand.'

'Not exactly cryptic. Indicators. But my guess?' Udolpho said. 'Can I offer you my guess?'

'Certainly.'

'He's been to see them.'

'Pellotte and Dean?'

'Direct, as he said.'

'He called on Pellotte at home?'

'I underline that this is a guess only.'

'Based on what?'

'To what purpose, this visit, you'll ask?' Udolpho replied.

'Well, yes.'

'My bet is he'd speak to them along certain lines. Words of this sort: "Adrian, Dean, there's been an unfortunate, accidental lapse, in no way caused by school fees or other pressures, a simple miscalculation on my part in a business sense, a delay in payment and other snags" – there's talk of forged notes, you know, Larry – "so, Adrian, Dean, please give me some mission, some task, to handle for you. Please. This will wipe out the problematical aspects of our recent relationship, which it would grieve me to see endangered." You'll be familiar, Larry, with the phrase *quid pro quo.* And, as the Bible has it, "Here am I, send me."'

'What kind of mission, task?'

'This would have to be something considerable, something almost definitely hazardous, or it would not fit the bill, would it?' Wentloog-Jones said. 'This has to be exchangeable against the very serious, very weighty, problematical aspects, which I don't know in detail, but which must be very serious and weighty or why is – was – Gordon so scared? They might not be serious and weighty in their own right, but serious and weighty as perceived. That is, as perceived by Adrian and Dean. The BMW parked right outside Gordon's house, you know. All right, it's on their way to some castle, a short cut, but just the same you have to wonder.'

It had perturbed Edgehill to hear Udolpho speculate like this. Larry felt a kind of regret, a kind of responsibility, as he'd describe it later to Esther: had he shoved Hodge into something 'almost definitely hazardous' by a refusal to intercede – by what Hodge would regard as indifference? And which, in fact, *had* been indifference, or very close. One drink only: 'must get along.' Contemptible? Inhuman? Yellow?

For the first time, he sensed in himself a Whitsun loyalty. Fellow feeling took hold. It linked up somehow with that excess of commitment he sometimes felt towards others, and tried to resist – did resist now and then. All right, cars and garages got savaged on Whit. So did people. All right, a lot of dog shit on the pavements. Cars and garages weren't everything though, and a degree of personal safety *was* possible if you kept alert and wily and had up-to-date door furniture. Dog shit could be stepped around, especially in daylight. Community ties existed. This Whit resident had come to another Whit resident for support and he had ignored the plea. Treachery? His relationship with Pellotte was slight to the point of skeletal, but, perhaps, after all, he could have used it to put in a word or two for Hodge. Which word, though, or two? If Hodge had been trying to defraud Pellotte, not much that Edgehill said would count. People like Pellotte ran their own judicial procedures, and Hodge might already have been condemned.

Just the same, Edgehill suffered now the type of guilt Hodge via
Wentloog-Jones said he shouldn't. He hated the idea that when
Udolpho and Hodge spoke about these things they excused the
failure by referring to his career: to his 'media executive position'.
Mr Larry Morethanmy Jobsworth Edgehill realized he felt not merely
a Whit bond with Hodge. This was about something simpler, vaster:
the obligation on one man, any man, to help another in distress.

It was around this spot in his morning talk with Udolpho that
Edgehill began to think he'd better search for some help himself
with things. He'd wondered about contacting Gerald Davidson's wife,
the Detective Chief Super.

Now, in Esther's office, he didn't feel sure it was a smart decision. Had he made the dire aspect of what might happen plain
enough to her? She listened but didn't seem gripped. He would
have to tell her about the gun soon. That might shake her, get her
concentration.

She said: 'It's vague, isn't it?'

'I don't know the full picture, no, but I sense something potentially very bad.'

'There's sometimes sense in sensing. Not always.'

Esther, eager to get out of him whatever he had, acted a bit
offhand, schemed to downplay the value of what he said, so as to
push him into saying more, force him into exactitude, drama, tact-
lessness, betrayal of someone, possibly. Force him into what he'd call
bravery – a snitch's bravery. These were routine tactics, well-tried
interview ploys. He wouldn't recognize them, as some old career
crook would. 'When you say you "sense something potentially very
bad", where did the information come from that got you sensing
like that?'

'A good source.'

'Yes?'

But Edgehill wouldn't name him. He trusted Udolpho, and owed
him confidentiality. This morning, after Wentloog-Jones had done
his ten or twelve minutes' worth, Edgehill should have gone for the
train. But he needed to hear whatever else was offered even guesswork. There'd been another break while Udolpho looked after his
livelihood and then: 'Luckily, I can put him in touch with useful
folk, Larry.'

'Ah.'

'Oh, yes. In an intermediary fashion.'

'What kind of useful folk?'

'You know – *really* useful folk.'

More obliqueness? 'Really useful in which way?'

'He's aware I have contacts. This is one reason he appeared here again. It would seem like just breezing in for an *Independent* and DIY mags, but there's more than that. Of course, he *did* buy an *Independent* and two DIY mags and he holds these prominent when he goes out to prove he'd only been here for papers. No, he'd been here for what in diplomacy they call "letters of credence" introducing, say, a new ambassador to a foreign government. Of course, I wouldn't give him letters, nothing written, for God's sake, but I'd say where to go and to let them know the introduction came from me.'

'Contacts of what sort? Hodge an ambassador?'

'But my contacts are not the *only* reason. Nor am I referring to the newspapers and mags. He realizes I'll be seeing you, doesn't he, and is keen for me to pass on that he's fine now, everything sorted, and he bears no grudge, not the slightest? Those kids – they'll be back at the same school next term, I'm certain.'

'I'm glad. When he's next in, tell him I'm glad.' Just the same, Edgehill was bombarded by fears and worries.

'In many ways, Gordon's a gent – not just because his kids are at a boarding school in that town famous for schools, or due to the interior decoration at his residence in Larch Street, but thanks to his core nature,' Udolpho said. 'By genes a gent.'

'I appreciate it.'

'He insists on paying me.'

'For his papers and so on? Yes, naturally.'

'For his papers *and* a fixer fee.'

'Fixing what?'

'The intermediary aspect. I said not to bother. I told him I know these useful, decently stocked folk in the ordinary course of business, and it's as easy as easy to put him in touch, though I've never used them personally as suppliers. I've never needed that kind of thing and never will. Wouldn't know how to handle one, anyway.'

'What kind of things?'

'They'll look after him,' Wentloog-Jones replied. 'But he says the labourer is worthy of his hire – again from the Bible, or similar. And he makes it a very elegant fee, I have to say. Not in proportion, actually – the fixer fee nearly half of what he'll pay for the item itself. But, once more, he won't be talked out of it. These things have come down in price with a real . . . Joke! . . . I was going to

say with a real bang! Have come down in price with an absolute
slide. It's well known. Ammo, too. Still a flow from Eastern Europe,
perhaps even more than when the Wall first tumbled.'

'You're talking weaponry – handguns?' Edgehill said.

'Why I said a mission.'

'A mission with a handgun?'

'Oh, yes, as I said – beyond the thinking and ideas stage. He's
readying himself in a systematic, careful fashion. Confident. That's
why I mentioned his morale is up. It's often the case: get a plan and
the world simplifies itself.'

'He's preparing to kill someone?'

'I gave him three, as it were, letters of credence,' Udolpho replied.
'He could make his own choice. I'm not going to point him – aim
him! – at any particular one, am I? Udolpho is not a controlling
person. This is just general information. I don't want anything coming
back on me if there's a cock-up, do I? I've got a business to cherish,
a newspaper business. But he says the fact he can mention to any
of them – any one of the three – that Wentloog-Jones sent him
smooths everything out, and they'll be careful not to sell him anything
a bit faulty and jammable or traceable. That's why the go-between
fee is so meaty.'

'You know armourers?' Edgehill replied.

'A lot of people come in here. I get told what some of them do.
All right, it might be rumour only, it might be wrong. I give Hodgy
the names and where they're at, and he can check for himself. It's
not like lining up in the army to draw a rifle. That's why I said
three. What we all know, don't we, is that there are obtainables around
on Whitsun and it's just a matter of finding who's flogging them
and who's reliable in all the reliabilities required? Price? Not really
so important. It's the reliability people are after. I'm sure there's
nothing worse than being in a dire spot with something in your
hand to help, but it can't or won't help because it's jammed.'

Four customers had come in more or less at once. Might one of
them be an armourer? Edgehill examined some of those home
improvement journal covers on a shelf. Hodge was house proud?
The last of the four went. Edgehill said: 'For clarity now, you're
referring to—?'

'Look at it like this: the Gladstone Milo Naunton death.'

'Of course, I've heard of that. A territory scrap, wasn't it? Is –
was – Hodge involved?'

'This is more guesswork by me, Larry.'

'Involved how?'

'Suppose he *got* himself involved.'

'How? It's a while ago, surely?'

'Right. Dead right.'

'So how—?'

'He goes retrospective, maybe. It's a while ago, as you point out, and nobody on Temperate knocked over for it. Nor any attempt, to my knowledge.'

'Maybe Pellotte has come to see vengeance as foolish.'

'He's not entitled to.'

'Not entitled?'

'He's part of a culture. Head of a culture. There are expectations. Extremely undodgable. Think of the Queen. She has to read that speech every year saying what the government will do. She's the head of state and top of the pile, but, because of this, she's got no option about turning up.'

'The death is unpunished?'

'So we ask, who's looking slow and weak because of that?'

'The police?' Edgehill replied. 'A street murder, with firearms.'

'The police! Do the police care which bit of lowlife shoots another bit of lowlife? They cheer. They shout, "Congrats!" They'd issue AK-47s if they could, as long as they knew the weapons wouldn't be turned on *them*. A killing wipes out a nuisance for the police. And then, if there's a tit-for-tat op – what's known in the community as a "requital sortie", meaning answer-back slaughter – if there's a requital sortie, perhaps another nuisance gets removed, or more than one. Officers lay on a champagne celebration party. Next thing will be they recommend gang leaders for knighthoods.'

'You're saying Pellotte should have acted?'

'You heard of *noblesse oblige* at all? Yes, such as the Pope: if you're boss you've got duties as well as perks. You know the Bible parable of the ninety and nine that were safely laid in the shelter of the fold? But one was missing, and the Good Shepherd had to search for who terminated that one, and wipe the fucker out.'

'Pellotte and Dean have dawdled?'

'Are they too busy poncing about at literature conferences? A lot of comment gets muttered around Whit. Hodgy would be aware of it. Estate commitments, company commitments, should get main attention from a leader like Adrian Pellotte, not fucking books. One of those commitments we've just discussed: Gladstone Milo Naunton. Forgotten about? Ignored? Back-burnered after the crem? Then there's Dean Feston and the girl Cornish, half accused of doing a reporter who wanted to know about the trade and the warfare and Naunton. Those two got released, yes, but was Adrian doing enough to keep the heat off them in the first place? Sloppy? Sleepy? Oh, sure, Gladstone had a great subsidized funeral, and Bert Marsh, his live-in, sweetly pensioned, to date. Those are only basics though. Where are the Temperate corpses? All right, it's too late to get Whit retaliation in first, but it looks to many as if it's not going to be got in at all. And, talking of Temperate, there's another topic. Is Adrian Pellotte so worried about his daughter's love life, as well as litera-ture, he can't be bothered with the firm's day-to-day health and duties, such as the Gladstone situation and home-patch blame for the dead journalist situation? Dione? We've discussed it, you and I – she being on the rebound to one of your people who lives on Temperate, isn't she – Rupe Bale? Pellotte's focused on that, and only that, except for the books? This is the mutter that goes around. It's not friendly.'

'And Hodge will see to all this for them?' Edgehill replied.

'Gordon's always been great at spotting niche opportunities.'

'Is he . . . is he familiar with that kind of work? Would he be putting himself at crazy risk?'

'The thing is, he thinks he's at risk anyway, doesn't he? They might have been slow going after who did Gladstone Naunton, but maybe they'd act faster against Gordon. Why he came desperate to you.'

'Misguidedly.'

'He'll accept that, I believe. Don't make yourself suffer. He's not going to broadcast you let him down. Like I say, a gent.'

But Edgehill did suffer and felt he'd been shifty, unlike himself. He wanted to put this to rights by protecting Hodge now – a bit late admittedly. So, he'd come to share the problem with Esther Davidson, perhaps shift the problem to Esther Davidson. That's what police were for, wasn't it – to give protection?

He said: 'Look, to get specific, I think Hodge is going to look for and slaughter – attempt to – someone on Temperate suspected of killing a Whitsun trooper, Gladstone Milo Naunton, during a frontier spat, and possibly the journalist, Tasker, as well. This would be Hodge doing a payback to Adrian and Dean for trying to siphon some business profits. People on Whit wonder why the firm hasn't answered in style for Naunton. Hodge will see to it for him, restore his reputation and grandeur. Perhaps they'll put a whisper around that whomever Hodge targets was the journalist's killer also, and you'll be able to close that file, give up harassing Adrian's outfit.'

'You're afraid Hodge will get killed, instead of killing?' Esther asked. Would Hodge go after Joel Jeremy North? Was the word around that she'd accosted and quizzed North herself? Was the word around that Tasker had met him also?

Edgehill said: 'I don't know whether he's capable of this kind of operation.'

'Nobody can know.'

'But it's got to be stopped, anyway, hasn't it?'

'If what you've "sensed" is true.'

'He's bought a gun.'

'How would you know that?'

'He has,' Edgehill replied.

'I'll have a look around Temperate. It's difficult. He's committed no offence, except possible possession of a firearm.'

'The idea is to stop him committing an offence, or having an offence committed against him, isn't it? Police don't actually want these people eliminating one another, do they? Do they?'

'I'll certainly have a look around Temperate,' Esther replied, 'and put some extra people on.'

And she did. As a result Esther missed the live showing of Gerald's performance on *A Week in Review*, though when she watched the film of it later she thought he came over as quite sane and nice-natured, regardless. She had gone again with him to the studios as support, but in the hospitality suite pre-broadcast was called away on her phone by one of the extra officers patrolling Temperate to the scene of that new, appalling death. She drove there at once. 'I have to leave,' she told Gerald, 'you'll probably need to get a taxi home.'

'Oh, thank you,' he said.

'It's important.'

'More important than my debut appearance on this television show, I suppose.'

'I can catch up on it later.'

'More important than my debut appearance on this television show, I suppose.'

'Yes,' Esther said, 'much more important, you daft prick.'

Gerald had been talking to the woman from News, Nellie Poignard, in Hospitality for another of her free drinks. Sacheverell Biggs had just topped her up.

'What is it?' she asked Esther.

'Something she's fucking manufactured because she hates to see me spotlighted,' Gerald said. 'She tells some minion to ring her here, create a stir, a diversion from me, something to prove she's the distinguished, indispensable chief of detectives. It's her standard ego aggression and cruelty.'

'Where?' Poignard said. She put her full glass on to a window sill. 'One of the estates? Which?'

Esther also put her glass down.

Nellie Poignard spoke briefly into her mobile.

'Best of luck, Gerald,' Esther said, blowing him a kiss. 'You'll be great.'

'As if you fucking cared,' he said. He was yelling. The room became silent for a minute. Perhaps his behaviour soured the evening, and prepared a route to the absurd fist fight between Bale and a panellist, Rex Ince. Esther heard about it later – Ince, a don from one of the Cambridge colleges, screaming that Bale had been offered a new programme series only because he was backed by his fucking girlfriend's gangster father, who'd fixed the fucking culture show of the year award and terrorized the television company bosses. Both Bale and Ince had to be smothered in make-up powder so their injuries would not be visible on camera. Less visible. Esther could see them well enough when she ran the tape. But Gerald seemed jaunty enough and was able to work in one of his jokes. They were discussing a revival of John Osborne's drama, *Luther*, which suggested the great reformer's personality was much affected by constipation. 'The play should have been called *An Immoveable Feast*,' Gerald said.

On her way to Temperate, Esther thought she might have a Volkswagen on her tail. The Poignard woman? Had she alerted a camera crew? Newshounds! They wouldn't, couldn't, rest. Or not until what happened to Tasker happened.

Eighteen

ON TV LAST NIGHT
by *Morning Express* critic, Tim Gold-Bravo

Pre-publicity for Nellie Poignard's documentary, *Powder Kegs*, about the two London estates, Whitsun Festival and Temperate Park Acres, said many months had gone into preparation of this film. Never can time have been better spent. This was a brilliant, thorough and thoroughly disturbing portrait of an enormous concentration of the capital's municipal housing and flats. And perhaps what the programme showed is typical of many other large cities here and abroad.

Apparently, the idea first came to Poignard – previous notable exposés on the box, *Drying Out* and *A Taste For Children* – two years ago in the winter of 1998 when she began trying to badger her bosses into allowing her to start building a film ready for the explosion of full-scale drug gang warfare between the estates, which she so rightly foresaw. An investigative journalist had already been murdered, and a Whitsun dealer shot dead in a turf battle for the resonantly named but continually fought over William Walton Avenue.

But it was the killing in 1998 of small-time pusher, Gordon Basil Hodge, that finally compelled Poignard's chiefs to give the OK. She began to collect and store what has turned out to be a magnificent, sensitive, eloquent series of glimpses into the two massive estates. She and her crew caught with marvellous skill, doggedness and, perhaps, danger the feel of these streets, the nature of the hatreds, plus the despair and suppressed anger of ordinary folk who live there and who find their existence constantly diminished and even threatened by the violence around them: this anger suppressed because of a constant fear of reprisals.

Among several dozen gripping scenes was the discovery on Temperate waste ground of Hodge's body, with the voice-over explanation that he had been on a frantic vengeance campaign, trying to compensate for offending an unnamed drugs baron on Whitsun. But, instead, Hodge himself became the target. Police presence had been increased on the estate following a tip-off, and the shooting was actually witnessed by a special patrol detective, who could not prevent it, but who arrested the gunman, Joel Jeremy North, later convicted and jailed for life.

By some fluke, or some astonishing intuition, Poignard and her camera and sound people had arrived just after the police and were able to catch the appalling misery of the death scene and interview other shaken, sickened witnesses immediately following the event. A sequence filmed at the conclusion of North's trial in 2001 showed Detective Chief Superintendent Esther Davidson announcing that police would not be looking for anyone else in connection with the murders of the reporter and Gladstone Milo Naunton, the Whitsun dealer killed in a territorial dispute. This gave a kind of completeness to the Poignard essay, though not necessarily a comforting one.

Some of the coverage of the outright open warfare between Whitsun and Temperate when it erupted as she had predicted, was on a par with anything we have seen from Vietnam or Northern Ireland. No, this was not a reassuring programme, but it had the resounding ring of continuous authenticity and, oddly, perhaps, of caring.

Nineteen

Karen Tyne likes to have a talk now and then with Dean Feston about things in general. Very regularly, so far, she, Dione, Rupert Bale, plus Dione's mother, Olive, when not abroad, go out to Marlborough Road Cemetery to tidy up the graves of Adrian Pellotte and Dean. Pellotte's other daughter, Clarissa-Mercedes, occasionally joins them, but she lives a long way off and can't always make it. In any case, Karen heard she married a Church of England rector, who probably disapproves of the visits, given the kind of special career followed by Pellotte and Dean. The graves lie not far from each other, reflecting the men's relationship in life. The women always place new flowers.

Karen enjoys briefing Feston via the white masonry chippings above him, invariably congratulating Dean on what happened to Dr Rex Ince. This morning she says: 'Nobody's been caught for that. The police keep trying to tie it on you. They want to close the file, don't they, and get their success rate up? How? Accuse someone who's not around to make denials. Easy.'

Today, Karen has brought with her a copy of Abel Vagrain's new novel, *On the Frontier*. She has pink-highlighted some passages in it which she feels would have interested Dean. 'The book's a mix of fact and fiction,' she says, 'known as "faction" – very fashionable. We're all in it, but disguised a bit and under different monikers, naturally. The estates are there, too, also with made-up names. He's done a very nice chapter describing how you and Adrian eventually died. There's honour in it, Dean. Well, I should hope so. He shows you and Adrian out there on the streets in person, fighting nobly for your territory around what the novel calls Thackeray Crescent, but which is really William Walton Avenue, of course. Although a business tycoon, the Adrian figure – Vince Caldrake, in the story – has to get to where the bullets are flying, to show he's still a worthy leader. Some have doubted this, because he had failed to avenge the death of one of his foot soldiers. And where the Adrian figure has to go, his bodyguard must go, too. That's you, Dean, but rechristened Grenville Lampoda. You get bopped when selflessly trying to protect your boss – which is really how it happened, isn't it?

'This next bit will really amuse you, Dean,' she said. 'In *On the Frontier* a university don, Norbert Gale-Hive is found murdered, apparently as punishment for a public slur on Adrian – Vince Caldrake, that is, and Gren Lampoda – you, that is – to do with a television awards incident. This is sure to make the reader think of the way that creep Rex Ince got slaughtered in reality, isn't it? The Hodge death is in the book, too, and there's a girl who might be me, giving pillow-talk tips during a one-night stand. Plus, we have a woman who makes a stir in a television arts show and then goes on to turn out art-house films that dispense with central characters. True name Sandine? I think so. At the end of the book, Dione and Rupert – or Angela and Cedric – are married and their house in Wandsworth is featured in a *Home and Gardens* three-page article. More near fact! It should be St John's Wood.

'And still more near fact? In chapter twenty-two, Lampoda and Caldrake go to a literary meeting where Lampoda is to give a keynote address. They are both loaded with money because they've collected from a pusher *en route*. Lampoda leans forward at one point and almost goes off balance because his suit is so full of cash. A nine mm pistol falls from his shoulder holster on to the lectern. Remind you of anything?

'There've been changes. Dione tells me the woman top detective has left London to take an even grander law and order job in Wales. You'll probably remember her reputation soared and stayed high after she schemed the arrest of a multi-killer on the estate where Rupe Bale lived. Dione thinks this officer somehow devised the battle in which her dad and you were so conveniently taken out by the other crew. I can't believe it. People's minds may be pushed off balance by grief. This might have happened to Dione, I fear. Admittedly, though, to choreograph such a smart, cleansing shoot-out is possibly the kind of ploy a big rank gendarme *would* get promoted to staff level for.

'Anyway, whether or not you sweetly nemesized Ince, dear Dean, I hope you appreciate that I'm the one who sent you unmistakably into a probably best-seller book, although he called you Grenville Lampoda. Vagrain changed the object of your literary fandom from Anthony Powell to Dylan Thomas, I don't know why. More disguise? The last-but-one book in the Powell *Dance to the Music of Time* series is called *Temporary Kings*, isn't it? That's how Whitsun and I will for ever remember you and Adrian.

'The estates are quietish without you, still a bit stunned by all that happened. There were such big losses on both sides, weren't there, Dean? No conquerors. No colonizers. The Olympics people are chuffed.'